The Morning After

The Morning After

Kendra Norman-Bellamy

and Hank Stewart

www.urbanchristianonline.com

Urban Books, LLC
78 East Industry Court
Deer Park, NY 11729

The Morning After Copyright © 2010 Kendra Norman-
Bellamy and Hank Stewart

ISBN 13: 978-1-60162-754-4
ISBN 10: 1-60162-754-8

First Mass Market Printing April 2013
First Trade Printing January 2010
Printed in the United States of America
10 9 8 7 6 5 4 3 2 1

*This is a work of fiction. Any references or similarities to
actual events, real people, living or dead, or to real locales
are intended to give the novel a sense of reality. Any simi-
larity in other names, characters, places, and incidents is
entirely coincidental.*

Distributed by Kensington Publishing Corp.
Submit Wholesale Orders to:
Kensington Publishing Corp.
C/O Penguin Group (USA) Inc.
Attention: Order Processing
405 Murray Hill Parkway
East Rutherford, NJ 07073-2316
Phone: 1-800-526-0275
Fax: 1-800-227-9604

Dedication

To all of those who are reading this book and know the pain of losing a loved one that meant the world to you; remember this:

. . . weeping may endure for a night, but joy cometh in the morning.

(Psalm 30:5b)

Kendra's Acknowledgments

To my Lord and Savior, Jesus Christ: You are my life, my breath, my everything. Thank you for continuing to allow me to "walk on purpose." I am humbled to be able to take the gift you've bestowed upon me and use it for your glory. How blessed I am!

To my husband, Jonathan: Thank you for being my loudest cheerleader and my greatest supporter. If you didn't do what you do; then what I do would be a much harder task. Brittney: I'm still trying to wrap my brain around the fact that the world now calls my firstborn child a national bestselling author. Thank you for choosing to follow in my footsteps and use your gift for God. To my baby girl, Crystal: You are so naturally creative and talented that it amazes me. Thanks for never allowing there to be a dull moment in our household. To Jimmy (1968–1995): Thanks for being my guardian angel year after year. Bishop Harold & Mrs. Francine Norman: Thank you for my righteous upbringing. Much of who I am is because of who you were . . . and still are. Crystal, Harold Jr., Cynthia and Kimberly: Thank you for just being the best sisters and brother a girl could have. I love y'all.

To Hank: Thanks for the concepts of *Three Fifty-Seven A.M.* and *The Morning After*. I enjoyed assisting you in becoming a bestselling published novelist through this two-book series. Aunt Joyce and Uncle Irvin: Thank you both for allowing me to continue to be your "little goddaughter" even at this stage of my life. Heather, Gloria and Deborah, you are my best friends forever. And ever and ever and ever. . . .

To Bishop Johnathan & Dr. Toni Alvarado: You are two of the most amazing preachers I've ever been blessed to meet. Thanks for the covering of Total Grace Christian Center. To my Anointed Authors on Tour sisters (Michelle, Vivi, Tia, Shewanda, Norma and Vanessa): Thank you for being my sisters of the pen. Working in ministry with you is a blessing. Dwan and Toschia: Thanks for being true author-sister-friends. To Terrance, Rhonda, and Carlton: Thank you for the intricate parts you play in the success of my career. I couldn't do it without you. Yulanda and Cooky: I just wanted to give a surprise shout-out to the two of you. Thanks for everything. To all of the creative talent who have joined me in The Writer's Hut, in The Writer's Cocoon, and on Cruisin' For Christ: Thanks for being a part of my expanded ministry.

To the women of the *Iota Phi Lambda* Sorority (especially Atlanta's Delta Chapter): You have become such a cherished part of my life. Thank you for adding more sisters to my life than I know what to do with. To my Urban Books family: Thank you for the opportunity to minister through fiction. To all book clubs and avid readers of my works: Thank you for being a constant blessing to my career. I appreciate each of you.

Finally . . . (y'all know I always go out on a musical note) . . . To Melvin Williams, Brian McKnight, Fred Hammond, India Arie, Antonio Allen, Melvin M. Miller, and Joss Stone: Thanks for the wonderful music that streamed from my stereo system and from my computer as the writing of this project took place.

Hank's Acknowledgments

I want to first thank the head and foundation of my life . . . my Alpha and Omega, my Lord and Savior, Jesus Christ! Without Him my life would be lost. I want to thank Kendra Norman-Bellamy, first for her friendship, and then our business relationship. Kendra, you are the best and I am glad the Lord allowed our paths to cross.

I want to take this time to thank Maureen Stubbs, my personal assistant. Mo, you know I can't do it without you. I believe people come into your life for a reason, a season or a lifetime. Well, Gwen Mason, I pray our friendship is a lifetime, you have made me better! You have taken The Stewart Foundation to another level, and with you as the Executive Director, it will go even higher. I also want to thank The Stewart Foundation Board, the volunteers, and all of my A.L.O.T. (A Leader Of Tomorrow) youth. This world is going to be so much better when each and every one of you share the gifts that God has put in you.

Now, I have the best mother in the world (Ruth Stewart) who is the source of my strength, and she has just celebrated her Eighty-first birthday. Momma, I love you! Thank you for telling and teaching me about God all of my life. Thank you for not only telling me to pray, but showing me how to pray. There are family members that if you had the opportunity to choose you would not choose them. Well, I have four brothers and sisters, and given the chance, I would choose them over and over again. Bobbie, Bernard, Valerie, and John, thank you for your continued support, I love you all. I love the word family and it comes in the form of friends and spiritual family. I have grown more being a member of Antioch Baptist Church North in Atlanta. Reverend Alexander, thank you for teaching the men of Antioch to be men. Thank you for supporting me and allowing Antioch Baptist Church North to be my first stage to share what God had placed inside of me. Thank you for being my spiritual father.

Now the Bible says "To be a friend you must first show yourself friendly." This shout-out is for all of my friends. I have so many dear friends who are always there whenever I call. Thank you for supporting me no matter what I come up with. Thank you for making even some of my bad ideas look like good ones. I only pray that I have been just as good of a friend to you as you have been to me. Thank you.

Last, but not least, I want to thank my son, Austin O'Connell Stewart. Austin, I am happy to be your father, and I want to continue to live my life as a true role model for you. You have made me see life with a new set of eyes. Austin Boston, I love you more than words can say!

The Morning After

Prologue

Ms. Essie was dead, but life still had to go on. How to make that happen, no one was exactly sure. Somehow the people she left behind had to find a way to pick up the pieces and move forward. In the short time that her neighbors had come to know her on a personal level, Essie Mae Richardson had become the glue that held them together. Now that she was gone, so was their adhesiveness. Slowly but surely, they were falling apart. She had lived a long, full life, but for those who had only recently gotten to know her, Ms. Essie had been taken away from them way too soon.

The morning after she slipped away peacefully in her sleep, all of the newly established friends of the seventy-seven-yearold woman tried to muzzle their emotions in order to honor their promises to her. Just a day before Essie went to join her beloved husband, Ben, in heaven, several of the residents of the Braxton Park subdivision agreed to put all of their plans on hold and go to Sunday morning worship with her. They'd had no idea that Essie wouldn't be there with them, but a promise was a promise.

It seemed like the entire city was mourning the death of the community's pillar; or maybe that's just the way it felt to the people who loved her the most. The funeral home where her body was still being prepared for burial had hung a beautiful black satin wreath on her door, and dozens of the people who lived in neighboring houses had placed roses, cards, and stuffed animals on her porch. It was clear that Essie was adored; loved, perhaps, even more deeply than she'd known.

Whether they had a personal connection with her or just remembered her as the wise old woman who sat on her front porch waving at nearby neighborhood children, knitting a new blanket, or swaying in her rocking chair as she sang songs or read her Bible; everyone who had been touched by Essie's life had also been affected by her death. At times, a sense of hopelessness seemed to encircle her former neighborhood. Her vacant porch, the car that no longer left the driveway on Sunday mornings, and the absence of the tantalizing aromas that used to seep from her kitchen all the way out into her front yard—all of them were signs that Essie no longer lived at 216 Braxton Way.

The morning after her death, the forecast didn't warn of rainfall, but right when that Sunday morning's service was just getting into full swing, water fell from the sky and delivered a wave of flash floods to the whole of Georgia's capital.

"Listen at that," Reverend Owens said, gazing at the ceiling of the church as he took the podium and opened his Bible in preparation to deliver the sermon of the day. "Jesus and the angels done shouted so hard in celebration of Sister Essie's homecoming, 'til heaven done sprung a leak!"

Those simple words immediately lightened the dismal mood that had encompassed the sanctuary from the moment the announcement was made that the church's oldest member had passed away. As soon as Reverend Owens had finished his declaration, the bow-tie wearing organist rolled his fingers across the keys of the ten-year-old Hammond 926 Classic Organ, and the music that burst forth seemed to light a fire under the behinds of more than half the worshippers. From the pulpit to the back door, men and women, old and young alike, began dancing to the music and the beat of the drums. All of a sudden, the gathering that had started out as a dignified service to honor Essie's memory turned into a shout-a-thon worthy of a video clip on YouTube.

Men sprinted around the building like they'd suddenly become Carl Lewis. Women danced out of their hats, wigs, and even a few half-slips. Most of the choir vacated the choir stand and congregated on the roomier pulpit so that they could get their praise on too.

"That's right, that's right," Reverend Owens urged into the microphone as he skipped his short, rotund frame across the pulpit in jubilance. "That's what Sister Essie would have wanted! Praise Him, everybody. Another one of God's children done made it in. Praise Him!"

That took the service to a whole new level. The few ushers who hadn't gotten caught up in the spirit themselves, raced to keep the runners from colliding into one another and the dancers from becoming an entangled pile of flesh. Even the children took advantage of the opportunity to scream and jump around energetically without being reprimanded or made to take a seat. The fact that Essie's death was no reason to mourn or weep had all at once become clear to almost everyone in the fifty-year-old edifice. *Almost* everyone.

In all of their spiritual rejoicing, the pastor and members of the Temple of God's Word didn't detect the still heartbroken first-time visitors who sat together on the padded pew in the rear of the church. With just over two hundred members, the five guests, four of which hadn't been on the inside of a church in years, went unnoticed. Neither the pastor nor the members saw Elaine's tears or Mason's confusion. They didn't realize Jennifer's despair or T.K.'s anguish at seeing the suffering of his friends. And not one of the dancing worshippers noticed the fourteen-year-old boy who was so angry at their joy that he couldn't stand to spend one more moment inside the walls of the church where Essie used to spend her Sunday mornings.

Before his mother could stop him, Jerrod dashed for the exit doors, removed his new dress shoes and ran barefooted; more than five miles toward home.

Chapter 1

One Year Later
Jerrod's Story

"Ma, I'm going next door to help Ms. Angel, okay?" he called from the front door of the home that he shared with his mother.

Jerrod turned around when he heard Jennifer step from the kitchen. She used a dish towel to dry her hands and said, "I thought you were gonna watch Austin while I got dinner ready."

"He don't need me to watch him no more." Jerrod pointed to Angel's sleeping one-year-old toddler while he spoke. "Ms. Angel's over there by herself and I know she needs some help. I'm done with my homework, so I can go help her pack up some of Ms. Essie's things."

"I don't know, Jerrod." A look of apprehension settled in on Jennifer's face. "I think it's real nice that you want to help, but packing up Ms. Essie's things could turn out to be a lot harder than you might think. Do you really believe you can handle being in her house again after all this time, and seeing all her stuff get packed away?"

Jerrod tightened his jaws and swallowed. He hadn't been inside Essie's house since the wee hours of that morning when they found her there, barely alive. Moments later, she was pronounced dead. That was a year ago. Ever since then, Jerrod had trouble just passing the vacant property where Essie used to live. Going inside hadn't even been a consideration—until now. This morning, Jerrod was determined to do it. He'd given himself the pep talk last night, telling himself that it was time to man up and stop being a coward. Just the thought of placing all of Essie's belongings in boxes and putting them away somewhere, never to see them again, was tugging heavily at his heart. But he couldn't let his mother see the strain.

Jerrod's claim that his plan was to help Angel was only partially true. In reality, he needed to do it for himself. He hoped that somehow, by helping to pack away the things that belonged to the woman that he'd come to love dearly, it would in some way help him bring closure to the pain of the loss of her, and bring an end to a year of restless sleep. If Angel, a woman who was closer to Essie than anyone else, could gather the courage to go inside Essie's house and dismantle her things, Jerrod reasoned that he could too. Essie would want him to be strong and do what he needed to do, and for Jerrod, it was important that Essie be proud.

"You ain't got to worry about me, Ma," he answered, trying to shrug his shoulders in as carefree a manner as he could muster. "It's cool. I got this."

Jennifer smiled, embracing her son, who over the past year had grown to a height that exceeded hers by two inches. "All right, then. When you get over there, let Angel know that her baby is in good hands, and tell her that she and Colin can eat dinner with us if they want to. It's already late, and I know she won't feel like cooking. My food won't be as good as Ms. Essie's, but it'll serve the same purpose."

"Okay." Jerrod had barely gotten the one-word reply out of his mouth before the front door of his house closed behind him. He'd had to rush out as soon as he could to keep his building emotions hidden from his mother. Hearing Jennifer mention their former neighbor's cooking seemed to smother Jerrod. He needed to breathe.

After inhaling deeply for the third time and releasing the breath into the comfortably warm spring air, Jerrod wiped a threatening tear from the corner of his left eye and walked down the steps of the front porch. His mother's home was only a few feet away from Essie's. As he climbed up the steps that would lead him to his former neighbor's front door, Jerrod stopped to mentally prepare himself to walk inside. He had gone through a myriad of emotions in the year since he watched the mortuary staff lower Essie's stunning white marble casket into the ground.

It had been a beautiful funeral despite the sad occasion. Essie didn't have any living family members, but no one would guess that from the crowd. Never before had Jerrod seen so many people try to fit in one church. Temple of God's Word was clearly too small to accommodate the demand, but Angel felt that it was the place of worship where Essie would want her service to be held. There were as many people standing on the outside as were sitting on the inside. Old, young, and middle-aged people; black, white, and Asian people; family, friends, and just plain nosey people. A few tears were shed, but most were too busy praising to weep. Even from the inside of the edifice, Jerrod could hear a frequent, "Hallelujah" and an occasional, "Praise our sho' 'nuff God" from those who could only listen to what was taking place on the inside.

In the early days following her demise, all Jerrod felt was overwhelming sadness. He refused to cry at the funeral, and he dared not fall apart at school. But, at home, it was a different story. Many nights Jennifer sat up with him, and sometimes she cried with him too. Those nights when it was too much for his mom to handle, she called for the assistance of T.K. Donaldson, Jerrod's track coach, who also happened to be his mother's steady boyfriend. T.K. had been a big source of support and strength. He had become Jerrod's hero, of sorts. But as much as Jerrod admired and respected the man that he simply referred to as Coach D, he tried not to get too close. Over the years, he'd seen his mother's boyfriends come and go, and the last thing he needed was to become too attached to T.K., and then have his heart broken, yet again, by a man whose relationship with Jennifer didn't work out.

After the devastating sadness eased, Jerrod found himself angry. Not at anyone in particular; just angry with the world. It didn't seem fair that Essie would be taken away from him at such a crucial time in his life. He needed her, and without her strong hand to set him straight when he found himself making the wrong choices, Jerrod feared that he'd slowly drift back into the old ways that he'd just broken away from shortly before she died.

"The best thing you could ever do to honor Ms. Essie's memory is to keep your determination to stay out of trouble, and keep your grades up. If you do that, you can always feel a sense of satisfaction because you will know that even from heaven, she's proudly smiling down on you."

That was what T.K. told him back then, and that was what Jerrod had been focused on doing. It was important to him to have Essie's approval . . . even from the grave. Jerrod had promised her that he would continue to respect his mother and do well in school, and somehow, no matter what, he had to keep his word. This school year, his grades were better than they'd ever been. For the first time in his life, he had made honor roll in the first semester. And this term, he'd not once been sent to the office for misbehavior. That was a milestone that even the principal had commended.

"Hey, Jerrod. Are you coming over to help out?"

Angel's voice broke into his thoughts, and only then did Jerrod notice that he'd just been standing on Essie's porch, staring at nothing in particular.

"Yeah . . . I mean, yes, ma'am." As far as Jerrod was concerned, Angel, who was still in her twenties, wasn't old enough to be categorized as a "ma'am." But Essie had taught him that it was just proper to show respect when talking to adults. "Ma said I could come over and see if you needed any help."

"I sure do." Angel smiled at him, but the whites of her eyes carried a hint of pink. Jerrod wondered if she'd been crying. If so, sadness wasn't detected in her voice as she added, "I never knew that Ms. Essie had so much stuff until I started trying to get it packed. I hate that Colin couldn't be off to help me, but you'll do just fine. Come on in."

He was a bit fearful at first, but as Jerrod stepped through the open door, he immediately felt at home; just like he did when Essie was there. As he continued to follow Angel, Jerrod couldn't help but take note of her flattering figure as she strolled ahead of him. When he was first introduced to her, Angel's belly was swollen with Austin growing on the inside of her. And for a few months following the delivery, she wore oversized clothing to hide her still bloated stomach and expanded hips. Now she had lost all of the post-pregnancy weight, and in Jerrod's eyes, Angel was as fine as any of the girls at his school who had never even had babies.

A stifled grin made the corners of Jerrod's lips quiver. *No wonder Mr. Colin is always so happy.*

"I've been working on Ms. Essie's bedroom, getting some of the clothes and other personal belongings packed," Angel announced, snapping Jerrod from his mannish deliberations. "There are two boxes in that corner over there. You can start taking the things from the shelves here in the living room and pack them away. The photos can go in one box, and all the other decorative items in the other. If you don't mind a little extra work, I need you to use pages from this newspaper to wrap each of the pictures before putting them in the box. I don't want to break any of the frames."

"A'ight," Jerrod said, his eyes scanning the shelves that lined the living room walls.

"You think you can handle that? I didn't give you too much, did I?"

Jerrod accepted the old Sunday edition of the *Atlanta Journal-Constitution* from Angel and almost laughed at the unnecessary concern in her eyes. "No, ma'am. It's all good."

"Great." She released a heavy sigh before heading back toward the bedroom. "Call me if you need help or if you have questions about anything."

The task of packing away all of Essie's what-nots and pictures took more effort and was more time-consuming than Jerrod first thought it would be. Sometimes it was his own curiosity that slowed his progress. He had seen many of the pictures on the shelves in the times that he had visited Essie's home, but there were several that he'd never noticed before, and he took the time to admire each one before putting them away. Each framed image seemed to tell its own story of a particular time in the elderly woman's life.

The photo of a youthful Benjamin and Essie Richardson had always been the centerpiece of the middle shelf. Though time had faded the photo a bit, it was still easy to see that Essie's soft, beautiful features and his strong, handsome ones made them an attractive couple. The wood framed picture was larger than all of the others, and that alone made it the automatic focal point. Jerrod began carefully wrapping it in sheets of newspaper, and he couldn't help but smile as he thought of how happy Essie must have been to be back in the arms of the man who had died so many years before her.

The next photograph that caught Jerrod's attention was one of Essie sitting in her rocking chair on the porch. His heartbeats quickened as he reached for the picture and held it in his hand. This was the way he would always remember her. With the possible exception of the kitchen, the porch seemed to be Essie's favorite place to be. That was where she was the first time Jerrod had seen her. It apparently brought her great joy to sit and watch the happenings in her community.

Jerrod sighed. He'd give almost anything to see Essie Mae Richardson again. Just to hear her voice, giving him a word of advice, would be a welcome sound. She often visited him in his dreams, but to come into contact with a strong presence of her while he was awake would be a wonderful experience.

Bong!

The sudden sound of the grandfather clock in the corner stunned Jerrod as it resonated throughout the house. The teenager's hands trembled, and the photo that he had been holding slipped from his grasp and fell to the floor. Had it not been for the plush area rug beneath his feet, the protective glass would have shattered.

"Jerrod, are you okay?"

Spinning around, Jerrod looked at Angel, who stood beside the living room sofa, looking at him with concerned eyes. He felt warm moisture on the sides of his face and realized that tears had begun streaming from his eyes. Using his bare arms, he wiped them away and then kneeled on the floor to pick up the photo and to hide his embarrassment.

"Jerrod?"

"Yes, ma'am, I'm fine," he said, without looking up. Jerrod hoped that Angel would just go back into the bedroom and continue with whatever it was that she was doing in there, but he heard her footsteps nearing him, and from the corner of his eye, he saw her sit on the La-Z-Boy where Essie often sat and watched *The Price Is Right*, the only show that she looked at on a daily basis.

"Jerrod."

It took all of the boy's strength to steady his trembling lips. Jerrod wasn't intending to be rude by ignoring Angel's call, but he knew that if he opened his mouth, he'd lose the battle that he fought to hold back a rush of tears.

Slipping from the chair, Angel sat on the floor next to him. Jerrod's vision was so blurred by the rising flood that he couldn't see clearly; but he felt Angel's hands cover his while he continued to hold securely to Essie's photograph. Complete silence dominated the room for a moment, and Jerrod wrestled not to even blink, knowing that doing so would be all the push that his awaiting tears needed.

"It's okay to cry, Jerrod," Angel whispered. "I do it all the time. I know how hard this is. Why do you think I waited a whole year to pack her things away? It took me that long to be able to come in here and do it; that's why. Ms. Essie wasn't a blood relative of mine, but I'd known her all of my life, and she had always been like a grandmother to me. It's painful for me to come to grips with the fact that she never got to hold Austin, and he will never get the chance to personally know the woman who was more influential in my life than even my own mother."

Despite his valiant efforts, silent tears slipped from each of Jerrod's eyes and ran down his cheeks. They met at his chin, and then dropped to the floor.

"None of us were ready for her to die, Jerrod," Angel continued. "And although every single time I cry, I feel like Ms. Essie is scolding me and telling me not to be sad because she's in a much better place . . . I still cry."

"Why didn't she tell us she was gonna die?" Jerrod's blurted the words and his voice trembled as he choked back the onset of heavier tears.

Angel squeezed his hand. "She didn't know she was going to die, Jerrod."

"Yes, she did." His reply was accusing. "Ms. Essie knew everything. She knew when people were coming by to visit, she knew when something was on your mind; she knew when it was gonna rain . . . she knew *everything*, Ms. Angel. She had to know she was gonna die. Why she didn't tell us?"

After a brief, thoughtful silence, Angel wiped a tear from her own eye, and then replied, "Let's just say she did know, Jerrod. Had she told us, would it have made a difference? Would you be any less hurt than you are now? Would you have been any more ready for her to die than you were then? I know I wouldn't have. And not only that, but if Ms. Essie had told me she was going to die, I would've been so sad that I probably couldn't have enjoyed Austin's birth. You probably would have been so sad that you wouldn't have been able to eat or sleep."

"Think about it, Jerrod. If what you say is true, and she really did know that God would come and take her early that Saturday morning, maybe she didn't tell us because she wanted us to be happy. Maybe Ms. Essie knew that the only way she could die happy was if we were all living happy."

It made perfect sense, but it didn't soothe his wounded heart. Jerrod decided that he'd have to deal with the embarrassment of Angel seeing him sob some other time. Conceding to the fact that he was neither man enough nor strong enough to keep his emotions in check any longer, Jerrod brought his hands to his face and wept harder than he had in months. He felt Angel's arms embrace him and pull him closer to her. He didn't see her tears, but he knew she was crying too.

Some days, Jerrod could go a full twenty-four hours without being overcome with sadness at the thought that Essie Mae Richardson would never again be a part of his life. Today wasn't one of those days.

Chapter 2

Elaine's Story

Four hundred eleven days . . . or was it four hundred twelve? She had lost track of the precise number. But whatever the length of time, it had been far longer than she'd expected.

When Elaine had the brief illicit affair that almost ended her then seven-year-old marriage, she knew that regaining Mason's trust would be an uphill battle. And she recalled very well the day that she told him that she was willing to wait as long as he needed. But Elaine had no idea of the punishment she had signed up for. She was afraid to check, but somehow she had the feeling that she qualified for inclusion in *The Guinness Book of World Records* for being the woman to go without intimacy for the longest period of time within her marriage. It wasn't a feat for which she'd want to take credit.

As she sat at her computer in her home office, typing the final lines to the health and fitness article that would appear in an upcoming issue of *Ladies Home Journal*, Elaine struggled to keep her focus. She loved her husband, and she felt deserving of being punished. But she didn't know how much more she could handle.

"At least we're still together," she mumbled, trying to focus on the positive. Zoning in on the good in every situation and minimizing the bad was something she'd learned from Essie, but sometimes Elaine wondered if remaining in such a strained relationship was a positive thing after all. It was beginning to take its toll.

Knowing that the bulk of the recent stress that their marriage had endured had been caused by her own infidelity, Elaine tried to remain patient while her husband dealt with everything at his own pace. Coming to grips that she had cheated on him had been very difficult for Mason, and Elaine had to admit that in spite of everything, he'd come a long way from where he was at the start of the mayhem. For weeks following the reveal of her adultery, he would barely talk to her, and when he did begin opening the lines of communication, he struggled to look at her when he talked. Now conversation was no longer an issue. They spoke with ease, even sharing laughs on occasion. But that was about all they shared. Elaine never dreamed that a year would pass with Mason still sleeping on the sofa. She was beginning to feel as though she had a housemate; not a husband.

In the early days of the sleeping arrangements that Mason had implemented, adding a mile to her morning runs seemed to relieve some of the frustration of not being able to spend any intimate time with the man she loved. But as those days turned into weeks and the weeks expanded into months, no amount of exercise was satisfying her physical and emotional needs.

"Elaine . . . you here?"

Mason's voice, calling from somewhere in the living room, took her by surprise. Elaine had been so absorbed in her own thoughts that she hadn't even heard him come in the front door. She looked at the clock in the lower right hand corner of her computer. He was right on time.

"Yes, I'm here." As she responded, she slid her rolling desk chair away from the computer and started down the hall to meet him. It was nearing seven o'clock. Her work had kept her so involved that she'd failed to finish preparing dinner. It would only take ten minutes to cook the boil-in-bag rice that would serve as a side dish to the peppered steak and gravy she'd cooked earlier.

Elaine came to a stop at the mouth of the hallway and watched Mason struggle to pull his shirt over his head. He always came home from hauling loads, smelling like a mixture of gasoline and sweat. Emerging love handles were evidence of the lack of exercise that his truck driving job allowed. But none of that doused Elaine's yearning to touch and be touched by him. Their marriage had seen some good days in years past. No one in her entire life, including the chiseled-framed Bermudian that she'd allowed herself to be swept away by, had ever loved her on the same level as Mason. It had been a long time since she'd been with him, but Elaine hadn't forgotten what it was like.

"Hey." Mason's single-word greeting shook Elaine from her mindless gaze.

"Hey," she replied, embarrassed that he had caught her longing stare. Her face felt flushed. "How was work?"

"Okay. What about you? You done with the story you were talking about last night?"

Elaine walked past him as she responded. "Almost, but not quite. I had to set it aside to meet a deadline on an article I was assigned. I'll be finished with both before the end of the evening though. Are you about ready to eat? It'll be a few minutes."

"No problem. I gotta shower first anyway."

"Everything will be ready by then."

Mason went into the bedroom and eased the door shut. The rule was unwritten and unspoken, but Elaine knew that anytime he closed the bedroom door behind him, she wasn't allowed inside. Most evenings when he returned home from his local hauls, he showered in the guest bathroom down the hall near Elaine's office, but today he wanted to use his own. The master bath's stall was more spacious, and unlike in the guest bath, this one's shower head had massage settings. Why should he have to be the one to get second best? After all, it was Elaine who had messed up everything by inviting another man to enter territory where he had no business.

"Okay, dude, cut it out!" Mason whispered harshly as he rubbed his eyes to try to wipe away the visual that often found its way into his mind. Every time he thought he was over it, mental snapshots resurfaced of Elaine and Danté pawing passionately at one another. For Mason, the thought of it served as a relentless form of torture.

"Listen, man, I know you don't want to hear this, but maybe it's time for you to seek psychological help along with spiritual counsel," T.K. had told him just last Saturday as Mason shared lunch with him and their mutual friend, Colin Stephens.

Ever since the morning after Essie's death, the three men had bonded. For Mason, the friendship had taken some getting used to, but it was one that he knew he needed. All of his life, he was accustomed to having friends who wasted away every non-working hour of the day, driving fast cars or sitting around playing poker, eating barbecue, and drinking beer. And breaking away from the bad company hadn't been easy.

Over the last year, Colin's and T.K.'s more productive lifestyles had been good examples for Mason. The banker and high school coach, respectively, had shown him that having fun didn't require him to spend large amounts of money that his blue collar job couldn't afford. And it certainly didn't call for him to spend hours away from home, leaving his wife to wonder about his whereabouts. But in all of their influence, Colin and T.K. hadn't convinced him to seek help for his inability to resume a normal marriage. Mason was already shaking his head before Colin could finish the sentence.

"Man, I told you before, that ain't for me. I ain't going to no quack. You can forget that, bruh. It just ain't gonna happen."

"If you stop seeing them as *quacks*, then you won't see it as a bad thing," T.K. insisted. "There's nothing wrong with seeing a professional. And if you can find one who is also a minister of God, why wouldn't you?"

"Forget it, Coach," Mason said, pausing to take a long sip from his glass of water. "I'm a man, and I'm not about to spill my guts to no stranger. I can handle my own problems."

"Oh, really?" Colin eyed Mason like he was daring him to lie for a second time.

T.K. tried again. "Going to a professional doesn't compromise your manhood, Mason. Plenty of *real* men see psychologists."

"It's been over a year," Colin added. "Do you know how long a year is? That's three hundred sixty-five days, man. And for you, you have to add another month or so to that. Man, it's been over four hundred days for you and Elaine. That's crazy." Colin slapped himself on the forehead for theatrical effect. "Actually, that's insane! I mean, I couldn't imagine going nearly that long without making love to my wife. Not by choice, anyway."

"Yeah? Well, I'll betcha you can't imagine your wife sexing it up with some other dude *by choice* either."

"Shhh! Keep your voice down," T.K. warned, taking a quick look around the room. "You don't

want to tell your private business to one psychi-
atric specialist, but you don't mind telling it to a
room full of spectators."

Before Mason could reply, Colin spoke again.
"Look, Mason, you're right. I can't imagine Angel
stepping out on me like that, and I'm not trying to
downplay what Elaine did. She was wrong, man,
and nobody's denying that. Even she knows that
she was wrong. But how long are you gonna keep
kicking her in the butt for her misbehavior? How
long do you plan to make her suffer?"

Mason shrugged as he took another bite of his
meal. "Man, Elaine ain't suffering. She's doing
just fine. I need just a little while longer, that's
all. She's waited this long with no problem, and
she'll be all right 'til I can work through this."

Colin and T.K.'s demeanors clearly indicated
that they didn't agree, but neither pressed the
issue any further, and Mason had been thankful
for that. But now, as he recalled the expression
on his wife's face as she watched him remove his
shirt, he wondered if they were right. Was Elaine
suffering? Behind that strong exterior, was she
yearning for him?

The questions in Mason's mind were tem-
porarily rinsed away under the pressure of the
pulsating water spewing from the shower head,

pouring over his tired body. Ten minutes later, when he finally emerged from the relaxing hot shower and stepped into the coolness of his bedroom, his thoughts returned.

Mason sat on the edge of the mattress and continued to use the towel to absorb the moisture from his skin. The strong smell of the smothered steak dinner that awaited him edged its way under the crack of his bedroom door and massaged his nostrils. Elaine had been trying very hard to please him since their reconciliation began all those months ago. She had been keeping a cleaner house, cooking on an almost daily basis, and giving him all the space he needed. Not once had she pressured him for intimacy. She'd kept her end of the bargain.

"Man, what's wrong with you?" Mason whispered to himself as he slipped on a fresh shirt and then stepped into a pair of blue jeans that were fitting snugger than usual around his expanding waist. He'd picked up fifteen pounds since Essie's death; a stark contrast from Elaine, who seemed to be shedding weight every week.

Mason's eyes fell to the ice blue night gown that lay draped across the bed. It must have been new because he'd never seen his wife wear it. He imagined that the satin fabric would fall beautifully over her new slimmer curves. Many nights as Elaine walked around the house in her sleep-wear, Mason would steal glances and long to reach out to her. His friends didn't understand the depth of his plight. They didn't know the half of it. It wasn't that he wouldn't make love to his wife. . . . He *couldn't* make love to her. As badly as Mason desired to be with Elaine, the haunting thoughts of her with another man had all but paralyzed him from the waist down. And it was frightening.

"Maybe it's time you seek psychological help along with spiritual counsel."

T.K.'s words ricocheted in Mason's head, begging him to comply, but he couldn't get himself to do it. The whole situation was just too embarrassing. What was he going to tell the quack? Was he actually supposed to admit to only being half a man? He wouldn't tell that to his own biological brothers, let alone a medical professional or a clergyman. Some things were just better kept unsaid, and this was one of them.

Mason suddenly shuddered as though a draft of cold air had burst through his closed bedroom windows. All his brothers were fathers whether they were husbands or not. Having babies was a big deal in his family, and of his mother's children, Mason was the only one who hadn't added any branches to the family tree. Until now, he'd escaped ridicule because of Elaine's multiple miscarriages, but if news of his new plight leaked out, Mason would become the shame of his mother and the laughing stock of his siblings. Even as he sat on the edge of his bed, Mason could almost hear the jokes of not being able to make his "soldier salute" or his "flag fly at full mast." His brothers loved him as much as they knew how to, growing up in a family as detached as theirs, but they could be ruthless. There was just no way he would admit to anyone that he couldn't get his body to respond to his desires. He'd just have to wait it out.

"I ain't the first man that's been cheated on, and I won't be the last," Mason said, keeping his voice level low so that Elaine wouldn't hear him. "I'm gonna get through this. I just need a little more time, that's all. I'm a man," he added, trying to keep himself convinced as he gently ran his index finger down the soft material of the gown that still lay on top of the bed comforter. "I'm a man, and I'll get through this. I *have* to find a way to get through this."

Chapter 3

Colin's Story

He held the phone to his ear and channeled all of his energies into remaining professional. "Yes, ma'am. . . . I understand, and I apologize on behalf of . . . Right. Right. I have everything I need in order to take care of it. You have been given every reason to be upset, Mrs. . . . Yes, ma'am. . . . Absolutely. I will give you a follow-up call next week. Yes, ma'am. Wednesday at the latest. Yes. Yes. All right. I under . . . Yes, I understand that, and we'll be in touch. Yes, ma'am, you have my word. Thank you, Mrs. Chambers. Have a good day. No, ma'am, I'm not trying to be facetious, I was . . . Yes, ma'am. I'm sorry that your day has already been doomed due to our incompetence. Yes, ma'am. The level of our stupidity staggers me as well. I fully understand your disdain, and I will take care of it personally. Yes, ma'am. You have my direct number if you need anything further. Sure thing. Bye."

Swear words that hadn't been a part of his vocabulary in years seemed to dangle on the end of Colin's tongue. Not the everyday, made-for-cable-TV words, but the *really* offensive kind. If he could just whisper them in the wind, he knew it would somehow relieve the insurmountable frustration he felt inside. Colin figured that if no one heard him, all would be well. No harm done.

But someone *would* hear him. And offending *Him* would be far worse than ruffling the feathers of any of his coworkers or the bank's clients. Even with the knowledge of it all, the temptation was still there. Colin had been saved for a long time, but submitting to God's will wasn't always easy; especially when everything around him seemed to be unraveling at the seams. Colin closed his eyes and prayed in silence. These days, he found himself doing a lot of that. When he was done, the desire to spit profanity had diminished, but the aggravation remained.

"That was thirty whole minutes of my life that I'll never be able to get back," he muttered while massaging his temples.

A bachelor's degree in accounting had trained Colin to be masterful when dealing with numbers, but it didn't prepare him to deal with irate customers like the woman with whom he'd just spoken. Although the call ended minutes ago, he could still hear Mrs. Chambers's shrilling accent ringing in his ears. The department store owner's voice was an annoying mixture of Fran Fine's from *The Nanny* and Karen Walker's from *Will & Grace*. It was enough to make any man lose his religion.

"Mr. Stephens, are you all right?" Her perfume marked her presence even before she spoke.

Colin looked up to see his new assistant, Nona Wright, standing in his open doorway with an armful of files that he hoped weren't being delivered to him. "Yes, Nona, I'm fine. Thanks." Colin rallied to assemble as genuine a smile as he could, then added, "Is it five yet?"

Nona laughed. "Not quite, but it's almost lunchtime if that makes it any better."

Colin shook his head and grunted. "I'm forwarding my phone to you for now," he informed Nona. "When you leave for lunch, just forward the calls into your voice mail. I'm going to need some quiet time to catch up on these accounts in my inbox."

"Will do." Nona disappeared around the corner, and to her boss's relief, the files in her hand disappeared with her. The perfume lingered.

It had been a rough year for Colin Stephens. What had been one of the happiest moments of his life—the birth of his son—had within hours, turned into one of the most traumatic. Shortly after Colin cut the umbilical cord and tearfully held his firstborn in his arms, he'd gotten the news of Essie's death. Mason had left the message on Colin's cell phone, and it was information that Colin kept from his wife for a full twenty-four hours. He knew that as soon as Angel found out that the woman she loved like a second mother had died in her sleep at 3:57 A.M., on the very same day and at the exact same time that Austin was born, she would be devastated. And she was.

Angel went into a deep depression immediately upon hearing the news, and for almost six months, Colin was forced to function like a celibate single father. It was the reason why he could relate, in part, to what Elaine must be going through with Mason. But Colin and Angel's situation had been different. Colin hadn't been celibate by choice, and his wife hadn't been denying him by choice either. At least, not spitefully.

Although he still had the demands of his nine-to-five job, Colin had become somewhat the sole caretaker of not only his son, but also his wife, who still hadn't healed from her labor and delivery. Neighborhood friends like Jennifer and Elaine had stepped in to help when they could, but for the most part, Colin, alone, bore the cross that Essie's death had delivered to his household.

"I feel like I'm enduring the calamity of a modern day Job." Three months into what had been the biggest trial of his adult life, Colin shared his heart with T.K. in a private telephone conversation. "I mean, I don't have the repulsive sores that the scriptures note that Job had. But every day that I roll out of bed to come to work, this sleep deprivation makes my body feel like it's been hit by a train."

From the other end of the line, T.K.'s reply had been, "Well, there's nothing wrong with feeling like Job as long as you handle the situation with the same faith that he did. Despite those sores and even the mocking of his wife, Job stood strong in his belief that God would work things out."

"Though He slay me, yet will I trust in Him," Colin had said in remembrance of Job's declaration in the biblical passage.

"That's what he said," T.K. agreed. "And although your wife is going through a hard time right now, you know she loves you, and she would never tell you to curse God and die, as Job's wife advised him to do. And for sure, you don't have Job's fair weather friends, who stood around accusing him of doing something dastardly to bring the trial on himself. You have people in your corner who are going before the throne of God for you daily, Colin."

"I know, and I appreciate that, man."

"God expects us to watch over our brothers in the time of need," T.K. had said. "You don't have to thank me or anybody else. I know you wouldn't even think twice about doing it for me."

"You're right," Colin had replied. "And I know that it's the prayers of the righteous that are keeping me sane right now. Keep praying for me, Coach."

"I will, Colin. As a matter of fact, let's take a minute to pray right now."

It was calls and prayers such as T.K.'s that eventually broke through the unseen barrier that for months had prevented Angel from enjoying her son or her husband. Colin still recalled the morning he woke up to the surprise of tender kisses being planted all over his face. At first he thought he was having an erotic dream. He'd had several of them over the months, with his wife in the starring role, so this one wouldn't have been the first. After a moment to gather his wits, Colin came to the pleasant awareness that this time it was reality.

Angel hadn't initiated any affection toward him since the moment she found out that her beloved Ms. Essie was dead. In that time period, their son had grown by leaps and bounds, and at a week shy of six months old, he was already holding up his head on his own, balancing his bottle without assistance, and even trying to scoot across the floor of his playpen to reach for toys. Angel's misery had caused her to miss it all, but it seemed that her recovery would make it all well worth it.

But Colin's celebration was short-lived. Aside from that early morning surprise rendezvous, Angel had given little time to anything else other than motherhood. As if she were trying to make up for lost time, she'd thrown all of her attention and energy into being the loving mother that she'd failed to be during all those months of misery. While Colin was glad that she was no longer in a deep depression, it almost felt to him as though she'd gone from one extreme to another.

To add more tension to his already stressful existence, a week after Angel regained some sense of returning to her normal self, the state of affairs at work began spiraling out of control.

"It has been determined that someone—most likely, someone on our staff—has been embezzling money from this branch of Wachovia Bank, and as of today, a major investigation is being launched. Everybody, myself included, is a suspect." Those were the words that the bank's president spoke at an impromptu Monday morning meeting with the managerial team.

Being that Colin knew he was innocent and had nothing to hide, he didn't expect to be affected by the investigation, but he was. A work environment that in the past had been a joy to be a part of, turned so uptight that Colin began to despise the very act of walking through the glass doors. And after four and a half months of rigorous inspections, investigations, and interrogations, Colin had had his fill and was all but ready to walk away from a $75,000 annual income. For him, it just wasn't worth it.

"But baby, if you leave, you'll look like you had something to do with the missing money," Angel had said to him after one of what had become their rare lovemaking sessions.

"It's not like I'd be the first to leave," he'd pointed out.

"No, but you'll be the first one to leave who had the inside track to commit the crime. Just be patient, baby. God will work it out."

Angel's encouragement and his patience eventually paid off when the investigation came to a thunderous close seven days later. Colin stood in his doorway and watched in awe as Ralph Snyder, his counterpart, the man he'd shared many lunches and several laughs with, was read his Miranda rights and escorted from the bank in handcuffs in the presence of his coworkers and the bank's midday customers.

The shake-up left a vacancy for a Senior Audit Manager that Wachovia didn't seem to be in any hurry to fill. According to them, a second audit manager wasn't an immediate need, and the current slumping economy wasn't giving them any encouragement.

Colin had little choice but to ready himself for the challenge. He had no idea that his one-time work acquaintance had left so many accounts, such as the one belonging to Mrs. Chambers, in such disarray. Taking on Ralph's accounts had almost doubled Colin's workload, leading to many days of working overtime. The bank had pacified him with a modest pay raise and by hiring him a personal assistant to replace Edna Shields, the fifty-something-year-old woman who'd served as assistant to both Colin and Ralph, but chose to leave the company during the chaos. Colin couldn't blame Edna for leaving, but he sure hated to see her go.

Nona Wright wasn't the first to apply or interview for the vacated position, but she was by far the most persistent. She followed up so often that Colin basically hired her just to shut her up. The way he saw it, anyone who wanted a job that badly, deserved a chance. It turned out to be a good move. Nona was a dedicated and dependable assistant who was just as efficient as Edna had been, but even with the administrative help, Colin's duties were still sometimes overwhelming.

"I'm getting ready to leave for lunch, Mr. Stephens." Nona overran Colin's thoughts as she knocked on the frame of his office door and stepped inside. "Are you planning to take a break for lunch?"

"I don't think I'll be able to today, Nona. Did you forward the phone into your voice mail?"

"I did." Nona paused. "I can stop somewhere and pick up something for you. If you're not gonna leave the office for lunch, at least you'll still be able to eat."

Colin looked up and smiled. "That sounds good. I'd appreciate it."

"Oh no, I'll take care of it," Nona said when she saw him reaching for his wallet. "You've been really patient with me these last couple of months as I've learned the ropes around here. The least I can do is treat you to a burger or something. What do you have a taste for?"

Colin wasn't used to being treated to lunch by any of his fellow coworkers, but the show of appreciation was a refreshing change. "Thanks, Nona. I'll have to return the favor one of these days." Tapping on his desk with the eraser of his pencil, Colin debated what to eat. Once upon a time, he could leave work and ride home on his lunch break to spend a few quality moments with his stay-at-home wife and young son, but those days had become distant fond memories. "How about a spicy chicken sandwich meal from Wendy's?" He liked those. "Does that fit your budget?"

"I think I can swing it on what y'all pay me," Nona said with a laugh while turning away and making her exit. "I'll bring it to you on my way back from lunch. Is that okay?"

"That's perfect," Colin said. "Close the door on your way out, will you?"

"Okey dokey."

With lunch taken care of and left in the quiet of his office, Colin focused his eyes on the pile of work that was displayed on his desk. The sight of his workload was sobering, and he leaned back in his chair and groaned. Needing a jolt of vigor that would help take him through the rest of the day, Colin picked up the phone and dialed. It would be a while before he'd again have the luxury of driving to his home on Braxton Way on his lunch break, but Colin knew that if he could hear his wife's voice, the second half of his day would be better than the first.

Chapter 4

T.K.'s Story

Thomas King. That was what his first and middle initials stood for, and nobody at Alpharetta High was privy to the knowledge of it. As a matter of fact, few people outside of his immediate family knew, and as far as Coach T.K. Donaldson was concerned, he'd like to keep it that way. Thomas King Donaldson was the name that belonged to his natural father—a man that T.K. never knew. His mother had been replaced by a new lover shortly after she told her boyfriend that she was pregnant, and for the life of him, T.K. couldn't understand why she still chose to name her child in honor of the bum. But she did. For a while, T.K. considered changing his given name. Even as a child growing up in Oregon, he recalled hating his legal identification and what it signified.

When T.K. completed seventh grade, his family relocated from Portland to Atlanta—clear across the map—and he seized the opportunity to make a new start. No longer would he be known to his peers as Thomas Donaldson. Instantly, he adopted his initials as if they were his legal name, and from that moment, everyone he met was introduced to T.K. Donaldson. Even his mother honored his wishes to change the way he was addressed. T.K. figured that she had lived to regret naming her son after such a worthless human being and was just as relieved to rid the name from her tongue as he was to rid it from his ears.

Regardless of the challenges that he'd faced as a child growing up in a single-parent home, T.K. had become one of the fortunate ones. His mother cared enough about him to place him in a mentoring program, and a higher force made sure that his mentor was also a man of God. By the time he was in high school, T.K. Donaldson was not only a thriving student, but he was also a dedicated Christian, heading an off-campus ministry where fellow classmates flocked on Friday nights for prayer and Bible Study. He was active in sports, playing basketball and competing in track and field. Running became a passion, and even after he graduated from high school, he continued the sport; only failing to make the 1992 U.S. Olympic team because of an injury he suffered in the qualifying meet. The United States would have swept the medals in the 400 meters relay competition had he been there; T.K. was sure of it.

The injury snuffed his dream of being an Olympic medalist, but his love for the track brought him full circle; back to the same high school—Alpharetta High—where he'd set many records as a teenager.

"Thirteen point four seconds, Jerrod!" the coach yelled as his favorite student crossed the 100 meter finish line well ahead of the rest of the pack. "That's a new record for you, kid!"

"Wooo-hooo!" Jerrod jumped up and down at the news, not even taking a moment to catch his breath after the high-energy sprint. "Yeah, baby; yeah!"

T.K. looked down at his stopwatch again and grinned. Jerrod's time was only three seconds longer than Dennis Mitchell's, the man who had taken the bronze medal in Barcelona in 1992.

"That's good, huh, Coach D?" the boy said as he jogged back toward his teacher.

"That's better than good, Jerrod." T.K. stopped short of telling him how close he was coming to national medal speed. Clapping his hands, T.K. looked out at the pack of boys and added, "Good job, guys, all of you are doing well. Keep up the good work." He was careful not to show favoritism; at least not in front of the others. "Get some water and take a fifteen minute rest. Then we'll do some stretching before you go home."

While the boys headed for the coolers, T.K. took to the track. Watching his students had stirred up a desire to take a few laps of his own. Every now and then, he envied the youngsters who had their whole lives and careers ahead of them.

T.K. was too old now, and he knew he'd never have the chance to realize his Olympic dreams. But he kept in shape, and at thirty-six he could still outrun some of his students. "Hey, Coach D. Wanna race?" But not Jerrod. He was the fastest of them all. The boy had just run from the water coolers to midway on the track where T.K. kept a steady pace, and he barely seemed winded.

"Not right now, Jerrod. You need to be taking advantage of this rest time," T.K. said between pants of breath. "You guys have to jog in place and do a few push-ups before we take it to the grass for your stretching."

"I'll be a'ight," Jerrod said, slowing his pace so that the drum of his shoes against the tarp beneath him was in rhythm with his coach's. "You coming over for dinner tonight?"

T.K. gave Jerrod a side glance. "Not that I know of."

"What you mean? You got somewhere else to be?"

"Nope."

"Then why you ain't coming over?"

Looking again at Jerrod, T.K. smiled. "I haven't been invited."

"Come on, Coach. You don't need no invitation. You always come over for dinner on Friday nights."

"That's because I'm always invited," T.K. said, bringing his run to an end after completing two laps. He took a moment to rest his hands on his knees and catch his breath. Then, standing to his full six-foot-three-inch height, T.K. looked down at Jerrod, who was five inches shorter. "A man should never take a woman's kindness for granted, Jerrod. Just because your mom generally invites me over for dinner on Fridays doesn't give me the right to start expecting her to cook for me every week. When she invites me, I gladly accept, but if she doesn't, I know how to cook for myself."

Jerrod pressed together his lips and slowly nodded, like he'd just been taught a valuable lesson about women. "But if she invites you, you'll come, right?"

T.K. beamed again. He knew that Jerrod had become quite fond of him over the past several months, and the feeling was mutual. He was grateful that God had chosen him to bring balance and provide a positive male influence in the life of a boy who had grown up much like himself. Before coming into Jerrod's life, T.K. knew the teenager had been fatherless and was starving for discipline and direction. He cringed to think what might have happened had he not been around for Jerrod after the death of Essie.

When Essie died, Jerrod began lashing out at those around him and showing strong signs of returning to a lifestyle that he'd barely been rescued from prior to her untimely demise. Losing Essie had been harrowing for so many people, and Jerrod seemed to have been hit harder than almost all of them. The aging woman had become the boy's lifeline, giving him guidance, wisdom, and understanding that he'd never known. It had been T.K. that God had given the strength to interrupt the setback that Jerrod had begun suffering. It hadn't been easy, but the results were rewarding.

"Will you, Coach? Will you come to dinner if Ma invites you?"

"Sure I will. But don't you go telling her that, you hear? I don't want Jen going out of her way to try and accommodate me. Besides, I was thinking of taking both of you out to dinner after church on Sunday. So if she wants to skip a Friday, that's fine."

The announcement seemed to please Jerrod. "Can we go to Benihana like we did the last time? I like watching them men cook the food in front of us. That was real cool. Ma liked it too."

T.K. knew Jerrod had thrown in the last part for leverage. The boy knew that if Jennifer was impressed, T.K. would most likely agree to the return visit. "Yeah, we can go back to Benihana. That'll be your reward for breaking your own record today; how about that?"

"That works," Jerrod said with his grin returning. "Thanks, Coach."

"You're welcome. Now get back over there with the other boys so you can prepare yourself for our final drill and cooldown."

As though T.K. had fired a starting pistol, Jerrod broke into a full sprint. Not since his own days as a young runner had T.K. seen a boy embrace the sport with such drive. Stopping at a nearby bench, the coach sat down to tighten his shoe strings. As he did so, T.K. came to another realization. Not since his college years had he been as enthralled by a woman as he was with Jennifer Mays.

Theirs was an instant attraction that T.K. found himself resisting, even though he didn't want to. Jennifer was beautiful and her heart was golden, but after his college relationship all those years ago, T.K. had promised himself that he would never again get involved with a woman who didn't know Christ as her personal Savior. It was just too hard to successfully sustain such a connection; not to mention that an unequally yoked relationship went against instructions clearly outlined in the Word of God.

T.K. and his college sweetheart dated for nearly two years, and their different priorities were a constant issue that kept their relationship strained. Like Jennifer, Deena was attractive, smart, and one of the kindest people he knew, but she hadn't dedicated her life to the Lord. Although they had openly discussed the parameters of their courtship, and Deena professed to be on the same page as he, T.K.'s vow of celibacy eventually became too much for her, and the woman stepped outside of their bond to find the satisfaction that her flesh needed. The experience was painful and embarrassing. They were both active and popular students on the campus of Georgia State University, so the breakup was a public one. It was an ordeal that T.K. promised himself and God that he would never go through again.

So when he met Jennifer shortly before Essie's death, the instant gravitation had red flags and whistles assaulting his eyes and ears. But only weeks after the funeral that brought droves of people to Temple of God's Word, Jennifer made a life changing decision at the very church where Essie had worshipped for decades. In many ways, T.K. felt like he owed Essie a posthumous deed of appreciation for putting him and Jennifer together. It had been the old woman's life that had been a beacon for Jennifer as well as many other people who lived in the subdivision of Braxton Park.

That was eleven months ago, and for nine of those eleven months, T.K and Jennifer had been frequent companions, seeing each other at least once a week; twice on weeks that either of them decided to visit the other's church on Sunday morning. And they spoke on the telephone daily.

Their relationship was ideal for T.K. Jennifer had her own life, her own friends, and a promising career working as an executive secretary at an insurance firm. She didn't smother him, and she didn't require that he spend all of his free hours around her. Jennifer treated him with the utmost respect, and T.K. returned the favor. Most importantly, she was his best friend. He could talk to Jennifer about anything, knowing that she would listen with unbiased ears. "Come on, Coach!"

T.K. looked up from the shoe that he'd been staring at robotically for a long while and saw several of the boys in the distance, waving their hands like they were ready to be done for the day. All of them enjoyed running, but few of them cared for the circuit training that he incorporated before they stretched their muscles.

Standing and taking the first steps that would eventually deliver him back to his awaiting athletes, T.K. focused his eyes on Jerrod, watching as the boy chatted and laughed with his classmates. What would Jerrod think if T.K. told him how he really felt about Jennifer? In front of her son, Jennifer had never kissed T.K. or even held his hand, so T.K. wasn't sure what Jerrod thought of their relationship. The definition of a girlfriend to a high school student was shallow compared to that of mature adults. What if T.K. told Jerrod that his affiliation with Jennifer wasn't just a casual one wherein they hung out on Friday nights or went to church together on Sundays? What if the boy knew that he thought about Jennifer during the day and dreamed of her at night? What if he knew that there was a little red box tucked away in T.K.'s nightstand that housed a ring that he was just waiting for the right moment to present?

T.K. smiled nervously to himself. *What will Jerrod say if I tell him that I love his mother?*

Chapter 5

Angel's Story

"Is it getting any better?" she panted, trying to catch her breath. "I mean, do you see any improvement at all?"

Ever since Angel Stephens recovered from what her doctor diagnosed as postpartum depression coupled with an overdose of dejection resulting from Essie's death, she had become a constant companion for her neighbor on mornings that Elaine went jogging. It was the only time she took advantage of the part-time daycare offered by the learning center two miles from Braxton Park. When the stay-at-home mom wasn't exercising, she relished the opportunity to saturate her son with love and attention. The regular workout schedule had been instrumental in helping Angel lose the pounds that her pregnancy had packed on, but even after reaching her ideal weight, she kept running to maintain her level of fitness.

"He rarely goes anywhere besides work and church, and we haven't argued in months, but what good is it to have him home if he's not being a husband? What good is a loving relationship without the loving?" The lines in Elaine's face were due more to aggravation than fatigue. "It's been over a year, Angel, and Mason is still sleeping on that doggone sofa. I used to love my living room furniture; now it makes me sick just to look at it. I feel like the sofa stole my man. The cushions on the couch get to have him lying on top of them every night, and he ain't been on top of me in ages. Girl, I'm jealous of my own sofa!"

Angel couldn't help but laugh. "Shut up, Elaine."

"I admit that I screwed up. Angel, I made a colossal mess of things, and I'm not even trying to say that my husband should have forgiven me overnight and been ready to come right back to the bedroom. If he had messed around on me, I know it would have taken me a while. As a matter of fact, if I'm really real about this thing, I can't even say that I would have even stayed with him. But Lord have mercy! If I were gonna stay, I sure wouldn't have been sleeping in separate quarters for this long, especially if I claimed to have forgiven him."

The conversation paused while the two women took their daily detour, cutting through a path that led them through a quiet community of houses that made up the Windward subdivision. Regardless of how many times Angel saw the houses in this area, she was astonished by their beauty. The massive five-and six-bedroom dwellings carried price tags that ranged from four to six hundred thousand dollars. They were like mini mansions.

Angel never asked Elaine why she chose to cut through the neighborhood, but she reasoned within herself that it was done to purposefully avoid passing the Goodyear shop where the man with which Elaine had had her brief affair, worked as a mechanic.

"Am I being unreasonable?" Elaine's voice forced its way into Angel's mental opinion, and it sounded pleading. "Am I expecting too much of Mason too fast? Tell me the truth, Angel. Am I being selfish? I really don't want to be selfish about this. I mean, when I got caught up in that mess with Danté, I took selfishness to the ultimate level. I don't want to sound like I'm still only thinking of myself in all of this."

"Okay, stop running." Angel had reached her limit. She didn't know how Elaine did it, but one thing was certain; Angel knew her lungs hadn't yet achieved the capacity of her friend's. When Angel first began running with her, the entire workout would only be two miles long. Now it was four, and Elaine could run every bit of it without a break. "I'm not the expert on this subject matter, Elaine," Angel said through huffs of air as they slowed to a brisk walk. "God has forgiven you of your sins, and from all outside appearances, Mason has too."

"Then why is he still having his love affair with the couch? And why does it feel like God is still punishing me?"

Angel took a quick side glance at Elaine and saw tears in her eyes that sufficiently explained the unsteadiness of her voice. Elaine was fragile, and while Angel knew that she had to be truthful, she was also mindful that she needed to be compassionate. "God is not still punishing you, Elaine. Don't let the enemy make you believe He is, don't let him make you doubt God's forgiveness."

Angel took a breath, and then added, "Men are so different from women, and just like they can't fully figure us out, we can't fully figure them out either. But one thing is sure; by nature, we are more nurturing and forgiving, and on the broad scale, they are more proud and egotistical than we are. And as long as these traits are used in the manner in which God intended them to be used, their pride and egotism is a good thing. Men need to be that way in order to protect and take care of their families like God intends for them to do. This could just be my own opinion, but I truly believe that because of our different genetic makeup, women can forgive and move on easier than men can. So while you very well might have forgiven Mason and would have moved back into the bedroom with him by now, he just may not be able to pick up the pieces as readily."

"*Readily*? This isn't readily, Angel, it's been a whole year."

"I know."

"And I'm a healthy, vibrant woman."

"I know."

"With *needs*."

Angel sighed and searched for something encouraging to say. "I know, Elaine. And God promised to supply all of your needs according to His riches in glory." It was the best that she could come up with on such short notice.

"Angel, I don't think God can fulfill this particular need; if you know what I mean."

"Yes, He can, Elaine. Not physically, maybe. But God made you, so He can adjust your mind and your desires so that you aren't feeling so lonely and empty and—"

"Hot?"

"Elaine!" Angel would have laughed had she not seen the tear that trickled from Elaine's eye.

"Well, that's what it is, Angel. Just call it what it is. My body's fields are on fire, and I need Mason to put out the flames." Elaine stopped walking, and Angel stopped with her.

"I know this is hard for you, Elaine."

"No, you don't. You have no idea. You're as clueless as a dumb blonde about this." The tears were streaming heavier now. "You may understand what it's like to want to be with the man you love, but that's as far as your understanding goes. The man you want to be with also wants to be with you, that's not my testimony. My man can't even stand to get in the same bed with me, let alone *be* with me. You've got this great husband who worships the ground you walk on, Angel. You can't even come close to understanding what it's like to have a husband that treats you like his college dorm mate or some other kind of platonic friend."

Angel reached out and touched Elaine's arm. She wanted to refute her accusations, and tell her that there had been times in her and Colin's marriage where they'd experienced what she was experiencing with Mason. But it wouldn't be the truth. Colin was always ready and willing. Although lately. . . .

"Angel, I know what I did was horrible."
Elaine's sobs flooded out Angel's reality check.
"If Mason had left me last spring, I couldn't have
blamed him one bit. But he didn't. He decided
to stay, and he agreed that we would work on
this together. We made a plan to get back in
the church and start praying more. We've done
all that. We go to church and worship together
every Sunday, and Mason prays just as much as
I do. I can't tell you how many times I've walked
into the living room and found him on his knees.
But even in all of that, he hasn't touched me."

Angel could feel Elaine's hurt and her sense of
abandonment. *God, give me something to say.*
Right now, Angel felt useless; like her presence
was of no benefit to Elaine's broken spirit. To
make matters worse, a feeling of hypocrisy was
nudging Angel. How could she encourage Elaine
when she had a husband who probably shared
Elaine's sentiment? Did Colin feel abandoned
too? Angel shook the idea from her head. This
wasn't about her; it was about Elaine, and her
friend needed encouragement. But Angel had no
idea what to say. Elaine, however, was not at a
loss for words.

"I thought that if I really made myself desir-
able, Mason wouldn't be able to resist me. I
purchased sexy clothes and racy nightgowns, got

myself this sassy new haircut, and even got down to my premarital, pre-pregnancy weight and . . ." Elaine gasped and put her hands over her mouth as if she were just mobbed by a horrid thought. "Is that it? You think he won't touch me because every time he's given me a baby I've lost it, and he just doesn't want to have to go through the disappointment again?"

"No!" Angel said the word as emphatically as she could. It was no secret that Elaine had suffered three miscarriages in her eight-year marriage to Mason, and it was no secret that Mason wanted children. But Angel refused to believe that it had anything to do with his rejection of her. "Now you stop that," Angel scolded. "You're gonna make yourself sick if you keep this up. You're just looking for a reason to blame yourself for this, and I'm not going to let you do that."

"Then what is it, Angel? If it's not that God is punishing me, and it's not that Mason hasn't forgiven me for being with another man, and it isn't that he doesn't want to take the chance on impregnating me again only to have me lose the baby; then what is it?"

"I don't know what it is," Angel blurted. "I wish I knew, but I don't. But one thing for sure is that none of this is your fault."

"How can you say it's not my fault? I'm the one who—"

"I didn't say you didn't screw up, Elaine. What I'm saying is after apologizing to Mason and after getting forgiveness from the Lord, your husband's decision not to touch you isn't your fault. There has to be a shortcoming somewhere else. Something that hasn't been addressed yet, maybe."

"There's nothing that hasn't been addressed. Mason and I have talked about everything." Elaine pointed at her fingers as she listed them. "I told him every sordid detail of my error. He told me why he'd gotten so involved with expensive cars and worthless friends. We talked about how our marriage got off track. I told him how much I couldn't stand his meddling mama, and he stepped in and stopped that old hag from calling me and asking me when I was going to give her a grandchild. He told me what he wanted out of this marriage, and I told him what I wanted out of it. We talked about what God wanted from us and what we wanted from Him. What else needs to be addressed?"

"I can't answer that, Elaine. Only God knows all things, but I really think that the two of you need to get into counseling and talk to a professional. Sometimes things get buried so deep inside of us that we forget that they're there. It's like trying to hide something from someone else, and you hide it so well that you can't remember where you placed it. so basically, you've also hid it from yourself. I'm not saying that's the case with y'all; I'm just saying that if there's a chance that there is a stone that's been left unturned or an issue that hasn't been openly discussed between the two of you, a therapist can probably pinpoint it over time."

"Mason would never go to a psychiatrist. He's way too proud . . . or way too stubborn. I don't know which it is, but I know he'd never go."

"What about a marriage counselor at the church?"

Elaine shook her head. "He'd never do it."

"How do you know? Have you asked him?"

"When we first began reconciling, yes," Elaine admitted. "But he wasn't feeling it then, said he didn't want to bring nobody else up in our business. I think that as a man, he was just too embarrassed at the thought of admitting to some stranger that his wife cheated on him. And after we started talking and getting along so well, I didn't think the humiliation was necessary either."

Elaine used her hands to wipe the remaining moisture from her cheeks, and then used the bottom of her shirt to dry her eyes completely. "I thought we'd be back to normal way before now, Angel. Ms. Essie died just days after all of this happened, but when I first told her what I had done, she told me that if I believed in God, He would fix my marriage, and when He was done, it would be better than it had ever been. At first, I thought it was gonna be as easy as it sounded. The morning after she died, when all of us went to church together, Mason knew how much I was grieving. He put his arm around me and comforted me during the service. I thought it was a start, but since then . . . nothing."

Angel shook off the onset of a sharp pain she felt at hearing Essie's name. She was closer to Essie and had known her for years longer than anyone else in the neighborhood. Yet everyone, except her, had had the opportunity to worship together at the church in Essie's memory and attend her funeral for a proper good-bye. Angel's inability to do either of these things had haunted her almost every day of the past year.

"I just don't know what to do," Elaine said, breaking the lingering silence.

"Ms. Essie was right, Elaine. All we can do is pray, and while God may not answer the way we want Him to or even *when* we want Him to, He always comes through for us in a way that is best for us. Ms. Essie always told me that God was always on time. His time may not be our time, but His time is *on* time. He knows how much we can bear, and He doesn't put more on us than we're capable of handling."

"Well, I think He got this one wrong." Elaine dropped both her arms by her side in despair. "I'm not nearly as strong as He apparently thinks I am. God must've gotten me mixed up with you. If this were you, you'd probably be able to handle it a whole lot better than I can. I know what I did was a horrible, unthinkable thing, and I know it was wrong on every level. But sometimes, Angel . . . Sometimes there are nights when my bed gets so lonely that praying doesn't work. And as wrong as I know it was, sometimes I think about stepping out and—"

"No, Elaine." Angel's voice had become stern again. "Don't you even let that come out of your mouth. You can't allow wicked thoughts like that to enter your mind, and you definitely can't let them slip from your tongue."

Elaine hung her head, and her words were only slightly above a whisper. "God must hate me right now, but I'm only being honest about how I feel."

"Look at me, Elaine." Angel used her hand to force Elaine to look into her eyes. "I wouldn't be your friend if I didn't tell you the truth, and I love you too much to stand idly by and watch you do this to yourself. What you're feeling is very normal, okay? God doesn't hate you. The flesh has desires, and God made it so that it would—it's natural. And you know what else? The Bible tells us that our flesh is always at war with our spirit, which means that we'll always be tempted to do wrong, but it's up to us to do right. If we fall, God is faithful, and He's there to forgive us. But we don't have to fall. I'm here for you, Elaine, and anytime you need someone to talk to, you can call me. We live two streets from each other, so you can come by and we can pray together whenever you need. But I don't ever want you to allow those words that almost came out of your mouth just now to reach the tip of your tongue again. Do you hear me?"

Two fresh tears—one from each eye—fell onto Elaine's cheeks, but it was her silence that was the most troubling for Angel. Essie had always said that silence was a calm, unspoken consent. But in this case, Angel wasn't so sure.

Chapter 6

Jennifer's Story

"I'm almost ready, Jerrod," she called to her son. Seeing that she hadn't yet decided upon which outfit she would wear to church this Sunday, Jennifer immediately realized that her pacifying answer to his fourth call to her was far from the truth.

Normally, it was she who would be waiting for Jerrod to finish getting ready. Countless times, Jennifer had impatiently stood at the front door or sat in the driver's seat of her car wondering what on earth could a fifteen-year-old boy have to do that required so much time. If they were late to Sunday morning worship today, Jennifer would have no one to blame but herself.

Standing half-dressed and with her hands perched on her hips, the thirty-one-year-old single mother looked over the two garments that had made it to the final round of her decision

making process. It would be a toss up between
the tangerine dress and the beige pants suit. But,
as pretty as both of them were, neither seemed
eye-catching enough to wear to T.K.'s church.
Not that the people at her boyfriend's church
were any more refined or well-to-do than the
folks at Temple of God's Word. In fact, neither
the church nor its members had very much to do
with Jennifer's dilemma. It was T.K. Every time
she was in his presence, Jennifer felt the need to
be her best self. For the first time in her life, she
was dating a man who treated her like she meant
more to him than what she could give him. T.K.
was the best man she'd ever known, and because
of that, he made her want to be a better woman.

"The dress," Jennifer said, making her decision vocal.

From somewhere in the front of the house,
Jerrod hollered, "Ma, can I—?"

"No." She didn't see a need in letting him
finish the request. Ever since turning fifteen
six months ago, Jerrod, without a permit to le-
gitimize or legalize his desires, had asked her at
least one hundred times if he could drive her car.
Jennifer's intuition told her that she'd just cut off
request number one hundred one.

With her dress finally on, Jennifer slipped her
feet into sandals that maximized the splendor
of her fresh pedicure, and then paused to take a

long look at herself in the full length mirror that was attached to the back of her bedroom's door. Using her fingers as a makeshift comb, Jennifer gently raked through her hair to revitalize the curls that had been disturbed when she pulled her dress over her head. In her reflection, she spotted a flash from the birthstone ring that she always wore on her left hand. Hastily, Jennifer removed it from her finger and placed it in the jewelry box that sat on the edge of her dresser.

"You'll feel naked, but only for a little while." She spoke the words to her finger as though it were a person, and then giggled at her own silliness.

When T.K. was leaving Jennifer's house on Friday night after sharing dinner with her and Jerrod, he whispered in her ear that he had a surprise for her and wanted to take both her and her son out to dinner on Sunday to present it.

"You sure you want Jerrod there?" she'd asked, her heart racing with anticipation.

"Yes," T.K. replied, still whispering and sending mounting chills down Jennifer's back. "This is big news and it involves him too."

Even now, as Jennifer recounted the moment, she found it difficult not to jump up and down with excitement. This was a moment that she'd dreamed about since she was a little girl, playing dress-up in her room to keep herself entertained while her parents had some petty, but loud disagreement somewhere down the hall. Jennifer would put on her best Sunday dress—the one her grandmother had made for her—and stand in front of the mirror holding plastic flowers; pretending that she was about to walk down the aisle to marry the man who would rescue her from her horrendous existence. It had been a long wait, but she could feel it in her bones; her Prince Charming was about to make his majestic entrance. And even though she'd risen from the life of poverty and abuse and made something of herself despite the statistics, Jennifer would still be ready to ride away into the sunset with T.K.

"Mrs. T.K. Donaldson," she whispered, rubbing her ring finger with gentle strokes. Jennifer used her fingers to silence the tears that screamed to be released from her eyes. She had to hold it together. When T.K. proposed to her today, she had to maintain a look of surprise. It wouldn't be right for T.K. to know that she'd already figured out his plan. *Men are so transparent.* She grinned at her own thought.

"Okay. One last look and I've got to get out of here." Jennifer wasn't totally satisfied with the image that stared back at her, but she was out of time. The church that T.K. attended was one of Atlanta's most popular, and on Sunday mornings, prime seating disappeared quickly. The drive from Alpharetta to New Hope Church in Stone Mountain was thirty minutes. Unless they encountered very little traffic today, Jennifer feared that her indecisiveness had already guaranteed that she and her son wouldn't get the opportunity to sit anywhere near T.K.

"We're gonna be late, Ma," Jerrod pointed out as soon as she rounded the corner from her bedroom to the living room where he waited. "Why you didn't just let Coach pick us up like he did the last time? He ain't never late. We would've got to church on time if we had been riding with him."

Jennifer knew that they were running late and had no need to be reminded. She was already unnerved enough, and now Jerrod was adding to it. "How many times have you made us late?" she snapped. "I run behind schedule one time and you want to gripe about it, but how many times has getting to church late been your fault, Jerrod? Huh?"

"That's different, Ma," he said in a matter-of-fact tone. "Everybody be late at Temple of God's Word. Ms. Essie used to say so herself. She was the only one who would get to church on time and would have to just sit out in her car and wait for somebody with a key to show up. So when we're late getting there, we're really on time, 'cause ain't nobody else gonna be there at eleven either."

Jennifer wanted to wallop him one good time, but Jerrod was too old for spankings now, and his words were way too accurate for her to contest. She used her hand to nudge him out onto the front porch, and then locked the door behind them.

"You sure I can't—"

"No, Jerrod." Jennifer knew that he would make one last plea for her car keys, and she'd prepared herself for it. "You get in Driver's Ed. next school term and get your learner's permit, and then I'll start letting you practice."

"Practice? I don't need no practice, Ma. I can drive. I used to do it all the time when I was a freshman. Big Dog Freddie used to let me—"

"Don't *ever* let me hear you say that jailbird's name again. Do you hear me? That's why he's doing time now. Because he's stupid. And you didn't have no better sense than to let him have you doing stupid stuff too. You used to do a lot of things you shouldn't have done when you were a freshman, Jerrod. That's nothing to brag about."

As she pulled out of the subdivision onto the main highway, Jennifer noted her son's sunken demeanor. She hated it when he made reference to anything he used to do when he was a part of that wannabe school gang last year. It had been a dark time in both their lives, and Jennifer didn't care to be reminded of it even now. Despite that, she knew that her tone had been excessively harsh. Jerrod had proven himself to be a good kid since being rescued by Essie's prayers and God's grace. He didn't deserve for her to take her tension out on him.

"I'm sorry," Jennifer said over the soft melody of Praise 102.5, the radio station that single-handedly prevented complete silence in the car for the first few miles of their drive. "I just don't like to hear you talk about Freddie or the Do-bermans. That bunch of hoodlums could have landed you in jail had you been caught driving without a license."

When Jerrod didn't offer a reply, Jennifer stole a brief glance, then turned her eyes back to the road ahead. In spite of it all, Jerrod was a sensitive child, and sometimes his tough ex-terior made Jennifer forget that. Her son had apologized for the deeds of his past, and Jennifer knew that she had no right to dredge up anything that had happened back then. More than a year ago, she had assured Jerrod that all was forgiven and forgotten, but this wasn't the first time she'd chosen to rehash it all.

Jennifer took another quick look in her son's direction. He hadn't moved an inch since she offered her apology. Jerrod continued to stare out the window, looking as if he hadn't heard a word she'd said. His stare was so convincing that Jennifer wondered if he had.

"I said I'm sorry, Jerrod." It was only then that she saw movement.

He shrugged his shoulders in a carefree manner. "It's a'ight, Ma. I'm cool."

The twenty-five mile drive seemed much longer with no dialogue flowing between them, but eventually Jennifer was navigating her car in the already congested parking lot of New Hope Church, a house of worship best known for its respected pastor, Reverend B.T. Tides.

When Jennifer and Jerrod pressed their way through the entrance along with other congregants who had barely made it inside before the praise and worship leaders took the stand, they had very little choice on where they would sit. The usher directed them to an exit row seating midway into the edifice. They weren't the best seats in the house, but at least the two of them weren't forced to get their best view of the pulpit from captured images portrayed on wide-screen monitors that hung from the ceiling. Those seats would be the reward of those who didn't make it in before the opening prayer that was soon to follow.

Jennifer loved the energy that immediately met her at the door every time she visited T.K.'s church. The services at Temple of God's Word were often spirited too, but for Jennifer, it wasn't to be compared.

"Do you see Coach?" Jerrod leaned in close so that Jennifer could hear him over the music.

"Among all these people? Are you kidding?" Jennifer laughed, mostly because she was glad to have her son speaking to her again.

Jennifer had barely gotten the words out when she felt a tug on her arm. Her heart fluttered just a bit when she turned to her left to see T.K. standing in the aisle motioning for her and Jerrod to follow him. Grabbing her belongings and her son's arm, Jennifer asked no questions. The three of them came to a stop at seating that was only four rows from the front of the church. T.K. had reserved two seats just for them.

"If you aren't standing already, let us corporately reverence the Lord by doing so at this time." Minister Jackson Tides, the pastor's eldest son, took the podium and gave his orders before leading the opening prayer.

Jennifer bowed her head as instructed, but she struggled to meditate on God. She found herself wishing that the service would suddenly shift into the speed of light and that this opening prayer would all at once become the benediction. Her palms sweated and her stomach churned, knowing what was about to take place over dinner this afternoon. *I wonder if T.K. is as nervous as I am.*

"In the matchless name of our Lord and Savior, Jesus Christ, we pray. Amen, amen, and amen."

It was the only part of the prayer that Jennifer had heard. Shamefully, she had to admit to herself that all other words that Minister Tides had uttered were as unintelligible as the "Wah, wah, wah, wah" dialogue of the teacher on every Charlie Brown movie she'd ever seen. Jennifer was remorseful that she'd allowed her mind to stray so far away from what was going on in the worship service, but there was no way that God didn't understand her excitement. No one knew better than He knew how long she'd waited for a decent man to share her heart, her home, and her son with.

Jerrod's finally going to have a dad . . . a real dad! Jennifer could hardly restrain herself. For more than fifteen years, Jerrod had been forced to grow up in a single parent home, and much of his life had been negatively affected because of it. With no help from Jennifer's parents, who expelled her from their home, or the boy she'd allowed to impregnate her, she and Jerrod had struggled for many years.

Jennifer remembered the process of having to relocate from her parents' dysfunctional home to an overcrowded group home for pregnant teens in Anderson, South Carolina; then to project housing that wasn't fit for human dwelling. Her time at the group home had run out, and the roach infested apartment was the best she could afford on a hotel maid's salary. They eventually moved to housing provided by the Department of Housing and Urban Development. It surpassed the living conditions of their previous dwelling, but not by much. Only after Jennifer relocated to Atlanta and obtained an associates degree, was she fortunate enough to net her current job and move her son to Braxton Way. By then, though, Jerrod had already been poisoned by his circumstances and environment, and it had taken a lot of prayer to turn his life around. A lot of prayer that only an old sanctified lady could deliver to God's ears.

That rescue had come compliments of Essie Mae Richardson. Now, Jennifer was ecstatic to know that their next step up would be a gift *she* could give her son. She had prayed for a testimony like this—one wherein she could glorify God because *she* had made a marked impact on her son's future. It would be because she had finally made a good decision on what kind of man to bring into her son's life that he would finally have a family complete with a mother *and* a father.

The praise and worship service was in high gear now, but Jennifer's mind took turns paying attention to the goings on in front of her and sinking into deep thought about what was going to happen later in the day. When the high-spirited music and singing ended, the service was turned over to the pastor.

"Before you take your seats," he said, "I want you to simply tell your neighbor that *all these other things will be added unto you.*"

Those seven words echoed through the sanctuary, followed by the scuffling noises of thousands of people being seated.

In mostly attentive silence, Jennifer listened as Reverend Tides expounded on Matthew 6:33, admonishing his listeners to put God first in every thing they did.

"So many times we find ourselves doing things at the wrong time and for the wrong reasons," he said. "But how many of you know that God is a jealous God? He wants to be first in everything we do. And while He will allow us to go on with our own agenda for a while, God will eventually make His presence known. He will shake us up with disappointment so that we will realize that it's not about us!" Reverend Tides scoped out the room for dramatic effect, then said, "Sometimes He has to do that so that we will allow Him to take His rightful place in our lives. Do y'all hear what I'm saying?"

"Amen," Jennifer's voice echoed amongst many others.

Reverend Tides was such a charismatic speaker, far more so than Reverend Owens. As Jennifer clapped her hands in support of the preacher's words, she surmised that she wouldn't mind a bit, having to transfer her membership from Temple of God's Word to New Hope Church once she and T.K. got married. As a matter of fact, at that precise moment, in the place where she sat, Jennifer made up her mind that she would do the honors next Sunday—one week after her engagement was official—to give T.K. a preview of just how spiritually in sync with him she would be as his wife.

A steady rainfall was being delivered from the skies as service dismissed two and a half hours after it began. Jennifer figured it would be the adjustment that would most likely be the hardest to make once she became a member of New Hope Church. Service at Temple of God's Word rarely ever exceeded ninety minutes. Each Sunday, Reverend Owens faithfully kept his message at thirty minutes, like his job was in jeopardy if he dared to go over.

"Stay here," T.K. instructed Jennifer and Jerrod as they stood in the foyer of the church. "I'll bring the vehicle around. It doesn't make sense for us go to the restaurant in separate cars. I'll bring you back to get yours once we're done celebrating."

Celebrating. Jennifer's heart delivered a massive thump that nearly made her lose her balance. *C'mon, Jen; keep it together*, she encouraged herself, leaning against the wall and lifting her foot to readjust her shoe in an attempt to mask her near blunder.

"Wait up, Coach." Jerrod shot out the door behind T.K. as though waiting for someone to bring a car around to avoid a little humidity wasn't a manly thing to do.

From the glass doors, Jennifer watched both of them take strides that were long and quick into the congested parking lot. She imagined that once she and T.K. were married, people who hadn't known them before would just assume that Jerrod was T.K.'s biological child. From behind, they shared like features. Both were tall and long-limbed with similar low-fade haircuts. They shared the same smooth brown complexion too.

Jennifer was pleasantly surprised when the burgundy Ford Escape rolled into view. T.K. favored his Corvette and drove it most often. Jennifer liked the sporty car too. It was sharp and sexy, just like its owner. But she preferred the newer and roomier Escape. T.K. must have planned for them to ride in the same vehicle all along, and that was probably his reason for driving the SUV today. The Corvette wouldn't have been able to comfortably accommodate all three of them.

The smile on Jennifer's face widened when she saw the driver's side door of the truck open and T.K. climb out with an umbrella in his hand. Other waiting women were making mad dashes to the cars that their men had only gone as far as bringing to the front door area. But Jennifer stepped out into dryness as T.K. walked all the way inside and then covered both their heads with the oversized portable shelter. He stayed with her until she was inside the car, then he closed the door behind her and returned to his place in the driver's seat.

"Thank you," Jennifer said, smiling as prettily as she could. "I'm sorry you had to get all wet."

T.K. returned her smile. "No harm done. The clothes are washable and the seats are leather."

"Coach D," Jerrod called, breaking the mood as he slid forward in the backseat and placed his head between those of the adults.

"Yeah, kid?" T.K. pulled out of the line of cars and headed for the highway as he answered.

"What's the big surprise? Why you being all mysterious and junk?"

Jennifer wanted to backhand him and tell him to sit back and shut up. The last thing she needed was for Jerrod to place any added pressure on T.K. and spook him into changing his mind. Jennifer knew men. It was hard enough for them to make a commitment without the interrogation.

"You'll see, Jerrod." The full beam on T.K.'s face didn't indicate any second thoughts. "Just sit back and buckle up, we'll be at Benihana in no time." He stole a glance at Jennifer and added, "I hope you guys are ready for this."

A lump rose in Jennifer's throat, and she swallowed back a joyful sob that fought to be released. Keeping her eyes straight on the road ahead, she rubbed the ring finger of her left hand. *I know I am.*

Chapter 7

Colin's Story

"Angel didn't go running with you this morning?" he asked into the telephone that he balanced between his shoulder and ear. With his free hand, Colin tapped his fingers against his thigh.

"No," Elaine replied. "She said she was taking Austin-Boston shopping. I think she heard about a sale going on at one of the outlet malls or something."

Austin-Boston was the nickname that Colin had given his son even before the child was born. Their friends were so accustomed to hearing him refer to the boy by the term of endearment that sometimes they did the same—especially when they were speaking to Colin.

"I know about the sale," Colin said. His scowl matched his irritation. "We went yesterday after church and purchased more stuff than he needed. What did she go back today to get?"

"Beats me, Colin. I didn't ask." Elaine let out a chuckle, and then added, "You know how Angel is with that child of hers. She'll probably come back with a trunk load of stuff that he'll outgrow before he can even use. You can catch her on her cell, I'm sure. She'll hate she missed you for lunch."

Not sharing the same humor, Colin's tone was dry when he said, "Yeah, okay. Thanks."

Hanging up the telephone, Colin sat on the side of his bed and released a burdened sigh. Today was the first day in weeks that he'd been able to break away from the shackles of his office to come home to spend lunch with his family. Friday, he'd toiled late into the evening to get additional work done just so that he could surprise his wife and son with a lunchtime appearance on Monday. But instead of being welcomed by the warm greetings of his family, Colin walked into the house to the animated sounds of a *Dora The Explorer* DVD, playing on the television set that had been left on in the living room. Austin's playpen was still set up in the middle of the floor, and a load of laundered clothes were jumbled in a basket on the sofa. The house was always in order when Colin got home from work in the evenings, so he could only deduce that Angel was in the middle of completing chores when she decided on the impromptu shopping spree.

"Surprise!" Colin yelled in a facetious manner, flinging his arms up in the air for theatrical effect. Then in mounting aggravation, he fell back onto the mattress and stared up at the ceiling.

This whole *I don't have time for my husband* attitude of Angel's was getting old as far as Colin was concerned. She was spending every weekday splitting her attention between counseling Elaine and coddling Austin; every Saturday cleaning out Essie's house; and every Sunday after church, too tired to do anything other than rest so that she could start the whole cycle over again on Monday morning.

"There's no sense in avoiding the inevitable any longer," Colin huffed. He sat up and picked up a spiral bound notepad from the nightstand table, then took a pen from the pocket inside his suit jacket. "Enough is enough. We're going to have to talk about all this and get some things clear." He didn't care that no one was in the room with him to hear his frustration.

Using quick, short strokes that mirrored his current temperament, Colin scribbled a note, telling Angel that he needed her not to be asleep or otherwise occupied when he got in from work this evening. There were some things that were weighing heavily on his mind, and he needed her to be available to have a heart-to-heart discussion. He didn't want the note to sound harsh, but at the same time, he needed it to have an overtone of urgency so that Angel would realize how important to him this request was.

Satisfied that his mission would be accomplished, Colin tore the single-page note out of the pad and placed it on the side of the bed where Angel slept. He secured the note's position by weighing it down with the pen that he'd used to write it with.

If he thought for a moment that Angel and Austin would return home soon, Colin would have waited for their arrival. But he knew that if shopping for the baby was on her agenda, it would be hours before Angel's task would end. Austin had more clothes and toys than any child his age needed. And while Colin wanted nothing but the best for his son, it was time for him to tell Angel that she was going overboard, causing a serious imbalance in their relationship.

Preparing to leave, Colin stood in front of the mirror and adjusted his tie. He'd loosened it on the ride home in anticipation of a relaxing afternoon of whatever tantalizing surprises that his unexpected visit led to. Thinking about it now, Colin almost laughed.

"Not today, boy," he told his reflection. "Apparently, it's still not your turn." With that, he snatched his keys from the dresser, set the house alarm, and headed for the front door.

When Colin pulled into his reserved parking space at Wachovia Bank twenty minutes later, he sat in his car for a moment to gather himself. What went on in his home, whether bad or good, was no concern of anyone at work. Colin made it a point to never mix his personal matters with those of his business. And the last thing he needed was to take out any temporary frustrations he had with Angel on colleagues or clients.

Help me make it through the rest of the day. Colin prayed the quick, silent prayer as his hand made contact with the button that would release the locks of his car. Within seconds, he'd put on his best all-is-well-with-the-world face, and after a few brisk strides, he was swinging open the doors of Wachovia and waving at nearby frequent customers on his way back to his office. Behind his closed door and his oak desk, Colin plopped in his leather swivel chair and took a deep breath before reaching for the file he'd been working on prior to leaving.

Three knocks brought his mind's attention to the door, but his eyes remained locked on his paperwork. "Come on in."

"Hey, Mr. Stephens. I was thrown off by the closed door for a minute. You're back already?"

Colin looked up at Nona entering his office with two files in her hand. "Yes, I'm back. What can I do for you?"

"Well, darn." She fixed her face into a pout. "Now I owe myself ten dollars."

With raised eyebrows, Colin responded with a clueless, "Huh?"

Nona laughed at his expression. "You were so eager to spend lunch at home this afternoon that I had placed a bet with myself that you probably wouldn't make it back to work at all. Not only are you back, but you're back early, so I lost the bet. I owe myself ten dollars."

Chuckling and shaking his head simultaneously, Colin replied, "I see." Then he added, "This may come as a bit of a surprise to you, Nona, but believe it or not, there are millions of better ways to entertain yourself that you probably should get exposed to. Talking to and making wagers with yourself . . . not to mention losing bets to yourself and actually paying yourself, can lead to long-term problems."

Nona broke into a jovial laugh. "You're probably right. I guess I need to get out more."

"That's all I'm saying," Colin said, raising both his hands in a manner of surrender.

"So are you back from lunch in every way?" Nona asked. "I mean, do you want me to send phone calls to you now or would you rather I keep the calls forwarded to me until you've at least taken a full hour?"

"That would help me make a little more leeway on everything—if you continued to take the calls, I mean."

"Will do," she said as she placed the files on his desk. "Plus it'll give your food time to settle. You ate way too fast today."

"I didn't eat." The words spilled from Colin's mouth without permission.

Nona had been heading for the door to leave, but his words caused her to turn back around. "You didn't eat?"

He'd already started, so Colin figured that he might as well finish. "No, I didn't. Angel had taken Austin shopping at one of the outlet malls somewhere, so they weren't home when I got there."

"I'm sorry to hear that, Mr. Stephens. I know how much you were looking forward to spending that time with the two of them."

"It's no big deal," he lied. "That's what I get for trying to surprise them, I guess. I'm the one who ended up being caught off-guard."

"So because they weren't home, you didn't even bother to eat lunch?"

Colin shook his head while chuckling at his own inanity. Until Nona mentioned it, he had actually forgotten about his physical hunger. Other, more prevalent, starvations overshadowed it. Today, he'd hoped for some possible intimate time with his wife to gratify his salacious appetite more than he was anticipating food to curb his bodily hunger. The former far outweighed the latter.

"Well, you want to run and get something now?" Nona asked. "I still have a little more than fifteen minutes before I leave to take my break. I can just keep answering any incoming phone calls until you return. Or if you like, I can bring you something back when I come back from lunch."

She had given him some good options and Colin sat back in his seat to mull over which was the better choice. He wasn't particularly fond of fast foods; they had a tendency to make him sluggish, and he needed to be fully alert so that he could get as much work done as possible before close of business. But he also didn't want to wait another hour before eating.

"I'll tell you what," Colin said, snapping his finger as an idea presented itself. "I owe you lunch anyway from when you bought mine last week."

Nona quickly broke in. "Oh no, Mr. Stephens. You don't owe me anything. I did that because I wanted to. I owed you for being such a great boss."

"Well, I'm a great boss because I want to be, so technically, you never owed me anything to begin with either. So here's how we'll settle the score. Let me buy you lunch today, and we'll call it even. How about that?"

"Well, I . . ." Nona looked around the office, then back at Colin. "What about here?"

"Here?" Colin echoed.

"Yes. Who's gonna run things here if both of us leave?"

Colin laughed out loud. "Believe me, Nona; as important as we all think we are to the everyday function of this place, Wachovia Bank will not have to close its doors simply because the two of us leave for an hour or so. Now do you want to go or not, because I'm starved and if I don't get some nourishment in my stomach in a minute, I'm gonna get cranky and when that happens, I'll no longer be the great boss that you've labeled me to be."

Nona laughed too. "Give me a minute to grab my purse, and I'll be right back."

Chapter 8

Elaine's Story

She corrected a typographical error, and for the next ten minutes managed to fight the thoughts that had disturbed her focus throughout the process and stay in writer's mode; focusing only on the project currently displayed on her computer screen. But as soon as she placed the period on the closing sentence, her thoughts wandered back to the plight of her unconventional marriage.

Elaine stood from her computer, deciding that now was a good time for an afternoon snack. She hadn't eaten since the half grapefruit she prepared for herself after her morning run. The walk down the hall was only a few feet, but on days like today, it seemed longer. Unhurried steps brought her into the kitchen where a fresh pot of coffee had been brewing. She eyed the box of glazed donuts that Mason had purchased from

Krispy Kreme on their way home from church yesterday and licked her lips. It had been over a year since she'd had one. Deciding that she had earned the reward, Elaine took one of the round desserts out of the box, quickly bit into it and moaned.

The taste was so pleasurable that Elaine felt as though she would cry. She made quick work of that one, then grabbed another before closing the box and filling her cup with coffee. Sweetening her drink with three packets of Splenda and flavoring it with a healthy dose of Vanilla Toffee Caramel nondairy creamer from International Delight, Elaine inhaled and relished the aroma before blowing through the steam and taking her first sip. "Ooh! Too hot." She placed the ceramic cup on the counter to give it a moment to cool.

As a part of her quest to shed the pounds that had invaded her body without consent, Elaine had rid her diet of a lot of things that online research had recommended, but she refused to deprive herself of her coffee. She had at least one cup every day—sometimes two, depending on her workload. The caffeine kept her attentive as she labored to meet the deadlines of her many literary obligations.

"Okay, Elaine. What are you gonna do about this man of yours? This foolishness has gone on way too long. You've got to use your feminine wiles to find a way to break through this tough barrier of his." She gave herself the motivational address while pacing back and forth on the tiles that covered her kitchen floor and nibbling on the remains of her dessert. In spite of the severity of the matter, Elaine broke into a laugh. She imagined that this was the same agonizing process that female groupies went through when they plotted to bed a big-time actor, recording artist, or NBA superstar. "This is crazy," she concluded. "I shouldn't have to go through these kinds of changes in order to score with my own husband."

Elaine licked residue glaze from her fingers and reclaimed her cup before walking from the kitchen into the living room. She stopped a few inches from the sofa where her husband slept nightly and tossed it the most hateful glare she could conjure. Hoping that doing so would somehow hurt the feelings of the inanimate object, she rolled her eyes as hard as she could, then blew again into her cup before strolling into her bedroom and closing the door behind her. Elaine took another sip of the liquid and determined that it was still too hot to fully enjoy. She placed the cup on the chest of drawers that was situated not five feet from the bed that she and

Mason used to share. From there, she walked into the bathroom to scrutinize her image in the mirror.

"Is it me? Am I still too fat? Is that it?" she grilled herself as she stood turning from side to side to see if there were more physical flaws that she needed to work on. "The scale says I weigh less than I did when we got married, but Mason sure isn't acting like it. There's something about me that he finds so offensive that it makes him not even want to touch me. What is it? Maybe I need to lay off the carbs," she said, pinching her waistline to see if she could grab more than an inch.

Layer by layer, Elaine peeled away the clothing from her body, looking for that one menacing imperfection or stubborn blemish that was making her husband abhor her most. Yes, she had breached their wedding vows in the worst way when she got swept away by Danté, but that was over a year ago, and Elaine believed that Mason had forgiven her. Had he not, she would have been single a long time ago. Mason wouldn't just keep her around to torture her. In fact, had her husband not genuinely pardoned her of her past sins, Elaine was sure that keeping her around would be more unbearable for him than it would her.

For a long while, she looked at her nude silhouette in the mirror, examining every inch of her physical makeup. The same image that had looked satisfactory to her yesterday, appeared repugnant today. Something about the revolting reflection in the mirror made her husband rather sleep alone.

Elaine's eyes dropped to the lower half of her body. That had to be it. *Every woman in the McKinney family has this big ole butt. Grandma Celeste had it, Mama had it, and now they've passed it down to me.* She scowled in indignation. If she wanted to save her marriage, she had to get rid of the "McKinney behind."

Elaine turned and faced the larger part of their master bathroom, knowing what she would have to do. She thought she'd gotten past this stage. She thought that she'd done it enough and could just eat right and exercise to maintain the progress she'd made. But apparently not. She had to continue the radical course until she had improved herself to the point where Mason would want to be her husband in every way. Turning again and looking at herself straight in the face, Elaine noticed a morsel of sugar in the corner of her mouth, left behind by one of the two donuts she'd devoured. She couldn't believe that after all this time she still hadn't built up enough willpower so that measly temptations such as pastries wouldn't overpower her. She almost felt sick just thinking about it.

"Greedy pig!" she scolded in ridicule of her actions. Regretful tears rolled down her cheeks, leaving hot trails of moisture. "See what you did? That's why Mason doesn't want you. Not only are you fat, disgusting, and barren, but you're also a pig." The tears were so thick now that Elaine could no longer see, but that didn't stop her from berating herself. "You're a fat, disgusting, barren pig!"

Running to the commode as if her life depended on how swiftly she could get there, Elaine stood over the gaping hole, stuck her fingers as far back in her mouth as she could, and braced for the release of the evils that had built a gargantuan wall between her and Mason.

Chapter 9

Jennifer's Story

When she kicked off her shoe, the force she used to do so sent the four-inch-heeled pump sailing clear across the room, only coming to a stop because the concrete wall of her bedroom wouldn't allow it to go any farther. Over the last twenty-four hours, Jennifer's emotions had gone through a continuous cycle of sadness, confusion, and anger. She was in angry mode now, but she could feel impending tears that would soon usher her back to square one.

"How could I have been so stupid!" she screamed, sending a shrilling echo throughout her room, followed by her left shoe on a jet-speed mission to join the right one. Plunking on the side of the bed, Jennifer buried her face in her hands. The exhale that she released was more of an animal-like growl. The tears were still building, but they weren't ready to break loose yet. There was still too much rage blocking the way.

Jennifer's disgust was more with herself than anyone else, and it was two-fold. She couldn't believe how totally convinced she had been that she would wake up this morning with an engagement ring on her finger. Even as she thought back, all outward signs pointed to the certainty that a bent knee proposal would take place at Benihana yesterday afternoon. There was absolutely no doubt in her mind that T.K. was going to ask her to marry him. Even as he reached in his coat to reveal the "surprise" that he'd been dangling over her and Jerrod's head like yarn for a kitten, Jennifer trembled with excitement. When he pulled out a folded slip of paper, opened it, and began reading an e-mail exchange that he'd had with an affiliate of Fox 5 News, Jennifer's heart plummeted.

That was the second reason that she was so aggravated with herself. Although what T.K. revealed wasn't the ring that she'd hoped—no, *prayed* for—she should have been elated at what the e-mail said. Jerrod, her son, who had known little else other than failure and trouble for the better part of his life, was going to be interviewed for a special news feature that would be shown on tonight's broadcast.

"I'm almost running at Olympic medal speed?" Jerrod's eyes had bulged in his head as he asked the question. "They're gonna put me on the news? Oh, man, Coach D, this is huge! This is cool, ain't it, Ma? Oh, man! We need to hurry up so I can go home and be straight for sho' by the time the news folks roll up."

"You don't have time for that, kid," T.K. had replied. "Fox 5 is coming here."

"Right here at the restaurant?"

"That's right. They'll be here in less than an hour. But before they come, I scheduled the—"

"T.K. Donaldson, my man. What it do, brotha?"

T.K. hadn't even finished his sentence before Hunter Greene, son-in-law of Reverend B.T. Tides, and owner of *Atlanta Weekly Chronicles*, walked into the restaurant with a photographer following close behind. In recent years, *Atlanta Weekly Chronicles* had grown to be just about the hottest weekly newspaper around.

Although it was based in Atlanta, it had hardcopy and online subscribers all over the country and as far outside of the U.S. as Croatia. By the time Fox 5 arrived, Hunter had not only interviewed Jerrod and had his photographer take photos, but he'd joined them for dinner.

All while the Fox 5 cameras were rolling and the brunette reporter shot questions to Jerrod and T.K., Jennifer stood quietly in a corner trying her best not to cry. She lost the battle when they insisted that she make an appearance on camera as well. As she answered the question of how she felt about her son's status and the knowledge of his inevitable future as a USA Track & Field star, Jennifer broke down. Now that it was all over, she found comfort in the fact that the thousands of eyes that would be watching the instant replay on tonight's news would draw the same conclusion as Jerrod, T.K., and the media had; that she was a proud mother who was just so overcome with joy that she couldn't form words. The truth of the matter was that Jennifer's heart was shattered by the disappointment that the same finger she'd left void of jewelry as she got dressed that morning would still be naked when she returned home.

The distress of it all had been so great that she left work an hour earlier than normal. All day long, Jennifer had managed to persuade her boss and coworkers that her dismal mood was because she was ill. She had never told a more precise truth. Ill was exactly what she was. Jennifer was sick with misery.

Four rings from her phone weren't enough to pull Jennifer from her bed. The fifth ring would send the caller to voice mail and she couldn't care less. She continued sitting on the side of her bed with her head lowered as her greeting blared over the telephone's speaker system, ending with a resounding beep, prompting the caller to leave a message.

"Hey; it's T.K."

Jennifer's eyes darted toward the phone, and for a second, they showed a trace of that glow that always sparked when T.K. called. An instant later, she had reclaimed her defeated pose— downcast eyes and all.

T.K.'s voice continued. "I've been trying to reach you all day, Jen; where are you? I got your voice mail at work when I tried to call you around lunchtime, and I just called again and somebody there told me you'd gone home for the day. I tried your cell a few minutes ago, but I got your voice mail there too. I guess you got off early to get prepared for Jerrod's big moment." T.K. paused to insert a chuckle, then he said, "It's been wild at school today. Everybody is excited for the kid, and he deserves it. Mr. Wright even called out his name over the intercom, and when you understand that the principal of this school isn't one for liberally handing out individual props, you know how major that is. Anyway, just about the whole school will be watching the six o'clock news, I'm sure. Call me when you get home, okay? Maybe I can come over and all of us can watch it together. Bye."

The angry Jennifer had disappeared at some point, and she had once again been replaced by the distressed one. A steady stream of tears began leaking from the young mother's eyes about midway through T.K.'s message, and in the silence that followed, the flow continued.

"How could I have been so stupid?" She reverted back to her initial question. "It all makes so much sense now. I don't know why in the world I thought he was gonna ask me to marry him. What made me draw that conclusion?"

Almost as if offering an answer to the question Jennifer had posed to no one in particular, her mind replayed the scene of T.K.'s insinuation of a surprise that he wanted to unveil over dinner. It wasn't what he said so much as the way he'd said it. When T.K. whispered the announcement in her ear, and then told her that Jerrod needed to be there too because of the impact, Jennifer couldn't imagine the surprise being anything other than a proposal accompanied by a matching ring. But when she thought back on it now, with a mind not cluttered by lovesick fantasies, it all made sense.

"Proposal? Why would T.K. propose to me? Don't you have to love somebody before you want to marry them?"

The impact of her own questions sent a sharp pain stampeding through Jennifer's body like a team of untamed horses. She wasn't sure when it happened, but at some point during their courtship, she'd fallen head over heels in love with the man that her son called Coach D. But not once had T.K. voiced the same for her. When she was around him, she *felt* loved. When they went to the movies without Jerrod in tow, he would hold her hand and allow her to snuggle up to him in the darkened theatre. The first time he kissed her, Jennifer could have sworn that she felt the earth rotating on its axis. That was eight months ago, but she recalled the night as if only eight minutes had passed since the brief, but momentous lip-lock.

It was a Saturday night, and T.K. had invited Jennifer to join him at an Atlanta hot spot called Café 209, where a local saxophonist by the name of Antonio Allen would be making a special live appearance. The celebrated musician was best known for the gospel/jazz flavor of his brass instrument, and on that night, he would be playing music from his popular romantic CD entitled *Forever & Always*. The restaurant's low lighting, coupled with the sound of the soulful serenade that filled the room, made for a setting more intimate than any other that T.K and Jennifer had experienced in their young relationship. Even now, in her saddened state, Jennifer couldn't help but close her eyes and savor the moment with fondness.

T.K. had stood from his seat, and with an extended hand, he nonverbally invited her to dance with him. Slipping his arms around Jennifer's waist, T.K. took the lead and the two of them joined many other couples who had been caught up in the moment of the ambiance. In the middle of the song, Jennifer felt T.K. pull away slightly. When she looked up at him, wondering why he'd stopped his rhythmic swaying, he placed both his hands on her cheeks, and then lowered his lips to meet hers.

The vivid memories of it all sent recycled chills down Jennifer's spine. They'd shared many kisses since that time, and for Jennifer, they all spoke an unmistakable love that T.K. never voiced. But now, there was little in her life that she was more unsure of than the way the high school coach felt about her. Literally overnight, she'd gone from thinking he loved her enough to marry her to thinking she was little more to T.K. than a passing fling. He was just like all the rest.

"It's your own dumb fault for jumping to conclusions," she mumbled while wiping away residue tears. Jennifer had been by herself for a long time, and it wasn't getting any easier. She desired to be married and a part of a family that came complete with a full-time father for her son. Several things made her believe that T.K. would fill that void. For one, he was everything she could ask for in a husband—both physically and spiritually. But that alone hadn't tipped the scale. Jennifer had been in love before, and she knew that she hadn't always had the best judgment where the opposite sex was concerned. But this time she had confirmation that she thought was infallible. Not only did she like T.K. Donaldson, but so did Essie Mae Richardson.

Jennifer recalled the first time she met her son's track coach. She and Essie had been standing on Essie's porch together when the tall, brown, handsome stranger parked his car on the curb in front of the elderly woman's home and got out with Jerrod shadowing him. He was bringing Jerrod home from school that day after the then troubled teen had stayed after school for a one-on-one chat session with his favorite educator. T.K.'s impression on Essie had been just as instant as it had been on Jennifer. While Jennifer might have questioned her own instincts, she would never have second-guessed Essie's intuition, and the wise widow had gotten good vibes from T.K.

"Did he fool both of us, Ms. Essie?" Jennifer scanned the white paint of the bedroom's ceiling as she asked the question. "You knew everything, so you would have picked up on it if he were gonna turn out to be just like all the rest, wouldn't you? You would have warned me if I were just gonna be strung along, right?"

Jennifer would have paid top dollar to hear Essie's wisdom-filled voice offer some form of insight, but she knew that God wasn't passing out that kind of supernatural fortune. Somehow Jennifer would have to figure this one out on her own. She hadn't been saved all that long, but even from her childhood days, she remembered her own grandmother telling her that God answered prayers. The old wheelchair bound woman would always say, "He may not come when you want Him, but He's always on time." Jennifer refused to believe that her time was not yet. She'd prayed for the Lord to fulfill her needs—to make her family complete. And in her spirit, she felt that He'd promised to grant her heart's desire. Could she have been wrong in her interpretation of God's confirmation?

A sudden thought terrified Jennifer, causing her to sit up straight for the first time in a long while. *Can it be?* And then speaking aloud with eyes filling with regretful tears, she concluded, "Maybe God *is* trying to give me what I need, but I'm allowing my own desires to block my blessing. I'm trying to make T.K. fit the mold, but maybe the fact of the matter is . . . he's just not the answer to my prayer."

Chapter 10

Mason's Story

"Brother Demps?" He stood at the sound of his name and extended his hand toward the man who had spoken it. It was Mason's first time personally meeting the famed Reverend B.T. Tides, and for a moment, Mason's heart swelled like he was meeting a Hollywood celebrity. In his own right, Reverend Tides was somewhat of an icon. His name, face, and voice were renowned not only in Atlanta, Georgia, but all over the United States. Until now, Mason had only seen the aging, but strikingly handsome pastor on television, in the newspaper, and on the covers of magazines. Glowing phrases like "highly respected citizen," "prayer warrior," and "powerfully anointed man of God" were used frequently when people referenced Reverend Tides. And all of that weighed in on Mason's choice to confide in him. But if he were to be honest with himself,

Mason would have to admit that the component that tipped the scales in his decision to walk through the doors of New Hope Church today was that he was as much a stranger to Reverend Tides as the preacher was to him. And for this particular problem, that was exactly what Mason needed—a counselor who knew nothing about him, his family, or the problems that had led to their problems.

"Pleased to meet you, Reverend," Mason said as the gentleman directed him into his study with an inviting sweep of his hand. Mason waited for the pastor to close the door behind them and point him in the direction of where he would sit. He said, "Thank you," as he eased onto the soft, buttery leather of the chair closest to the preacher's massive desk.

"Would you like a cup of water?" Reverend Tides offered.

"No, thank you." Mason watched the leader of New Hope Church grab a nearby chair and move it closer to where he sat. He'd expected Reverend Tides to sit behind his desk like all the preachers in the movies did, but he didn't. Mason set his face and tried not to look as uneasy as he was beginning to feel. "I guess you're wondering why a man who's not a member of your congregation would call on you for counsel, huh?"

A slow smile crossed Reverend Tides's face as he sat back in his chair, ran his fingers through his short, naturally curly hair, and crossed his legs. He shook his head from side to side and said, "Not really, son. I counsel many people who aren't members of New Hope. The wisdom that God has given me is not only for those who sit inside these four walls every Sunday; so please don't feel out of place here. You're at home." The preacher readjusted his chair so that he was sitting face-to-face with Mason, and then leaned forward and extended both his hands. "Before we begin, let's pray together."

Nervous moisture was beginning to build in Mason's palms, but he wasn't given time to wipe the embarrassing clamminess away. Mason concluded that although Reverend Tides didn't react to it, he had to have felt the dampness when their hands came in contact.

"Heavenly Father, we come before you this evening, asking that you let your commanding presence rest in our midst. I haven't been where this brother has been, Lord, but you are omnipresent. I don't have all the insight to his troubles, but you are omniscient. I don't have the power to change his situation, God, but you are omnipotent. Let Brother Demps know that you are a God who is able to do above all that we ask or think, according to the power that worketh within us. Give him comfort and let him know that his quandaries, whatever they are, are no challenge for you. Give him trust in your servant, and let him know that he can open his heart and speak to me with confidence. And when he speaks, Lord, give me the wisdom to understand and the words to say that will encourage him. Let him know that you are God. You are the alpha and omega, the first and the last, the beginning and the ending, and with you, he is more than a conqueror. We speak victory in every aspect of Brother Demps's life in the matchless name of your son, Jesus Christ. Amen."

"Amen," Mason whispered through a throat that had become more parched than ever. *Lord, I wish I'd accepted that water.*

"Are you sure you wouldn't like something to drink? I have plenty," Reverend Tides said, pointing toward a water cooler that was positioned near a door that provided an exit to the outside.

The eerie follow-up offer shook Mason, and for a split second, he stared blankly at the pastor. A moment later, upon finding his voice, Mason rubbed his chin and said, "Well, I guess a cup of water would be good. Thank you."

"You're quite welcome, son."

Mason watched Reverend Tides bounce up from his chair without strain. He didn't know the exact age of the pastor, but Mason knew that he had three adult children, the oldest of which had to be nearing forty; so Mason figured the preacher to be at least sixty. Whatever his age, Reverend Tides had very few strands of grey in his hair, and his steps were as vigorous as any thirty-year-old.

"Tell me a little bit about yourself, Brother Demps."

"Please, call me Mason." Mason noticed the slight tremble in his own hand as he accepted the cup from Reverend Tides. He immediately brought it to his lips for much needed relief.

"Okay, Mason. Tell me about you."

The cool water felt good going down Mason's throat. "What is it that you want to know, Pastor?"

"Just who you are in general," Reverend Tides said while again making himself comfortable in his chair. "Who are you? What do you do? Where do you worship? Tell me about your family. That kind of thing."

Mason wondered what all that had to do with the reason he'd come to talk to Reverend Tides, but he followed the instructions given. "Well, let's see. There's not much to tell, really. I'm a thirty-three-year-old ordinary guy who likes sports and cars like most men. I live in Braxton Park in Alpharetta. I'm a truck driver, and I've been married for a little more than eight years."

"Do you know the Lord as your personal Savior?"

"Yes, sir."

"Both of you?"

"Yes, sir," Mason repeated, assuming the preacher was referring to him and Elaine.

"Wonderful." Reverend Tides's grin gave away his pleasure in hearing it. "How long have you been a born again Christian?"

Mason drank from his cup, then said, "We were both saved a while back, right after we got married, and then we kind of lost touch with God," he admitted. "We stopped going to church and stuff and kind of lost our way, really. But we rededicated ourselves to God about ten or eleven months ago."

The pastor nodded his head. "Amen, amen. And you have a place where you worship regularly?"

"Yes, sir. Temple of God's Word in Alpharetta."

Reverend Tides's facial expression said that he wasn't familiar with the church. Mason wasn't surprised. It was more than thirty miles from

New Hope, and unlike Reverend Tides, Reverend Owens wasn't a household name.

"Good, good." Reverend Tides seemed to approve despite not knowing Reverend Owens on a personal level. "Any children?"

"No, not yet." Mason took a moment to drink more water.

"Ah," Reverend Tides said with a knowing smile. "I hear a strategy in there somewhere. You and your wife plan to have children soon?"

Mason took another sip. "Uh, well, uh . . . no. I mean, yes, I suppose. I mean, it's not that waiting this long was a strategy, it just hasn't happened yet. We've tried, but . . . well, none yet."

"I see." The pastor's eyes turned serious, and then he smiled again and quickly changed the subject. "My oldest son is a minister, but he's a truck driver too. He shares many of his onthe-road stories with me. It's a very interesting job. I suppose one would have to love to drive in order to choose to do it professionally. Jackson is sometimes gone for a week or two before coming home to spend time with his family. It's a bit of a sacrifice, but the job pays well, and God has blessed him with a very supportive and understanding wife. Does your job keep you away from home like that?"

"I don't do long hauls," Mason explained. "The farthest I travel is Gainesville, Florida. I take the haul there, help the company unload it from my truck, and then come back to Atlanta. So I'm home every evening, and I also get every other weekend off."

"Your wife must be delighted about that."

Mason shrugged and then readjusted himself in his seat. "I don't know. I guess." He turned up his cup and drained the remaining water in his mouth before sitting up straight, clutching the Styrofoam between his hands and looking at the empty bottom.

Without pause, Reverend Tides took the cup from Mason's hands and stood. "Can we talk about your wife for a few minutes?" he asked en route to the water cooler to replenish the supply.

"What about her?" Mason felt comfortable and uncomfortable at the same time. A part of him wanted to talk about Elaine. Talking about her meant he didn't have to talk about himself.

"What does she do?"

"She's a writer."

"A novelist?" Reverend Tides's eyebrows rose with piqued interest as he brought the newly filled cup to Mason.

"Thank you," Mason said. "She's writes columns and short stories for magazines. But she claims that she's going to write a novel about Ms. Essie one day."

"Ms. Essie?"

Mason smiled for the first time since being seated in the pastor's office. "Ms. Essie . . . Essie Mae Richardson . . . was this lady that lived in our neighborhood for years. She was like some kind of angel or something. She was the person that Elaine . . . that's my wife . . . would go to when she needed to talk. Not always. I mean, Elaine didn't get to know Ms. Essie until a few weeks before Ms. Essie died. None of us other than Colin and Angel—those are two friends who live in Braxton Park—knew her personally prior to then. Until then, we just knew Ms. Essie as the old lady who sat on her porch knitting, singing, and reading her Bible." Mason felt like he was babbling.

"Sounds like my own mother, rest her soul," Reverend Tides said with a chuckle.

"Not mine," Mason mumbled. Then to avoid any probable oncoming questions about his up-bringing, he hurried to resume his speech about Elaine and Essie, especially since Reverend Tides seemed to be enjoying it. "Anyway, Ms. Essie was the reason that we got back in the church."

"You say she passed away?"

"Just over a year ago. It really crushed us all, because even though she was pushing eighty, she just seemed so full of life. We weren't expecting it."

"Sounds like she was a true soldier for the Lord," Reverend Tides said. "She won souls for the kingdom. That's a beautiful legacy to leave, and I'm sure the angels rejoiced upon her entrance."

"Yeah." Mason's eyes dropped. "But ever since the morning after . . . seems like something went wrong."

"The morning after?"

"The morning after Ms. Essie died."

"When you say things went wrong, what do you mean?" Reverend Tides was sitting forward in his chair, with his hands and fingers linked together in his lap.

Mason was feeling far more comfortable than uncomfortable now. "I mean, right before she died, all of our lives were coming together. Colin and Angel were expecting their first baby, Jerrod was doing better in school and had broken free from the gang he had gotten involved with, Jennifer and T.K. were starting a new relationship, and me and Elaine . . . well, although her affair was still kind of fresh, I thought that I was on the road to being able to resume my role as her husband."

Mason knew that for the most part, Reverend Tides didn't have a clue of the people whose names he'd just rattled off, but it was clear from the pastor's response that the only names that immediately meant anything to him anyway were Mason's and Elaine's.

"Is that what you are here to speak to me about today? Elaine's affair?"

It really wasn't, but Mason figured that it was a good place to start. If he didn't start with the affair, he'd end up having to talk backward to get the pastor up to speed anyway. "That's a part of it," Mason said. "That's where it all began." He looked down in his still-full cup and realized that he was no longer dying of thirst, and rattled nerves no longer caused his heart to race. In the few minutes of conversation, he had developed a level of trust in Reverend Tides.

The pastor rested his back against the cushion of the chair and resumed his crossed-legs position. He placed his right elbow on the armrest and struck a pose that was similar to the ones Mason had seen of Dr. Martin Luther King on the church fans at Temple of God's Word. The pastor's index finger was directed toward his ear and his other fingers rested below his chin. "If that's where it began, then let's start there—with Elaine's infidelity."

A bit of Mason's discomfort returned as he revisited the darkest moment of his life. Reverend Tides sat quietly while he told the story of how Elaine had befriended Danté Prescott, and later betrayed their marriage vows when she consummated the extramarital relationship by sharing a bed with the Bermuda-born mechanic.

"The actual sexual part of the affair was a short one," Mason said. "It only lasted for a week, and they were only together a couple of times, but still, she slept with him." He had to take a break to drink from his cup. Mason felt the need to wash down the vile aftertaste that the words left behind.

"I imagine that it was very disheartening to find out she'd betrayed you in such a manner," Reverend Tides put in. "Did you confront this other gentleman?"

Mason scowled. "First of all, he was no gentleman, and I did way more than confront him. I whooped his—" Mason caught himself just in time, and immediately, his brewing anger fizzled into a sea of embarrassment. He lowered his eyes to the carpet near the pastor's feet. Taming his tongue had probably been the biggest makeover that God had done after he'd rededicated himself, but when Mason thought of Elaine and Danté, it tested him on a whole new level. "I'm sorry," he whispered, bracing himself for the pastor's reprimand of his near-blunder inside the house of God.

"Apology accepted," Reverend Tides simply said. "Please, go on, son."

Mason looked back at the counselor, and with a slight smile, expressed his nonverbal appreciation for his kindness. And then he continued. "We fought. It got real ugly, and to tell the truth, as much as I'd like to say I won that fight, I was the one who had to get stitches, so I don't know who got the best of whom." Mason paused to point at the reminder that could still be seen above his eye. "The dude was solid—probably can bench press three-fifty—but I gave it all I had. I probably would have killed him if I thought I could have done so and gotten away with it. I probably would have killed both of them."

"But you didn't. God was watching over you even then."

"Is that what it was?"

Reverend Tides returned Mason's smile. "You'd better believe it. You probably think that you didn't kill him because you weren't strong enough and didn't kill her because you still loved her in spite of it all. But rest assured; the reason you didn't kill them was because God wouldn't allow you to."

Mason's smile faded. Those were the exact reasons that he'd always thought that he hadn't killed the two of them. How the preacher had been able to detect his year-long thoughts, Mason had no idea.

"You and Elaine are still together, right?"

"We're still married, if that's what you mean."

"That's not what I mean," Reverend Tides said. "I mean, are you still together? Are you, or were you ever estranged?"

Mason shook his head. "No. We actually never separated. At least, not in the sense that we ever lived under separate roofs."

"Go on," Reverend Tides urged.

"She slept in the bedroom, and I slept on the living room couch, but we were still under the same roof."

"I see. And how long did it take for you to forgive her?"

"A few weeks. A couple of months. I don't know exactly."

"But you *have* forgiven her?"

Mason paused and searched the preacher's face. He didn't even know how to answer the question. He thought he'd forgiven her; he honestly had. But maybe he hadn't. That's why he was here—he was confused. "I don't know. I told her I forgave her, but I really don't know if I have, Pastor. There has to be some reason why I can't . . ." Mason's voice trailed. "I don't know if I've forgiven her or not."

"Why do you doubt yourself and the validity of your forgiveness?"

A sigh escaped Mason's partially separated lips, and he felt the build-up of unanticipated tears gathering behind his eyes. With a slight tremble in his voice, he answered, "Because it's been over a year, and she's still sleeping in the bedroom, and I'm still on the couch."

An uncommon quietness blanketed the office space, and Mason couldn't bear to bring his eyes up to meet the preacher's. He could only imagine the shock that was on Reverend Tides's face. To Mason, even the sound of the words coming from his own mouth resonated as stupid. A whole year had passed and he hadn't slept with his wife. He could only imagine the thoughts that were running through his counselor's head.

"Why have you not moved back into the bedroom?" Reverend Tides's voice was steady and his tone was sympathetic, but Mason still couldn't look at him.

"I don't know."

"Mason, why have you not moved back into the bedroom?"

Closing his eyes and swallowing, Mason repeated, "I don't know."

"Look at me, Mason," Reverend Tides said, suddenly sounding more like a concerned father than a pastor. Reluctantly, Mason complied. In a slow rhythmic manner, the preacher said, "Why have you not moved back into the bedroom with your wife, son?"

The pastor's face became a cloudy, distorted mess as Mason's eyes overflowed, sending silent tears streaming down his cheeks. "I don't know," he said with a tone of exasperation.

Reverend Tides scooted forward in his chair and placed one hand on Mason's knee. "I want my prayers to be specific, Mason. Throw away your pride and your humiliations, and trust in the God that abides in me. I'm going to ask you this one last time, and I need you to answer me honestly. If you have forgiven your wife of her misdeeds, why haven't you become her husband again in every way?"

Tears had blinded Mason. He hadn't cried this hard since the day he found out about Elaine's affair. He felt the cup he'd been clutching being removed from his grasp, and with his hands now

free, Mason used them to cover his face as he
sobbed uncontrollably. He was a man. How was
a grown man supposed to admit to something
like this and still walk away with dignity? He had
the feeling that Reverend Tides already knew the
answer to his own question anyway. Saying it
would just mortify Mason even more.

"Give him peace, Father." Mason heard Reverend Tides say the words just as he felt the
pastor place firm, but gentle hands on both
sides of his head. "I come against every demon
that rises to torment him and prevent him from
getting the breakthrough that he so desperately
needs. Still the hands of the enemy, Lord, and
give him peace!"

Chapter 11

Angel's Story

She was putting away the last of the leftover dinner when her husband finally decided to come home. When she heard the security alarm beep, signaling someone's entrance, Angel's eyes immediately locked onto the numbers on the stove's built-in clock. It was almost nine-thirty. Colin had been working late many nights since the arrest of his associate, but this was a full ninety minutes later than he'd ever arrived before.

"Hey, babe, I'm home," he announced, sticking his head in the kitchen only momentarily before disappearing again. Angel didn't even have time to respond before he was gone.

"It's about time," she whispered.

On the other side of the wall, she could hear Colin walking down the hall, and Angel figured that he was going to their son's room to check on him. She'd had a tough time getting Austin to sleep and hoped Colin didn't wake him. No sooner than the thought had passed through her mind did she hear him returning to the living room with the child in tow.

"How's Daddy's Austin-Boston?" Colin asked.

"Da-da-da-da-da-da-da," Austin replied. He'd been stringing the sounds together since he was nine months old. It was the closest he'd come to saying "Daddy" and Colin relished every time he did so.

"That's right, big man. Daddy's home. You missed me? Daddy missed you."

"Da-da-da-da-da," the one-year-old replied. His groggy voice gave way to the fact that he'd been awakened.

Angel dried her hands on a paper towel and retired to the living room to join them. "I'd just gotten him to sleep, Colin. Now, he'll be awake for hours."

"That's fine," Colin replied without even looking at her. "I'll stay up with him if you're tired and want to go to bed."

Angel tossed a look at him that was as uncommon as Colin's words. Usually, her husband was vying for her attention, wanting to spend time with her when he got home from a rough night at work. She wasn't accustomed to him encouraging her to go to bed while he sat up with the baby. Plus, for a man who wanted to talk, he sure didn't seem in any hurry to do so. "Why are you rushing me off to bed tonight?"

Colin looked at her for the first time since her entry. "I'm not, baby. You can stay up as long as you want. I was just saying that I'll take the responsibility for waking up Austin. I mean, I'd understand if you were tired from all the *shopping* you did today."

Angel noted the snide manner in which he had said the word. She had seen the note Colin had left for her on the bed, and she knew he was probably a bit upset that she and the baby weren't in place when he came home to spend lunch with them. "We did more window-shopping than anything else. I only purchased a few things that I saw on sale. I'm sorry we weren't home when you stopped by this afternoon. Every now and then I just need to get out of the house, see some other grown folks—maybe some other shopping mothers— and have some adult conversation. You know what I mean? It can be weird doing nothing but talking to a baby all day."

"We'd just gone shopping Sunday, and if adult conversation was what you were looking for, you could have come by my office."

Angel shifted her feet. Colin had invited her to his office many times, but she'd only taken him up on the offer a few. And she hadn't been there at all in the past year. "I know. I hate feeling like I'm disrupting your work. I know how far behind you are."

"Have you ever heard me complain that you're interrupting me?"

He knew the answer to that question, so Angel didn't know if it were a rhetorical one or not. She decided to answer. "No."

Colin grinned at Austin, and then added, "And if you were worried about disturbing me, you could have gotten adult conversation while walking with Elaine. Apparently talking to an adult wasn't all that important today since you decided not to workout with her this morning."

Angel was blindsided by his comeback. She had been so busy playing catch-up and trying to be sure the house was in order by the time her husband got home that she hadn't had time to talk to Elaine since telling her friend that she wouldn't be walking with her today. So until Colin's remark, Angel wasn't aware that he knew she'd skipped her regular morning exercise routine with their neighbor.

"Sometimes I feel like I'm slowing her down," Angel answered, not sure that the reply was the real reason she'd avoided this morning's routine. "Elaine likes to run the whole four miles, and I'm just not up to doing that yet. So every time I go with her, she has to slow down to accommodate me. I don't like feeling like I'm a hindrance."

"You don't like feeling like a disruption, so you didn't visit me. You don't like feeling like a hindrance, so you didn't walk with Elaine. So what adults did you talk to while shopping who made you feel so at home?"

The measure of Colin's cynicism rocked Angel to the core, rendering her speechless. The man who sat in front of her had the face of her husband, but that's where the resemblance ended. Everything else about him was unfamiliar. Was he accusing her of something? Did he think she was with another man? It couldn't be. But why was he being so petty?

Snapshots of her wedding day flashed a slide-show through Angel's mind. During the celebratory reception that followed, Angel remembered Essie taking her to the side, tossing a look across the ballroom floor at Colin, and saying, "He's a keeper, sho' nuff. God done blessed you with a husband that most women can only dream of. But as beautiful as everything is today, just as sho' as God is God, there's gonna come a day when your love and your marriage is gonna be tried. But don't you worry none, 'cause the same God that got y'all now is gonna have y'all then. And while you can always talk to Jesus, I just want you to know that Ms. Essie gonna always be here for you whenever you need to talk to me too."

In the moment of newlywed bliss, Angel could not even fathom the appearance of that trying day that Essie prophesied about. But now it was here. Boy, was it ever! Only problem was . . . Essie Mae Richardson wasn't. In the likeness of a child, Angel's mind whimpered the words, *But she promised.*

Without Essie to help her, all Angel could do was stare at this familiar stranger in disbelief as he so generously fussed over their son. Colin didn't even look at her as he unleashed his obvious disdain; nor did he break his cycle of colorful facial expressions that kept Austin's giggling unrestrained.

"Are you upset that I didn't walk with Elaine?" Angel asked. "I mean, I never knew you cared one way or the other whether I walked with her or not."

Colin released an annoyed sigh, like he was tired of trying to break down his language to a level that a person as dumb as she could understand. "Baby, why in the world would I be upset that you didn't walk with Elaine?"

"Then what's your problem?" Angel's voice rose. She didn't know what kind of game her husband was playing, but she didn't want to be a contestant. "Why are you acting so, so, so . . ." She couldn't even think of a word to describe Colin's actions that wouldn't offend him.

"Acting so what, baby?" His relaxed facial expression showed no signs of agitation, which frustrated Angel even more. She felt like he was taunting her. This was not the man she'd married four years ago. "Acting so what?" he repeated. The innocent look on his face deserved a Tony Award.

Angel flung her arms into the air, and then let them fall by her sides. "You know what? I'm going to bed."

"Fine." Colin remained calm as he kissed his son's forehead. "I already told you that I'd take care of Austin, and you could turn in if you wanted to."

Deep, anger-induced lines creased Angel's forehead, and she planted both her hands firmly on her hips. "Yeah? Well, you also told me that you wanted me to wait up for you so we could talk," she reminded him. "Which is it, Colin? Do you want to talk or not?"

Standing from the sofa, holding their child close to his chest, he replied, "I did. But my plan

was to have a rational conversation, and this one
has already crossed that line. I'm not gonna ar-
gue with you in front of my son. He doesn't need
to see or hear that. I don't get to spend enough
quality time with him as it is. What time I do
have to be with him won't be tainted by argu-
ments."

Angel's hands slipped from her hips and
dangled freely on both sides of her body. She
could feel the build up of tears forming somewhere behind her eyeballs. "What about me?"
she disputed. "You don't get to spend a whole lot
of time with me either, but you seem okay with
arguing as long as it's outside of the presence
and ear-range of Austin. How much sense does
that make, Colin? You're willing to fuss in front
of me, but not in front of him. What's the difference?"

Shaking his head from side to side, Colin's
lips vibrated under the pressure of the wind that
propelled his newest sigh. "Baby, I don't want to
fuss with you period, but it's clear that an argument is what a conversation tonight would turn
into. It's already at that point right now, and it'll
only get worse. So let's just drop it, okay?" He
turned to walk away, but then stopped, snapped
his fingers like he'd forgotten something, and
faced her again. "Oh yeah. You asked for the dif-

ference, so here it is. Austin's limited time with me isn't within his control. Yours is. He's a baby. You're not. He can't decide to drive to my office for a visit, or be at home on days I make the sacrifice to spend time with him in the middle of the day. You can. He never opts to spend his free weekend times shopping for stuff he doesn't need or visiting friends that he could see any day of the week. You do. He hasn't reorganized his personal files so that everybody and everything in his life comes before I do. You have. That's the difference, Angel. That's the difference."

Chapter 12

T.K.'s Story

He turned up his plastic bottle and gulped down the last of his water. The cool liquid served as much needed replenishment for T.K.'s thirsty body. "Jerrod, you got a minute?" Track team practice had just ended, and the warmer than normal temperatures had made today's a more grueling session than usual.

"Yeah, Coach D." Jerrod had defied the heat and run an additional lap around the track. So as the others dispersed to the school to take their showers or meet awaiting guardians, the team's lead sprinter continued to lie with his back flat against the grass, holding his knees to his chest to stretch his quadriceps.

T.K. smiled and grabbed another bottle from the cooler. Those little extras were what made the difference between Jerrod's speed and the charted time of the others. When Jerrod made

no effort to stop what he was doing, T.K. occupied the space beside him, laid the unopened
bottle on Jerrod's stomach, and began stretching
his own legs. "I hear you're a celebrity around
these parts," T.K. joked.

It was enough to make Jerrod sit up and
laugh. He took a moment to twist off the cap
and refresh himself before responding. "Nah.
I ain't no celebrity." Using the hand towel that
lay on the ground beside him, Jerrod wiped his
mouth. "It's just that everybody got a kick out of
the news thing, that's all. It's all my teachers and
friends have been talking about for the last three
days. But it'll die down after a while."

T.K. continued to stretch; not that he really
needed to. "Stop being modest, kid. You're doing good in the classroom and on the track, and
everybody's proud of you. I know I am."

Jerrod sported a subdued grin and shrugged.
T.K. could tell that he was embarrassing the
boy. "Thanks," Jerrod responded. "Getting good
grades is cool 'cause I know I'm freaking out
all the teachers from last year who were used
to me doing bad. Especially that geeky old Mr.
Greene."

"Mr. Greene?" T.K. dropped his leg to the
ground. His first thought went to his pastor's
son-in-law, and right away, Jerrod read his
mind.

"Not the guy who met with us at Benihana that's doing the newspaper feature on me," he clarified. "That Mr. Greene is tall and good-looking. I'm talking about the stumpy, ugly dude who teaches freshman English." Jerrod frowned as he spoke of his least favorite freshman instructor.

"That's not a very nice way to describe anybody."

"It might not be nice, but it's true. I bet you knew exactly who I was talking about as soon as I said it."

Jerrod was right, so T.K. didn't even try to dispute him. Instead, he chose not to respond at all.

"He was the worst teacher ever," Jerrod proclaimed. Then mimicking the teacher's cranky voice, he added, "'Can you tell the class what a complex-compound sentence is, Mr. Mays?' I used to hate the way he called me *Mr. Mays*, like I ain't had no first name."

It was hard not to laugh at the boy's antics, but T.K. managed. "Teachers do that sometimes, Jerrod. He probably didn't mean anything by calling you Mr. Mays. I mean, it's a respectful title, right? At least he wasn't calling you something rude."

"Well, he wasn't trying to be respectful, that's for sure," Jerrod insisted. "In his mind, he probably was calling me something rude. If he was,

I don't care. Every time I called his name, I was thinking something rude in my mind, so if he did the same, it would just make us even."

T.K. shaded his eyes from the overhead sun and looked at Jerrod in concern. "You sound bitter. I thought we'd gotten past all those grudges."

"I am past it, Coach D. Most of it, anyway." Jerrod scanned the distant trees, avoiding eye contact with his mentor. After draining the rest of his water, he added, "It's just that every time I see him in the hallways, he cuts his beady old eyes at me like he wishes I'd just disappear or something. I know I gave him a hard time last year, but that was then and this is now. The other teachers don't diss me like he does. I mean, they don't run up and hug me either, but at least they don't act like I'm some kind of fungus. It don't matter to Mr. Greene that I ain't still doing all the stupid stuff I did as a freshman. It don't matter to him that I'm making better grades, got a better attitude, or that my skills on the track made the six o'clock news. He's always gonna see me as Puppy J."

It had been months since T.K. had heard Jerrod refer to himself by the name he'd been given during his stint in the now dismantled Dobermans school gang. The boy had been so tame lately that it was easy to forget his wild days.

"Look, Jerrod, you're never going to please everybody, so don't even try. There are some folks in all of our lives who will choose to forever know us as who we were, regardless of who we are now, or what we will become in the future. Pleasing people isn't what we should be concerned with anyway. Remember? We've talked about this before. It would be a lost cause, because we could never please everybody, even if we tried. It's all about pleasing God, kid. As long as we do those things that satisfy Him, we're good to go."

"You sound just like that dude at your church," Jerrod pointed out.

"What dude?"

"That preacher that had the fine, dark-skinned lady with him when he came over and spoke to us after church last Sunday."

T.K. chuckled at Jerrod's reference. "You mean Reverend Tides's son?" Jerrod nodded. "Yeah. Not the one who sits in the pulpit all the time. The real cool one."

"Jerome."

"Yeah, Jerome; that's his name."

Being compared to "the cool one" caused T.K.'s smile to linger, even as he reverted back to the original subject. "Jerrod, the point I'm trying to make is that you have to get beyond people like Mr. Greene. Whether he likes you or not shouldn't even matter. You made some mistakes in the ninth grade—big deal. What kid didn't? It's what you do from this point forward that matters. So what if you didn't know what a complex-compound sentence was then? You know now, don't you?"

Jerrod looked down at T.K. and waved off the comment. "Pshhhhh! I knew what a complex-compound sentence was then too. I just used to fake like I didn't just to get him going. And he fell for it every single time."

Finally sitting up, T.K. gave Jerrod a side glance. "Did you really know what it was?"

Jerrod smacked his lips as though T.K.'s doubtful words were insulting. "A complex-compound sentence is a sentence with at least two independent clauses and at least one dependent clause," he said with ease. Then he pursed his lips, cocked his head, and gave his coach a look that said, "Now what?"

T.K. patted Jerrod on the back. "Okay, okay, I stand corrected. That was good. Very good, actually. What I don't understand is why you couldn't have just answered the man's question so he would have known that he wasn't wasting his time on you."

"As far as I'm concerned, he was wasting his time. Mr. Greene is lame. He ain't taught me jack. He ain't taught nobody nothing for that matter. I ain't need him to teach me junk that I learned in middle school. We knew that mess way before we ever got in his class."

T.K. made a mental note to work with Jerrod on his grammar, but for now, it wasn't the most pressing issue. "Well, that's even better, Jerrod. You should have told him that, so he would know that you not only knew what he was teaching, but you were beyond it."

"Why?" Jerrod challenged. "He ain't expected me to know it anyway."

"All the more reason to show him that you did," T.K. stressed. "Put your thinking cap on, kid. If he really didn't expect you to know, and you acted like you didn't, then you validated his expectations. You let him get the best of you when you had all the ammo needed right in here"—he poked Jerrod's head with his index finger—"to win the battle."

Still in a seated position, Jerrod pulled his knees close to his chest and wrapped his arms around his legs. T.K. watched as the boy stared across the field in the direction of the school. Shrugging, Jerrod said, "I wasn't thinking like that. I guess when you know that people ain't gonna believe in you no how, you just don't feel like putting forth the effort to give them a reason to. When they tell you that you ain't nothing long enough, you start to feel like nothing."

Jerrod had grown a great deal over the past year; both physically and mentally, but as T.K. looked at him now—shoulders slumped, chin resting between his knees—the fifteen-year-old had the demeanor of a boy half his age.

"Well, I'll bet the little stump doesn't know what to make of you now, huh?" T.K. needed to say something to revive Jerrod's deflating spirit, and it worked.

With a wily grin, Jerrod looked at him and replied, "Oh, that little stump didn't know what to make of me *then*. I fixed him real good. I got the last laugh."

T.K.'s eyebrows shot up, and his mind reverted to the Dobermans, who would do just about anything to get back at teachers they disliked. Ms. Shepherd, a young, first-year administrator who was Jerrod's freshman Algebra teacher, had been forced to resign from a profession she'd dreamed of since childhood, after she was gang raped and brutally beaten by members of the Dobermans who thought she'd mistreated Jerrod. It wasn't until Jerrod and other boys in the group who had played no part in planning or executing the attack, testified against the guilty members during a trial that sentenced them as adults, that Jerrod was able to forgive himself and put the ordeal behind. Ms. Shepherd had forgiven him too, and that helped.

"Got the last laugh, how?" T.K. asked through a held breath. He needed to know that Jerrod hadn't done anything to harm Mr. Greene. "What did you do to get back at him?"

"I aced the test," Jerrod said to his coach's relief. "I proved my knowledge on the final exam. We had to give several examples of complex-compound sentences on there, and the last one I gave was a good one if I must say so myself."

This was the first time T.K. had heard this confession. "What kind of sentence did you write? Nothing improper, I hope."

"I didn't cuss or nothing," Jerrod said, like cursing was the proverbial line that divided what was seemly and what wasn't, "but he still sent me to Mr. Wright's office."

"Then it was inappropriate in some way, I gather."

"Not to me, it wasn't," Jerrod defended. "He asked for a complex-compound sentence and I gave him one. He didn't say it had to be a sentence he liked. Even the principal couldn't punish me. How could he? I did my assignment and gave a correct answer. Mr. Wright had me to sit in his office for the rest of the period just to pacify Mr. Greene, and that was cool with me, 'cause I woulda rather sat in doggy doo than sit in that English class."

In the brief silence that followed, T.K. twisted his mouth to prevent himself from laughing. Then the suspense of it all became too much. He asked his next question with caution. "What was the sentence, Jerrod?"

A new smile spread across Jerrod's lips like he had been hoping T.K. would ask. He raised his head high and proclaimed, "Many amphibians live in wetlands, but the boy's English teacher, who is human by most definitions, is shaped just like a bullfrog, but gets to live in a house anyway."

T.K. didn't want to laugh at the example that Jerrod had given, but he had been caught too unprepared to stifle the eruption. Mr. Greene's peculiar, dumpy, elfish appearance could, in fact, be described as frog-like, making it all the more amusing. Jerrod joined in, and they both had a hearty laugh at the teacher's expense.

"That was so very inappropriate," T.K. managed to regain his composure and say.

"Maybe, maybe not. But it was still a complex-compound sentence. And I didn't call no names, so Mr. Greene couldn't prove that I was talking about him."

"But you were."

"His word against mine."

T.K. shook his head, but residue laughter lingered in his belly. For a while, only the voices of horse-playing children in the distance filled the empty space around them. Jerrod's voice ended the swelling silence. "You wanted to talk to me about something?"

T.K. hadn't forgotten the real reason he'd asked for some of Jerrod's time. He just needed to talk about something more light-hearted before getting into it. "Yeah; I did." He squirmed a little and cleared his throat. "Is Jen okay?"

"Ma?" Jerrod's nose crinkled. "She's fine. Why you asking me that? You just saw her a couple of nights ago."

Monday evening was the last time T.K. had seen or communicated with Jennifer. That was when he'd made the drive to Braxton Park so that they could watch the special news feature together. While both T.K. and Jerrod had been overly excited to see themselves being interviewed on the major network, Jennifer barely responded. Every smile, every accolade, every emotion of any kind that she showed, had to be wheedled out of her, and each one of them lacked authenticity. Jerrod had probably been too immersed in his own exhilaration to notice, but T.K. hadn't been ignorant of her distant behavior. The warm affection that he usually felt around Jennifer had chilled to the point of nonexistence.

"Today's Friday, Jerrod. That was four nights ago when I came over."

"I'm not talking about then," Jerrod explained. "I'm talking about Wednesday. Didn't y'all hang out the night before last?"

T.K.'s head snapped in Jerrod's direction. What was he talking about? Unless there was a special occasion, like the one wherein they watched the televised report on Jerrod's impressive track record, T.K. never saw Jennifer on a weeknight. They both had jobs that required early reporting times, and they'd agreed that weekends were best. "Jen went out Wednesday?"

Jerrod looked clueless. "Yep. She got a phone call around seven, left around eight, and stayed out until around eleven-thirty, I guess. I'd just gone to bed when she got home. I just figured it was you, but I guess it wasn't."

Licking his dry lips with a sandpaper tongue, T.K. struggled to appear unfazed by this new revelation. Questions bounced from his left temple to his right, prompting a rhythmic annoyance. What was she doing out until near midnight, and who had she been with? Was Jennifer seeing someone else? Is that the reason she'd been so cold toward him Monday and hadn't returned any of his phone calls this week? Was she preoccupied with a new admirer? T.K. didn't want to drag Jerrod in the middle of something that he had nothing to do with. This was grown folks' business. Whatever issues he and Jennifer might be having weren't really the child's concern.

In as nonchalant a voice as he could imitate, T.K. said, "No, it wasn't me." Then forcing a smile, he added, "She probably just went to see Elaine or Angel. Probably Angel. Jen has gotten pretty attached to little Austin."

Jerrod relaxed into a smile that was far more genuine than T.K.'s. "Yeah. Ma loves it when Ms. Angel lets her babysit. I wouldn't be surprised if she was at their house."

T.K. wished he'd been as convincing to himself as he'd been to Jerrod. But he knew better. There was no way that Austin was up at that hour of the night. No way Angel would keep him up that late just so Jennifer could spend time with him. But if Jennifer wasn't at the Stephenses' house, where had she been? And if Austin wasn't the name of the male who had her attention, what was?

Chapter 13

Jerrod's Story

B*ong!* He jolted into an upright position, heart pounding like a bongo in his chest. A morning time of six o'clock illuminated from the digital clock on his nightstand. Remnant moonlight was peeping through Jerrod's blinds, revealing shadows of wall poster images of his track hero, Maurice Greene, who, between the 2000 and the 2004 Olympics, brought home two gold, one silver, and one bronze medal.

"Not again," Jerrod whispered.

This wasn't the first time he had been jarred by what sounded like the magnified chiming of the pinewood grandfather clock that stood in the corner of Essie Mae Richardson's living room. The first time the sound interrupted his sleep was just a few minutes before Essie's unconscious body was found lying peacefully in her bed. And just minutes after that, she was gone.

Jerrod had experienced the unsettling occurrence only twice since then. The first time was the day before the news broke that everyone at Colin's job was under the microscope as a suspect for embezzlement. At that time, Jerrod made no connection between the sounding of the clock and Colin's dilemma. Then it happened again.

The day before Jerrod was subpoenaed to testify at the trial that ultimately sent Big Dog Freddie Townsend, leader of the Dobermans, to prison, the echoing bong jerked him from his sleep at about this same time of morning. That was when he began identifying the clock with life-altering happenings. Jerrod had hoped to never hear it again, but here it was for a fourth time.

Fatigue enveloped him, but Jerrod was too frightened to remain in bed. With a single sweep of his arm, he removed his covers and slid onto the floor, kneeling. The whole scenario behind the grandfather clock terrified him. There was no way that he was really hearing it chime. Not when the clock was in the house next door. The homes in the Braxton Park development were well-constructed concrete dwellings, and Jerrod's bedroom was on the end of his house that was farthest from Essie's house. The likelihood of him actually hearing the clock's chiming was practically impossible.

But make no mistake about it; he was hearing *something*. And whatever it was, Jerrod had come to believe that when he heard it, major things would soon follow.

"Lord, please don't let nobody that I love be getting ready to die, and please don't let Freddie or none of the other big dogs be done busted out of jail and looking for me," he prayed. The thought of the latter brought micro beads of sweat to Jerrod's brow. He remembered very well the "mean mugging" that Freddie, Devion, and Adrian had given him from their seats in the defendants' chairs as he sat on the witness stand, trying not to wet his pants.

Before she died, Essie had promised Jennifer that the Lord would be with Jerrod if he were called to testify. But to the then fourteen-year-old, although he saw his mother and T.K. sitting in the courtroom supporting him, it felt like he was all alone with a big red target drawn between his eyes. While Jerrod gave up all the information he knew regarding the Dobermans, fear gripped him like an eagle carrying his doomed prey in clenched claws. But in the midst of his turmoil, something good resulted. Without even realizing it, Jerrod was introduced to effectual fervent prayer.

During the weeks of that trial, he prayed harder than he'd ever done in his life. Not the regular "Now I lay me down to sleep" prayers that Jennifer had taught him as a toddler; but Jerrod poured everything he had, including his tears, into his words as he kneeled beside his bed at night. Some nights after he talked to God, he'd sit on the edge of his mattress and talk to Essie. Jerrod had been such a wayward boy that he couldn't help but wonder if God was even listening to him. He didn't know if Essie would listen to him either. He'd been deeply hurt and angered by her sudden passing, and the result of that rendered times that he reverted back to his former self—days that he lashed out at his mother, T.K., Colin, Mason, his teachers, and everybody else who dared to try to tell him that "God doesn't make mistakes," or "It was just time for Ms. Essie to go."

Everything he'd promised Essie that he'd do: behave in school, study harder, obey his mother, respect his elders . . . all of it was tossed in a hole, much like the handful of dirt that Angel's parents ritualistically sprinkled in the six-foot-deep ditch that Essie's casket had been lowered into.

"Ms. Essie," Jerrod had said one night, eyes full of tears, as he looked upward through the darkness of his bedroom, "I know you all happy up there and everything, being that you done been reunited with Mr. Ben and all, but can you take a break away from him long enough to go talk to God for me? Please, Ms. Essie. You gotta know that I wouldn't disturb you if it wasn't important, but I really need you to do this for me. Please ask God if He'll help me through this. I'm scared. I ain't never been scared like this before. I know a lot is riding on what I tell those people in the courtroom. If I get so scared that I don't say all the stuff that needs to be said, Big Dog Freddie will be let go. And if he don't get locked up, I know he'll kill me. He'll probably kill my mama too. Please ask God to help me, Ms. Essie. *Please*. If He gets me out of this, I swear—" Essie had taught him never to swear. "I mean, I promise I won't never get involved in nothing like this no more. I won't never let nobody call me Puppy J or even Big Dog J. And you know how all the dudes at school call each other dog just in regular conversation? Well, I won't call nobody that, and I won't let them call me that either. Shoot, Ms. Essie . . . if you get God to get me out of this, I won't never in my whole life even own a dog as a pet."

He rambled out those promises months ago, but Jerrod remembered it like it was yesterday. He didn't know if Essie had actually gone to the

Master on his behalf, or if God had heard his prayers directly. But when the court convened again, Ms. Shepherd, still bruised and barely able to talk through her constant flow of tears, was wheeled into court by her fiancé and took the stand to testify against her attackers. The jury only took an hour to bring back their guilty verdicts. Freddie and his partners in crime had gotten twenty-five years to life for the gang rape and brutal assault of Ms. Shepherd.

Jerrod was glad that God had answered that prayer, and he was happy that Colin escaped punishment for the misdeeds of his colleague too, but now he had heard the chime again, and the knot in the pit of his stomach told him that the next big thing was about to happen.

"Lord, I done kept all my promises." From his bent-knee position, Jerrod yawned, but his prayer was sincere. "I been doing good in school, obeying Ma, respecting my teach—" His mind darted to Mr. Greene and the things he'd said about him just yesterday as he sat and talked with T.K. Was God getting ready to punish him or somebody he loved because of what he thought about that old geezer? Jerrod didn't know what to say or do. He could tell God that from now on, he'd have nothing but nice words and thoughts concerning Mr. Greene, but who would he be fooling? Not God; that's for sure.

"Okay, Jesus, here's the deal." Surely with him being a minor, the Lord would be a little bit flexible. "I'll try to do better about Mr. Greene. I won't make no promises I can't keep, but I'll make an effort to do like Coach D says and just not let him get under my skin. I promise to do that. Please . . . just don't let nothing bad be getting ready to go down."

At some point during his prayer, fatigue took over and Jerrod fell asleep. Knocks to his bedroom door awakened him two hours later.

"Jerrod, are you up yet? Are you dressed? Can I come in?"

Jerrod scrambled to his feet at the sound of Jennifer's muffled voice coming from the other side of his door. He massaged his aching knees, and then slipped back into the bed, pulling up the comforter so that it hid him from the waistband of his boxer shorts down. "Come on in, Ma."

When Jennifer walked in, Jerrod was confused by her stylish appearance. She wore a floral, silk, strawberry blouse and black slacks. Her hair had been neatly styled in an updo that showed off her high cheekbones, and her face was softened by the hairs of her bangs. It was Saturday morning. Jennifer never dressed up on Saturday morning unless. . . .

"You and Coach going somewhere?" Jerrod asked.

"Going out to breakfast," she said. "You know it's after eight o'clock, right? Are you gonna help Angel finish packing up Ms. Essie's things?"

"Oh!" Jerrod kicked away the covers and jumped up. He had told Angel that he'd meet her over there at seven-thirty this morning. They were going to get some things boxed up to be placed in the storage space she'd rented until she made a permanent decision on what to do with them. "I'm coming. I just gotta brush my teeth and wash my face. Tell her I'll be over there in a minute, will you, Ma? I overslept." Jerrod darted past his mother and into the bathroom across the hall.

"Well, don't kill yourself." Jennifer laughed. "Wish I could get you that excited about cleaning up your own room."

"I'm gonna clean that up today too," Jerrod vowed while looking at his red eyes in the bathroom mirror. His room was almost always messy. "I'll do it when I get done with helping Ms. Angel."

"You don't have homework?"

"I only had science," he reported through the closed door. "I did it last night."

"Okay," Jennifer called back. "I have to get going, but on the way out, I'll tell Angel that you'll be over soon."

Jerrod was just about to put his toothbrush in his mouth when he stopped to ask, "You ain't gotta keep Austin-Boston today?"

"Colin has him."

"He ain't had to work today?"

"Angel said he went into the office, but he's not really on the clock. Colin's just catching up on some stuff and insisted on taking Austin with him, saying it wouldn't be a problem. No babysitting for me today."

"Oh. Okay."

A moment of silence passed, during which time, all Jerrod could hear were the bristles of his toothbrush grinding against his enamel.

"Jerrod?"

Jerrod winced a little. He thought Jennifer had already left. Spitting the mint-flavored paste from his mouth, Jerrod answered, "Ma'am?"

"I may have a surprise for you when I get back."

"Surprise?" Speckles of white foam jumped from his mouth and landed on the mirror as he spoke. Jerrod used his washcloth to erase it. "What is it?"

Jennifer's laugh could be heard echoing from somewhere near the front of the house. "Now if I told you, it wouldn't really be a surprise, would it?"

Jerrod smiled to himself. He wasn't as clueless as his mother thought, but he played along anyway. "I guess not."

"See you in a couple of hours," she said.

"A'ight."

It only took Jerrod a few minutes to freshen up and pull on a pair of shorts and a T-shirt that showed his track team spirit. It tickled him to think that T.K. and Jennifer didn't give him more credit than they did. He wasn't a kid anymore. Approaching sixteen and with only two years to go in high school, he'd have to be pretty dim-witted not to know that his mother and his track coach were a serious item. Although Jerrod had made a conscious effort not to build up false hope, Jennifer's little *surprise* was one that he'd been wishing for ever since it became clear to him that she and T.K. were more than friends. He wasn't stupid. Jerrod knew that what his mother was going to bring back home with her was T.K. And what the two of them were going to announce was their engagement.

"That would be so cool!" Jerrod's voice bounced off his bedroom walls. He would like nothing more than to see the two of them make it official. T.K. would make a great addition to their family, and Jerrod would finally have the father he'd always wanted. "I'll bet that would make Ms. Essie smile."

His spoken words brought him back to the reality that Angel was waiting. As soon as he finished tying his shoestrings, he bounded out the front door and scurried up the steps of what used to be Essie's home. He stopped on the porch and looked up into the sky. This time, it wasn't about having reservations about entering the house; he was just noting the rain clouds that loomed above.

"Hey, Jerrod." When he entered the house, Angel greeted him with kind words, but her smile was void of its usual warmth. She still looked good though. Jerrod couldn't remember a time that he'd seen her in shorts before.

"Hi, Ms. Angel," he said, making an effort to keep his eyes fixed on her face and away from her perfect legs. Her solemn look made Jerrod wonder if she were displeased with his failure to keep his word. "I overslept. I'm sorry. I didn't mean to be late."

"It's okay, sweetie." Jerrod basked in the sound of her term of endearment. If he were a few years older, he'd give Colin a reason not to like him. "You're just in time," she continued. "I've been working on putting away all of Ms. Essie's towels and washcloths." Angel pointed down the hall that led to the open linen closet. "I had no idea she had so many of them."

Jerrod shrugged. "Well, maybe she bought them for other folks."

"What other folks?"

"I don't know. Whatever other folks needed them, I guess. I told you she knew everything. Maybe she knew people like me would be coming over and would need towels."

Angel tilted her head. "People like you? What do you mean? You and Jennifer needed towels?"

"No, not me and Ma. Just me." Jerrod couldn't help but laugh a little at the recollection of it all. "Ma had locked me out of the house one night when I stayed out past my curfew."

Angel sat on the couch in the living room, making herself comfortable, like Jerrod was getting ready to tell a long and gripping story. Her eyes were wide with anticipation. "Really? What happened? You came over and stayed with Ms. Essie?"

"Believe me, I didn't want to. But I didn't have much of a choice. Like I said, Ma locked me out, and this was one of those times when she really did what she said she was gonna do if I didn't get home in time." Jerrod sat too. "It was raining so hard that night that I saw animals walking down the street in pairs, headed for the ark."

Angel giggled. Jerrod was glad that she wasn't as somber now as she had been when he arrived. "What happened? Did you have to settle for knocking on Ms. Essie's door?"

Shaking his head in protest, Jerrod said, "Nah. I probably would've slept on the porch before I did that. Ms. Essie heard me calling for Ma to open our house door. I guess since I wasn't getting the message that it was never gonna happen, Ms. Essie came out and told me to come over. I ended up crashing here that night."

Angel looked at the phone that still sat on a stand near the grandfather clock. "Why didn't you just call your mother from here? You know . . . to wake her up so she would open the door."

"Ms. Essie wouldn't let me," Jerrod revealed. "She said it was too late to be calling anybody that time of night. I think we both knew that Ma wasn't really asleep. She heard me knocking; she just wouldn't open the door. It was her way of putting her foot down, I guess."

"So Ms. Essie let you sleep here? That was nice of her." Angel's eyes smiled. Jerrod could tell that she was having other fond memories of Essie.

"Yeah, it was," he agreed. "That's when I found out that although Ms. Essie was old and all, she was still cool. She brought out fresh towels, let me bathe in her guest bathroom, lent me something to sleep in, gave me some peach cobbler, talked to me for a while, and then let me sleep right there." Jerrod pointed at the couch where Angel was sitting.

"One thing I've never known Ms. Essie to do is to let anybody go to bed hungry," Angel said.

Jerrod rubbed his stomach. "Ms. Angel, that peach cobbler was *slammin'*." A rush of sadness threatened to cloud Jerrod's pleasant memories, but he smiled it away. "I sure do miss talking to her."

Standing from the sofa, Angel smoothed out her shorts and turned away from Jerrod. "Me too." Jerrod was sure that he heard sadness in her tone, but before he could say anything, Angel spoke again. "I put a big empty box in her closet. You mind taking the things from the hangers, folding them up, and placing them in the box?"

"Sure, Ms. Angel," Jerrod said.

She never did turn back to face him before walking down the hall. "Thanks," she called over her shoulder. "Call me if you need me."

Jerrod stepped out onto the porch for a bit of fresh air. Things sure felt different without Essie around. The rocking chair she used to sit in daily remained on the front porch, but now, it always sat still. If he concentrated hard enough, Jerrod was certain that he would be able to hear Essie humming. All of her favorite songs seemed to surround the theme of God's perfect timing, but Jerrod couldn't recall any of the words. He wished that he'd asked Essie to teach him some of those songs before she died. Had he known she was going to go, he would have.

The pounding of feet against the sidewalk snatched his attention and he turned to see Elaine rounding the corner of Braxton Way. She must have been finishing up her Saturday morning run.

"Hey, Ms. Elaine." With her Walkman strapped to her arm and with earphones plugged into her ears, Jerrod knew she hadn't heard him, but his waving arms got her attention.

"Hey, you," she said, breathless, slowing her pace to a brisk walk and pulling the plugs from her ears. "You and Angel still packing?"

"Yeah. Yes, ma'am," he corrected himself. "We were gonna load some things in Ms. Angel's car and take them to storage. Looks like the rain might catch us though."

Elaine looked upward. "Looks like," she agreed. "Tell Angel that she can call me if she needs any additional help. I can break away from the computer for a little while if she needs me to."

"A'ight. I'll tell her." Elaine never stopped moving, and by the time Jerrod gave his last response, she'd already passed the house.

Jerrod watch Elaine's hips sway in quick, choppy motions as she pumped her arms and eventually disappeared down the hill that would lead to her home. He had to admit that Elaine had a nice shape too, but not like Angel's. He had never viewed Elaine to be as pretty as Angel, but there was a time when Jerrod thought Elaine's body had the better curves. But that was before Angel lost her post pregnancy weight, and when Elaine was probably fifteen pounds heavier than she was now. Now, to Jerrod, Elaine was too small, bordering on skinny. As an athlete, he believed in staying in shape as much as the next person, but everybody had an ideal weight, and as far as he was concerned, Elaine had crossed over her line at least ten pounds ago.

Wandering back into the house, Jerrod headed straight for his duties. He hadn't been inside Essie's bedroom since the night she died, and he found himself beleaguered at the sight of the bed in which she drew her last breath. Jerrod closed his eyes, swallowed, and then escaped to the closet. Though the confined space was much smaller, it wasn't nearly as smothering. One by one, he took each garment—mostly dresses—down and gingerly folded each before placing them in the open box.

The closet smelled like Essie. The air in it carried that same hint of a lightly scented perfume body lotion that Essie used to wear. The aroma seemed to percolate from the fibers of her clothing, awakening Jerrod's nostrils and filling his head with more memories. One item of clothing, in particular, demanded his undivided attention. He pulled it from its hanger and held it for a long while.

"Everything okay in here, Jerrod?" Angel asked. He hadn't even seen her approach the closet doorway.

"Yes, ma'am," he answered. Then turning to her, Jerrod held up the article and added, "Can I have this?"

Angel stepped closer and pulled the material from his grasp. Her inspection was brief, having identified the faded grey garment almost immediately. "This used to be Mr. Ben's nightshirt," she said. "It has to be sixty years old, at least. Ms. Essie made it for him and kept it because it helped her feel close to him. You like it?"

"It's the shirt she let me wear the night she called me in from the rain and let me sleep on her couch," Jerrod revealed. "She told me that I was the first man to wear it in over sixty years. I guess that means I was the last man to wear it too. I'll pay you for it if you want me to," he offered. "I'd just like to have it, if you don't mind."

Angel embraced Jerrod and smiled upon releasing him. "Of course I don't mind, Jerrod. But I wouldn't dare let you pay me for this. It was just going to get stored away just like everything else. I'm sure Ms. Essie would want you to have it."

"Thanks." It was at that moment that Jerrod noticed the colorful mass that was draped over Angel's shoulder. He gasped. "The blanket!"

"Yeah." Angel smiled and held up the knitted pink and blue blanket that Essie had finished crafting just before her death. "I found it in the closet with the towels and bed linen. I think Colin placed it there. I know he came here a day after she made her transition and did some cleaning. He washed the bed linen that she died on and then placed it back on the bed once he pulled it from the dryer. He told me that the blanket was crumpled on the bed along with her covers when he came in, so he must have washed it too, and put it away."

Remembering clearly, Jerrod nodded. "Yeah. I had put the blanket over her body when the paramedic announced that she was dead. I guess when they moved her they just left the blanket there." He looked at Angel with hopeful eyes. "Are you gonna keep it?"

"Why? Do you want this too?"

"Oh, Ms. Angel. I'd love to have the blanket if you don't want it." Jerrod reached out and touched the linked yarn as he spoke.

After a slight pause, Angel said, "I'll tell you what. When Ms. Essie was living, we were all touched by this blanket in some way. So instead of any one of us keeping it, why don't we all share it?" She handed the blanket to Jerrod. "I'll let you take it first. You and Jennifer can keep it for a while, and then you can pass it on, how's that? That way this will be like the tangible link that we all have to Ms. Essie's memory."

Jerrod could barely contain his excitement when he took the blanket from Angel's grasp. When his hand made contact with it, he almost felt like he had just touched Essie . . . or that she'd just touched him. "Cool! Thanks. I promise to take good care of it."

"I know you wi—"

An unexpected knock at the screen door, accompanied by a roll of thunder, invaded their conversation, and Angel headed to the front of the house with Jerrod following close behind.

"Hey, guys." It was T.K.

"Hey, yourself," Angel said, unlocking the screen door and allowing him to step inside. "What blew you on our side of town this morning?"

"You act like you never see me on this end or something."

T.K. laughed. "I got reasons to be in Braxton Park now, you know."

Snickering, Angel replied, "I know."

Jerrod held his hand out. "'Sup, Coach D?"

"Not too much, kid. How's it going?"

Jerrod wasn't nearly as surprised to see him as Angel was. He knew his favorite teacher was going to show up, but so as not to mess up the little scheme that T.K. and Jennifer had cooked up, he kept his excitement under wraps and acted unprepared. "It's all good. Just helping out Ms. Angel."

"I see." T.K. accepted Jerrod's handshake, and then pulled him in for a quick hug.

Clearing his throat, Jerrod stifled a grin and hoped that his voice wasn't sounding anxious. "So y'all back already, huh?" T.K.'s eyebrows furrowed.

"Y'all, who? Back from where?" Okay, so T.K. was going to make him work for it.

"You and Ma, silly. I was expecting breakfast to last longer than that. Y'all ate pretty fast."

"What are you talking about, Jerrod?" The lines in T.K.'s forehead deepened. "I didn't have breakfast with Jen. I came here looking for her."

Chapter 14

Colin's Story

"Tell Ms. Nona hello," he instructed, handing his son off to his doting secretary.

"He is absolutely adorable," Nona said, placing her lips near Austin's ear and kissing him. "Oh, my goodness. Look at those eyes, look at that handsome smile. He's the spitting image of you, Mr. Stephens."

Colin felt himself blushing. "Thanks. That's my Austin-Boston."

"He's yours all right," she said, pressing her cheek against the child's. "You couldn't have denied this one if you wanted to."

Colin could hold back his grin no longer. "Most people say he looks like me. He's got his mama's nose though."

"Maybe," Nona said, looking from Austin to Colin in careful comparison. "I know one thing. He's a good baby."

"Yes, he is." Pride illuminated Colin's face.

"He's so quiet that I didn't even know you had him in here." She ran her fingers through the child's curly hair.

"Austin's generally not fussy," Colin bragged. "If he cries, either he's sick, hungry, or wearing a soiled diaper. He doesn't cry just to get attention or just to be picked up. He doesn't even cry when he's sleepy."

"He's my kind of baby," Nona said. Then looking at Colin, she added, "What are you doing here anyway? I thought you said yesterday that you were off today."

"Technically, I am, so don't send any calls or any walk-in clients my way." Colin sat behind his desk, picked up a pen, and motioned for Nona to put Austin in the playpen he'd brought with them. "Had a few things I wanted to catch up on, so I thought today would be a good day to do it."

After placing the child down, Nona took the liberty to sit in one of the empty chairs across from Colin's desk. "After you missed your wife and son when you went home for lunch the other day, I'd figure that you'd take any day off to, well . . . be off. This couldn't wait for Monday?"

Colin pretended to be too involved in his note writing to answer right away. He was buying time to think of a response that wouldn't expose the trouble that had been brewing in his house, but one that wouldn't be dishonest either. "Let's just say, I improvised." He closed the folder he'd been writing in and opened another. Not once during this time did he look up at Nona for fear his eyes would betray him. "I brought Austin in so that I could spend time with him and get some work done at the same time."

"And Mrs. Stephens?"

Nona was treading on waters that she'd never approached before. She'd never probed into his personal affairs. Still, Colin opted to answer. "Angel had some busy work to do this morning that would keep her away from the house for several hours anyway. So it's not like Austin and I abandoned her."

"Busy work? Does that mean she's shopping again?"

It was then that Colin looked up and across his desk at his assistant. He'd probably said too much during their recent chats. It wasn't Nona's business that Angel had picked up a habit of shopping unnecessarily, but talking about it with someone lessened Colin's anxiety. Nona was too busy making faces at Austin and drawing laughter from the child to see Colin's stare.

He looked back at the paper on his desk. "No, she's not shopping. Remember her grandmother's friend that I told you about?"

"The one who passed away last year?" Nona asked, now giving him her full attention.

"Yes, Ms. Essie. For the past two or three Saturdays, she's been spending time over there packing away her belongings."

"What's she gonna do with the house? Ms. Essie left it to her, right?"

"Yeah." Colin couldn't recall telling her that, but there was probably a lot he'd said in that state of mind that he wouldn't recall now. He pulled a bottle from Austin's bag and stood to hand it to him. It was time for a nap, and he knew the milk would do the trick. "Angel was pretty much left everything. Ms. Essie didn't have any surviving blood relatives."

"None? How's that possible? She wasn't that old that *all* her relatives were dead."

The disbelieving scowl that distorted Nona's face made Colin chuckle. "She was knocking on eighty—not terribly old by today's standards, I don't guess. But I know that both Ms. Essie's parents were deceased, and both her sisters passed away some years before she did. Her husband died very early in their marriage, and they had no children. So yes; she outlived everyone in her family."

"Her immediate family, maybe," Nona said, "but what about nieces? Great nieces? What about cousins . . . nephews? She had to have some blood relatives left, I would think."

Colin shrugged his shoulders. "Nope. At least, none that she ever spoke of. And no cousins, nephews, or nieces ever came around, so I'm guessing they didn't exist. I never asked, but she never mentioned any either. That's why she took so fondly to Angel. She was her closest thing to having a biological family. Angel's grandmother died when she was pretty young, so since Ms. Essie and Angel's grandmother were such good friends, Ms. Essie became sort of a surrogate grandparent to Angel."

Nona readjusted her position in her chair, then changed the subject. "So, why are you letting these folks in corporate America own you, Mr. Stephens?"

"What do you mean?"

"I mean, you said that Ms. Essie left your wife a ton of money, right? Is it locked away so that you can't gain access to it or something? That's the only way I'd get out of my house on a cloudy day to report to a job that I didn't need."

Colin looked at Nona again. He didn't realize what a boatload of grief he'd unloaded on her when he unburdened himself as they shared coffee at a nearby Starbucks after work a few days ago. It was the reason he'd gotten home so late

the night that he and Angel had the disagreement. He'd needed a listening ear that night,
and Nona's had been perfect. Colin didn't feel
that his issues with Angel were topics that he
could discuss with T.K. or Mason. Mason was
going through his own storm, and T.K . . . well,
he thought Colin and Angel had the perfect marriage. Colin didn't want to tarnish his friend's
image.

"Did I say something wrong?" Nona had become concerned by Colin's unresponsiveness.
"I'm sorry. I just—"

"You didn't say anything wrong," Colin said.
"But can you not say it so loud? I don't need anyone else in the office knowing my business."

Placing her hand to her lips, Nona lowered
her voice. "Was I talking loud? My grandmama—
God bless the dead—used to tell me all the time
that my voice carried. She was always telling me
to shut up. Said I talked too loud and too much."
She sucked her teeth like the recalled chastise-
ment brought back old childhood wounds, then
said, "I'm sorry. I'll be more mindful of the volume."

Rubbing his forehead, Colin released a sigh.
"This is just not the kind of information I want to
become common knowledge, that's all."

"Oh, don't worry, Mr. Stephens," she assured him. "I'd never do that to you. I know you confided in me in the strictest of confidence, and I want you to know that you can trust me like a big sister. None of these folks around here will ever hear me repeat anything you've said."

Colin chuckled. "Like a big sister? You think you're older than I am?"

Nona flashed a flattered smile. "I know I am."

"How do you know that?"

"What are you, Mr. Stephens? Twenty-five . . . twenty-six?"

It was Colin's turn to be flattered. Her guess didn't surprise him though. Most people thought he was younger than his age. When he and Angel first got married, they'd often be mistaken as teenaged newlyweds. "I'll be thirty-two before the end of the year," he said.

"Really?" Nona looked surprised. "When you first introduced yourself on the day I interviewed, I kept thinking of how odd it was going to be to have to refer to some kid who was fresh out of college as *Mr.* anything."

"I've been out of college for ten years," Colin bragged.

"Well, I'm not telling my age, so don't even ask," Nona said, grinning. "I'm not as much your senior as I thought, but I still qualify to be your big sister. So if you don't have a biological one, you can adopt me. I'll still work like a regular employee," she added through a giggle.

Colin came back with, "If you want to be paid as one, I suggest you do."

They shared a laugh.

"Well?" Nona pitched.

"Well, what?"

Nona rolled her eyes and shook her head. "I might be older, but you've got the worst memory. Why are you working when you don't have to?"

Reaching into his top drawer to switch from the black writing pen he had used earlier to one that contained blue ink, Colin said, "For starters, everything Ms. Essie left Angel wasn't cash money. Her home, property, and some personal valuables were included in that."

"Still, it's enough for you to tell these folks who are overworking you to kiss your behind. You don't have to be here."

Colin laughed. "I don't think a half, or even three quarters of a million dollars is enough to retire off of. If I were twenty years older, maybe it would be a thought. But at Angel's age and my age, and with so many years ahead of us, God willing, I don't think it's enough to live comfortably off of for the rest of our lives. Not with a growing son who, seventeen years from now, will need money for college. Despite how much money my wife has, I'm still head of household, and I have a family to take care of. Even the Bible tells us that a man who doesn't work shouldn't eat."

"I can think of at least a dozen men, right off the top of my head, that you need to talk to," Nona said with a grunt. "If all brothas thought like you, there wouldn't be so many single sistas in the world. Mrs. Stephens is a lucky woman, but I know she doesn't need me to tell her that."

Colin curled his tongue to keep his mouth from forming the words that it begged to. *Please tell her.* That's what he wanted to say. Maybe if Nona told Angel how lucky she was, she'd appreciate him more; give him more love and affection.

"So how late are you going to be working today?" Nona asked, standing. She crept toward Austin's playpen and reached down. When she returned to her full height, she held a near-empty bottle in her hand.

Colin stood and looked over his desk. "Is he asleep?"

"Out like a light," Nona answered.

Taking the bottle from her hand, Colin placed it in the middle of his desk, just above the file he'd opened several minutes earlier. Looking at his watch, he said, "I'm not sure how late I'll be here today. Probably only for another hour or so."

"Well, if you're still here at lunchtime and want to grab a bite to eat before going home, it's my turn to treat."

"I don't think I'll be here for three more hours, but I appreciate the offer. Even if I am, I've got Austin."

"So? Bring him along," she said, turning toward the door. "As they say, the more the merrier. It's not like he's gonna run up my tab."

Laughing, Colin said, "True."

Just before turning the doorknob to let herself out, Nona turned back to face him. "I mean it, Mr. Stephens. I'd love to have both of you join me for lunch. You're a great boss, and I enjoy your company. Plus it'll give me more time to play with my new little nephew."

Colin hadn't felt like his company was appreciated in some time. With his parents living so far away and his wife's lack of interest, these days he hadn't felt like he had much of a family either.

"Just give it some thought," she added with a blithe wave of her hand. "If I don't see you again before you leave, enjoy the rest of your weekend. Unlike you, I have to be here until closing."

Chapter 15

Elaine's Story

The massage setting on the shower head was just what her tired body needed. Elaine faced away from the rotating jet stream and allowed the water to beat on her back like a set of trained hands. Today's run was more difficult than usual. Her lungs didn't have the same wind capacity as normal. A routine that had become almost effortless for her over the past several months had been a worthy opponent today. Every hill, every winding way, every mile that she ran was a challenge.

"I've got to get to bed earlier tonight," Elaine told herself just before shutting off the water. She couldn't workout at full intensity if she didn't get the proper rest.

For the past two nights, she'd labored late into the night to keep pace with her writing schedule's growing demands. She'd prayed for her writing to capture the eyes of other magazines, and it had. As of yesterday, she was now writing for two major magazines. The editor for a third one had left a message on her voice mail requesting a return call.

"I've got to make that a priority today."

Elaine often had these self-chatting sessions in the morning before she began her day. They kept her focused on what things were most pressing. She'd discovered long ago that if she gave her day a schedule, more of the items on her daily list got accomplished.

She was already behind on today's agenda. Running hadn't been a part of Elaine's plan, and doing so had set her back an hour. She hadn't run on a Saturday since she reached her ideal weight. Or at least, what she *thought* was her ideal weight. Mason's continued detachment from her had put things in their proper perspective. Nothing like a man's repulsion to bring out the truth, and her husband's distance told Elaine that she still had a long way to go.

"Let's see here," she said, examining her nude form in the mirror of the master bath that was connected to her bedroom. Her stomach was flat, her waistline was trim, and when she held her arms out and shook them, there was barely any jiggle. Her inherited hips remained, but

Elaine could see a little improvement in them since she resumed the habit of purging herself at least once a day. Sometimes, she did it twice. But only when it was absolutely necessary. She didn't dare lose control and get like those silly women who did it after every single meal.

"Elaine . . . you here?" It was Mason's voice, and it was coming from the open doorway of their bedroom. It was his Saturday off, and he'd come home from getting his truck washed.

Elaine stood up straight and took in a breath that thrust forward her breasts. Striking the sultriest pose that she could, she purred, "Yes, Mason; I'm here. I'm in the bathroom. Just got out of the shower."

"Oh. Sorry. I'll see you when you come out."

The bedroom door closed and Elaine's chest deflated in synchronized fashion. She would have given anything for him to walk in on her. Maybe if she hadn't indicated that she wasn't dressed, he would have chanced coming in.

"You're so pathetic," she scolded her reflection while snatching her silk robe from the counter and covering the hideous sight that was her body.

Mason hadn't seen her unclothed in over a year. Elaine had seen him once, but that was only because she'd invaded his privacy without his knowledge. Elaine imagined that Mason would be livid if he knew that she'd stood, like a common voyeur, peeking through the small opening in the guest bathroom door one morning as he prepared for work, and watched as he dried the water from his freshly bathed body. She wondered if lusting was a sin if the "lustee" was her husband. Elaine knew that Mason wouldn't approve of what she'd done, but she needed something to hold on to. Something to remind her of what used to be. Something to give her hope of what she might be able to look forward to again.

"Hey." She put on her best smile when she emerged from the bedroom.

"What's up?" Mason was sitting on the sofa removing his second shoe. "Why are you showering so early? You going somewhere?"

Elaine sat on the loveseat opposite him and intentionally exposed the fullness of one of her legs. "I ran this morning, so I needed to freshen up."

"Oh." Mason's eyes lingered on her, but not in a good way. Elaine felt uneasy under his stare. "Listen," he said, "how would you feel about missing services at Temple of God's Word tomorrow?"

"Missing service? Why?" They had been very faithful in their church attendance over the past year, and they still needed all the divine intervention that they could get. Elaine wasn't at all sure about agreeing to Mason's yet unexplained plans. "You don't have to work tomorrow, do you?"

"No. Nothing like that. I was just thinking that maybe, for once, we could do something . . . I don't know, different."

Elaine reconsidered her apprehension. Maybe Mason wanted to take her somewhere romantic, where it would be just the two of them. Or maybe on such short notice, he had something less dramatic in mind, like a lazy day at home—never getting out of bed. Just the thought of it sent ripples up Elaine's spine. A quiet day alone could be just what they needed. Missing one Sunday service wouldn't hurt them. In fact, if they were creative and spontaneous enough, it would help them.

"I know you . . . I mean, *we* made a commitment to attend Temple of God's Word regularly, but—"

"No, it's okay," Elaine quickly put in. "We can do something . . . *different.* I'd love to, as a matter of fact." She tried not to sound too anxious, but her body was already tingling.

"Really?" Mason's whole body relaxed, like he had been expecting the worst.

Elaine smiled. She was glad that she'd pleased him with her answer. "Really."

"Wow, babe. I owe you an apology."

This was already looking like a winner. Mason had called her babe and had mentioned his need to apologize in the same sentence. She hadn't heard either one of those words from him in months. Elaine was just about to put on a naïve front and ask him what on earth had he done to warrant an apology when she found out that had she "played dumb," it wouldn't have been an act at all. Her assumptions of what Mason had in mind had been way off base.

"I told Reverend Tides that it would be like pulling teeth to get you to go to a church other than the one Ms. Essie went to," Mason said.

"What?" Elaine felt like a fool. "What? Where? What? Huh?" She sounded like a fool too.

"Reverend Tides. B.T. Tides," Mason said, still smiling with relief. "You know, the preacher that got kidnapped a couple of years back. The one with the big church over in Stone Mountain."

Elaine knew very well who Reverend B.T. Tides was. *Everybody* knew who Reverend B.T. Tides was. Although his church wasn't as large, Reverend Tides's celebrity status, in recent years, had grown to challenge that of Bishop T.D. Jakes. What Elaine couldn't understand was how Mason had gotten close enough to the revered preacher to see him, let alone talk to him.

"What do you mean you *told* him it would be like pulling teeth? You know Reverend Tides?"

At first, Mason appeared to be thrown by her question. "No . . . no, I don't know him. I mean, I know him, but I don't *know* him know him. You know he's T.K.'s pastor, right?"

"Yeah, but what does that have to do with you?"

"Nothing, really." Mason shifted his feet. "I just . . . well, I ran into him the other day, and of course, he didn't know me, but I knew who he was, so I spoke to him."

"And he actually talked to you?" Elaine had never met the pastor personally. She'd heard Jennifer mention him and rave at how much she enjoyed the Sundays that she visited the church with T.K., but Elaine had never imagined that a pastor of his caliber would be so personable as to talk to common folks.

Mason laughed at her question. "Yes, he talked to me. Why wouldn't he?"

"I hear he has bodyguards and stuff." Elaine frowned. "Jennifer says that the church has a security staff and they're always standing somewhere near him when church adjourns."

"Well, I'm sure they do," Mason replied. "If I were him and some crazy dude kidnapped and tried to kill me, I'd have some bodyguards too. But they ain't with him twenty-four-seven. They weren't with him when I saw him."

"Where'd you see him?"

"Out near his church," Mason said. "Why does it matter where I saw him, Elaine? That's not the point. The point is that I saw him and we spoke. He invited me to stop in and visit some time, and I thought tomorrow would be a good day to do it since it's not pastoral Sunday at Temple of God's Word."

"Oh." Elaine had nothing against New Hope Church, but this wasn't the *different* plan that she hoped Mason had in mind.

"Well, don't get too excited," he noted in sarcasm. "What's wrong? You got a problem with going with me to visit his service tomorrow?"

Elaine tried to smile through her disappointment. "Of course not. Sure, we can go there if you want to. Just to visit though. I'm not crazy about churches whose memberships run into the thousands. That's just too many people for me."

"We're just going to visit," he assured her.

"Okay. Fine." Elaine pulled her robe close to her body. Mason was staring at her again. That same strange, almost perplexed stare that made her uneasy the first time. She was about to ask him why he was looking at her in that manner, but his answer came before her question.

"What's going on with your weight?"

"My weight?" Without thinking, Elaine pulled back the leg that she'd left exposed for the purpose of bait, and hid it beneath her robe. "What do you mean?"

Mason stood from the sofa and took cautious steps toward her, looking her over like a paid inspector. Elaine squirmed. Why was he looking at her like that? "I mean, your weight," he said. "What's going on? What are you trying to do?"

"What do you mean, what am I trying to do?" Elaine blinked back tears. She was trying all she knew to lose the extra pounds. What more could she do?

"I mean it's too much," he said. "It's too much, Elaine. You need to slow down or stop doing whatever it is that you're doing all together."

Elaine's lips trembled as she tried to form her next words. The ringing of the telephone interrupted them, and Mason excused himself to answer. His walking away gave Elaine the opportunity to escape. She scuffled to the bedroom and back into the bathroom where she secured herself behind the locked door and wept silently.

What did he mean by saying she needed to slow down? She was already ignoring hunger pangs and barely eating as it was.

"*. . . or stop doing whatever it is that you're doing all together.*"

The end of his sentence rang in her ear. Stop all together? Did he want her to stop eating period? Starve herself?

With water still dancing in the corners of her eyes, Elaine looked at her blurred reflection in the bathroom mirror. "If that's what it takes, then that's what I'll do."

Chapter 16

Jennifer's Story

For ten minutes, she'd been sitting in her car hoping that the downpour from heaven would at least lighten up so that she could get from her driveway into her house without getting drenched. "I thought for sure that my umbrella was in this car," Jennifer muttered with regret while looking into the backseat. "Of all days to leave it at home."

She glanced at her watch; her third check for the time since parking. An unconscious smile tugged at her lips as she ran her index finger over the glass face. The watch reminded her of T.K. He'd given her the gold Guess timepiece for Christmas last year. She'd never had a more beautiful accessory to grace her wrist. He had great taste and always seemed to know exactly what she wanted.

"Apparently not," Jennifer scolded, shoving the pleasant memory from her mind. "If he *really* knows what I want . . . *wanted*," she corrected in a tone that was meant to be convincing, "I would have had another, more defining piece of gold jewelry by now." She rubbed her temples. This was no time to think of T.K. In fact, he was the last thing that needed to be on her mind right now. Thinking about him only confused the matter. He'd had his chance.

The rainfall had lightened, but still fell steadily. Whether it stopped or not, she had to get out. Jennifer was on a schedule; had a plan. And if there was any chance of everything going as smoothly as she hoped, her getting inside the house and having ample opportunity to prepare her son was her only option.

"Lord, if this boy messes this up for me . . ." Jennifer left the sentence open. As much as she'd like to believe that this conversation with Jerrod was going to be easy, the knot in the pit of her stomach indicated differently.

On second thought, he might just surprise her. Jerrod had matured by light-years over the past twelve months. The stubborn, temperamental, unruly Jerrod hadn't been seen since he came to accept Essie's death. If he could keep his cool and help pack away Essie's things, with the full knowledge that Angel was preparing the house for the market, then surely Jerrod could make other substantial adjustments.

"He's gonna do just fine. As a matter of fact, this could be something he's secretly wanted his whole life. What boy wouldn't?" The pep talk was working, and a smile sneaked across Jennifer's face. "God works in mysterious ways. Everything happens for a reason." It was a notation that she'd heard Reverend Owens make during more than one Sunday morning sermon. "And if everything happens for a reason, and God is in control of everything," Jennifer rationalized, "then God had to have His hand in this one. This is just too major to be a coincidence."

The last of her declaration was muttered through wet lips. Jennifer had abandoned her car and dashed up the steps as quickly as she could. Despite her best efforts, her blouse clung to her body by the time she reached the shelter of her porch. It had been some time since Alpharetta had gotten a good soaking like this one. Jennifer pulled open the screen door, then fumbled with her keys in slippery hands.

"Jerrod!" The sight of her son standing directly on the other side of the front door shocked her. She wiped her hand across her flattened hair, and then proceeded to place her wet purse on the floor near the door. "Boy, don't scare me like that. If you were standing right here and saw me struggling to unlock the front door, why didn't you just open it?"

When she got no answer, Jennifer turned to see Jerrod still standing quietly, looking at her as though she were some uninvited guest. An invader, even. "Did you hear me, Jerrod?"

He nodded. "Yeah, I heard you."

His uncommon less-than-reverent response took Jennifer aback. He hadn't responded to her with a *yeah* in months. Instead of addressing his backslidden behavior directly, Jennifer aimed for the root of the problem. "What's wrong with you? If you heard me, then why didn't you answer me?"

Jerrod hunched his shoulders. "I wasn't standing here the whole time. I just walked up to the door right before you opened it."

"Oh." She didn't know if she quite believed him, but Jennifer let it slide. Still, she had an eerie feeling that something had happened in her absence. If she kept talking, maybe she'd find out. She softened her tone. "What did you do today? Did you and Angel get much done, or did the rain interfere with your work?"

Jerrod stepped away from the spot he'd been occupying and walked to the nearby couch and sat. "We packed some stuff, but we didn't make it to storage." He crossed his right foot over his left knee; a pose he'd definitely gotten from his coach.

T.K. sat like that whenever he was in deep conversation; especially with Jerrod—when they had those man-to-man talks.

Jennifer shook thoughts of T.K. from her head for the second time, and then walked around the bar and pulled several sheets of paper towels from the upright metal holder that sat on the counter. As she dried her arms and face, the hovering silence felt as if it were closing in, threatening to smother her.

Jennifer searched for a way to introduce the topic of conversation that needed to be addressed. The clock was ticking, and her grace period would soon end.

"Where you been, Ma?" His question could have been the perfect segue, but Jennifer didn't like the tone in which it was posed.

She looked up and across the way toward where Jerrod still sat scrutinizing her for a reason she still hadn't figured out. "What do you mean, where have I been?" Jennifer tried not to sound defensive, but she could hear it in her own voice. "I told you where I was going this morning. I know you heard me."

"Yeah, I heard you. But Coach D stopped by looking for you, so you wasn't with him like you said you were."

Hot flashes couldn't have been more uncomfortable. An overbearing heated feeling traveled from the base of Jennifer's neck to the roots of her hair, forming beads of sweat around the edges. She wiped them away with the paper towel she still held. Of all the Saturdays for T.K. to make an unannounced visit, he chose today. What was he stopping in for? Actions spoke louder than words, and his actions had proven that she hadn't meant very much to him. At least not as much as she thought she meant. "I never told you that I was with T.K., Jerrod. I told you that I was going to breakfast."

"With Coach D." His voice was accusing.

Jennifer shook her head in denial. "Jerrod, I never said I was going with T.K. I said I was going to breakfast, and you *assumed* that I was going with him."

Jerrod uncrossed his legs and stood to look at her. His voice didn't call her a liar, but his face did. "Ma, I sat right there in the bed and asked you if you and Coach were hanging out today, and you said you were going to breakfast."

Jennifer knew that she'd misled her son, but she found vindication in knowing that her response to his accusation would be the truth. "I said that *I* was going to breakfast. I didn't say I was going with T.K."

"But I asked you if you were going with Coach."

"And my reply was, 'Going to breakfast.' Not once did I say I was going with him." Even to her own hearing, she sounded like a deceiver.

Jerrod flailed his arms in the air, and then allowed them to fall by his side. "Fine." His concession clearly wasn't by choice. "So who were you with, then?"

Jennifer cocked her neck. "Don't you take that tone with me, Jerrod D. Mays. Who do you think you're talking to? I'm the mama. I don't have to answer to you."

Plopping back onto the cushions of the couch, Jerrod immediately picked up the remote control and turned on the television set. Jennifer watched as he stared at the screen, watching some show that he probably had little or no interest in. This was not the way she'd planned for this conversation to go. How had things gotten so off-track? With her eyes resting on the digital clock that was built in to her oven, Jennifer knew that she had to work fast. She had less than ten minutes to start the conversation over and make it work to her advantage.

Quick steps delivered her from the kitchen to the living room where she gently took the remote from her son's hand and sat beside him, placing the television on mute. She shivered a little in the damp clothes she still wore, but there was no time for a wardrobe change. Jerrod's eyes darted away from her, aiming for the front door that she'd left open. The pitter of the spring shower was almost rhythmic.

"Jerrod, please look at me." When he complied, she continued. "Listen, I need to talk to you about something. I need to ask you some questions so you can tell me what you think about some things."

"Ma, how you gonna not answer my question, but then you got questions that you want me to answer?"

"Because I'm—"

"I know you're the mama," he said through a sigh. "You ain't got to keep telling me that, Ma. But just 'cause you the parent, that means I don't get to get no answers? I ain't earned your respect yet?"

Jennifer swallowed hard. The last thing she wanted was for her son to think his feelings didn't count. She squeezed his hand. "Of course you have my respect, Jerrod. As a matter of fact, answering your question is what I'm trying to do here. It's just not as cut and dry as you want to make it. I need you to let me explain."

"A'ight. I'm listening." His left leg resumed its place; crossed over his right knee.

Jennifer squirmed on the leather couch. "I, uh . . . I've been seeing someone."

"I know that, Ma. You and Coach can't think I'm that stupid that I don't know what's up."

"I don't mean T.K." With those words, Jerrod stiffened, and Jennifer felt that if she didn't keep talking, she'd lose her nerve. "I mean, I *was* seeing T.K., but not anymore."

"What you mean, not no more? Since when did this happen? We was all just together less than a week ago."

"I know, Jerrod, and that's when I realized that our relationship—mine and T.K.'s—wasn't going anywhere. Listen," Jennifer said, interrupting another oncoming outburst from Jerrod. "I prayed about this, and I think God sent me my answer."

"What answer? Coach D done been with us through everything, Ma. Ms. Essie's death, my trial, everything. How you gonna just dump him like this?"

"What makes you think I dumped him? Why do you automatically assume that I'm the villain here? T.K. has made it clear that—"

"Coach D just left here not that long ago, Ma. He came here to see you, so I know this ain't his idea. You had to be the one to walk, 'cause if he had ditched you, he wouldn't have been coming here to visit. Does he even know that you're seeing some other dude?"

Jennifer felt trapped. Her tongue was so pasty that she wanted to go back outside and stand with her face to the sky; mouth wide open. "Listen, Jerrod. It's not that sim—"

"He don't know, do he?" Jerrod was up and pacing now. "I can't believe you dissing Coach like this."

Jennifer stood too. "I'm not *dissing* anybody, Jerrod. If you'd just listen for a second, I can explain everything."

"Explain what, Ma? I knew you were gonna do this. I just knew it."

"Do what?" Jennifer placed her hands on her hips and dared him to say something foolish. He was taller than she, and he was too old for her to whip, but she wouldn't think twice about banishing him to his room without dinner.

"*This*," Jerrod stressed. "I knew that if I got to where I really liked Coach, you'd find some way to run him off."

Tears burned in Jennifer's eyes. How could he say such a thing to her, like she got her kicks from breaking up with men just to add misery to his life? "I didn't run anybody off, Jerrod. It just didn't work out, that's all. Relationships fail all the time, and ours just happened to be one of them."

"Don't a relationship take two people? How is it gonna fail when don't but one of y'all know it done failed? Coach don't even know he been dumped. And for who? Some man you just met?"

"I didn't exactly *just* meet him. I—"

"You might not have just met him, but you had to just start seeing him this week, 'cause before now, you ain't been seeing nobody but Coach." He had a point, and Jennifer couldn't think fast enough to respond. Instead, it was Jerrod who continued his rant. "What's so good about him that he was worth leaving a man as great as Coach D? He can't be a better man. There ain't no better man than Coach D."

"He's a *very* good man, Jerrod, and it's very unfair for you to judge him when you haven't even met him yet."

"I don't want to meet him. He's your choice, not mine. If you marry him, he'll be your husband, but he ain't gonna be my daddy; that's for sure."

"Jerrod!" Jennifer rebuked.

"Well, what you want me to say, Ma? That I like him? I don't. Like you just said, I don't even know the man."

Jennifer looked up at Jerrod with pleading eyes when she reached out and touched his arm. "I want you to meet him and get to know him, Jerrod. I know if you get to know him, you'll like him. It's important to me that you like him. Your opinion matters."

"It must not matter. You ain't talk to me before you ditched Coach, and you ain't talk to me before you hooked up with this other dude. If it didn't matter then, how come it matters now?"

"Because there's a very good chance that Devon is going to be a part of our family." The words had exited Jennifer's lips before she had the chance to block them. This wasn't the way she wanted her son to find out. Nothing was going as she'd planned it.

"*Devon*?" Jerrod's face twisted and his brows puckered. "His name is Devon?" Before she could reply, his third-degree continued. "What you sayin', Ma? I know you ain't talkin' marriage? You just met this dude and I, the person whose opinion you say matters, ain't *never* met him. How you gonna even be thinking about making him a part of the family? You ain't pregnant, are you?"

Jennifer's palm burned from the solid connection it made to Jerrod's cheek. The blow was so intense that it nearly sent the boy falling back onto the sofa. Somehow, he steadied his footing, and with a look that exuded anger and disbelief, rubbed the place where Jennifer's hand had made impact.

Jennifer saw a look in her son's eyes that she hadn't seen in over a year, but the memories of it were too recent to be totally forgotten. It was that glare he used to give her back in his rebellious days. A look that would send terrifying chills down her spine and make her fear that he was capable of harming her. She took a step back, suddenly feeling the need to guard herself against the worst.

The sudden opening and closing of the screen door caused both of them to turn and face the front of the house. Jennifer looked from Jerrod to Devon. He was right on time, yet his timing couldn't have been worse. She didn't know how much he'd overheard or what he'd witnessed, but it was too late to take any of it back or explain any of it away.

"Hello, Jerrod."

Devon's warm greeting seemed to escape Jerrod's hearing. Jennifer held her breath as her son's eyes narrowed, and then slowly widened

as he turned back to face her. She didn't know
what to say. What could she say? From Jerrod's
expression, Jennifer knew that no introductions
were needed. Jerrod's eyes told her that it all
made sense now. Why Jennifer was taken in so
quickly by this "new" man, why she was considering marriage after such a short courtship, and
why the figure standing in the doorway had the
same first name as Jerrod's middle name.

Chapter 17

Mason's Story

He'd never stood up this much in church, but there was something about the praise and worship service at New Hope that kept Mason on his feet. The songs were spirit-filled, and the praise team sang with elevated conviction. If heaven truly had a choir, this must be close to what those cherubic voices sounded like.

Mason felt like he was in the presence of God now, but the morning certainly hadn't started out that way.

He'd basically had to beg Elaine to keep her word. She had agreed that they would go to New Hope Church instead of Temple of God's Word. Yet, Elaine got up Sunday morning with a case of amnesia, pretending that she was mystified when he mentioned their plan for the day. By the time they finished arguing as they got prepared for service, Mason was about ready to wave the white towel of surrender. Fussing with Elaine was physically draining. Literally.

Mason sweated through two dress shirts during their hour-long heated discussion. It was as though Elaine felt like missing a Sunday at Temple of God's Word was a cardinal sin that came with no forgiveness. A one-way ticket to hell to spend eternity with the devil and his goons. Knowing that most of it was her need to feel as though she was keeping her promise to Essie, Mason made a valiant attempt to be understanding. But Elaine had only promised Essie that they'd go to church with her the Sunday following her conversation with the elderly woman. They hadn't signed in blood that they'd go to Temple of God's Word and *only* Temple of God's Word for the rest of their lives. But one would have thought so with the way Elaine carried on.

In the end, Mason won. There was no TKO. He'd had to go the full twelve rounds, and his win was definitely a split decision. Nothing unanimous about this one. And he didn't get through it without feeling the body aches of a man whose endurance had been pushed to the limits. Elaine had proved herself to be a worthy challenger. The verbal combat had exhausted him, but the win still made him want to break into one of those tap dancing routines that he'd often seen the WB frog do on television back in the day.

But he didn't.

When the couple finally arrived at the church, they'd both been a bit intimidated by the throng of people who were pressing toward the entrance door. The parking lot alone was unsettling. Cars belonging to people who went to the early morning service were pulling out, while new arrivals for the second service vied for the precious spots.

Mason saw his wife look at her watch as they pulled onto the church property. "It's barely eleven-fifteen, and the parking lot is already just about filled. I thought you said they started at eleven-thirty. Are we late?"

"We're not late, Elaine. They're just more prompt than the people we normally worship with."

"We probably won't even find a good seat in this big old church," Elaine grumbled.

Mason climbed from the driver's seat and slipped on his suit jacket. She was trying his patience, but he remained silent. The sunglasses he'd worn while driving were still covering his eyes. He peered through them at Elaine as she rounded the trunk of the car. The melon-colored dress and matching high-heeled sandals that she wore was a sharp ensemble that he'd not seen her in before today. It must have been new. She'd been shopping quite a bit recently, buying new clothes that would fit her slimmer figure.

Shaking his head and turning away was all that Mason could do to keep from making a remark that he knew he'd regret. He was all for being fit. Heck. He'd pay good money if he could find a pill that would make his expanding midsection shrink overnight. But Elaine had adopted more than just an active lifestyle; she'd become fixated with the whole idea of weight management. Gone were the steep curves that he used to love, and the ample behind that made his insides quiver was performing a disappearing act that he didn't find entertaining at all.

If he thought his opinion mattered to her, Mason would tell Elaine not to lose any more weight. Going back and recovering some of what she'd already shed would be even better. But why should she change for him? He hadn't touched her in years. Okay, it wasn't years. But it sure felt like it.

God, please restore me. Make me whole again. I need my manhood back. I need to be a husband. Help me to forgive . . . forget . . . do whatever needs to be done to find healing. He'd been praying that prayer in his heart ever since his meeting with Reverend Tides.

"Well, are you coming or not?" Elaine's voice snapped Mason back from wherever his mind had traveled. He didn't even realize he'd been staring mindlessly at her. It was almost 80 degrees, but Elaine used her arms to hug her body like she was cold as she continued to reprimand him. "We're already not gonna get a good seat, Mason. If you move any slower, we won't even be able to get in the church period. You're the one who wanted to come here today, so why are you standing there looking at me like you're having second thoughts?"

She still wasn't thrilled about coming to New Hope and Mason knew it. "I'm coming." He pulled his brush from the cup holder in the armrest that divided the driver's seat from the passenger's and raked it over his head a few times for good measure. It was almost time for a haircut, but it would wait until next weekend. "Okay, I'm ready."

The two of them walked side-by-side toward the entrance-way and were met by several greeters who handed them church bulletins, offering envelopes, and one even offered them a Bible.

"We have one." Elaine sounded offended, and Mason gave her a side glance as they walked toward the wooden doors that would place them inside the sanctuary.

"What's wrong with you?" he whispered.

"What's wrong with *him*?" She nodded toward the greeter as she whispered back. "What makes him think I need a Bible? I don't look holy enough for him or something? How is he just gonna assume?"

Mason's forehead creased. "I think he was just being friendly, Elaine. Lighten up."

He heard her harrumph and then say, "These people who go to these big ole churches that got famous pastors, think they're so much closer to Jesus than everybody else."

Mason clenched his teeth to keep from telling her to shut her piehole, but something needed to be said about her unwarranted bashing. He'd developed an unexplained closeness to Reverend Tides; trusted him more than he trusted his own mama, not to mention his absent daddy. No way was he not going to defend the man of God's honor.

Mason waited until they were seated before responding, and when he did, he kept his voice as low as possible to be sure the others seated near them couldn't easily hear. "Why would you make a judgment call like that? You just called that usher judgmental, and now you're doing the same thing. That man don't know us from Adam and Eve. He don't know what size church we go to, so how would he know to treat us differently because of it? New Hope ain't the biggest church in metropolitan Atlanta. For all he knows, we could go to that mega church over in Decatur whose pastor has not only been seen on televised ministry broadcasting, but in actual movies and music videos. This church ain't got nothing on the size of that one."

"Umph," was Elaine's reply.

When she folded her arms and sat back, Mason knew he'd won another one. Two bouts in one day. Two marks in the win column. He was on a roll. And anyone who knew Elaine knew that winning one round against her wasn't an easy feat, let alone winning the whole match. He had recuperated enough from this morning's bout with her to carry out that frog dance now.

But he didn't.

Mason looked around them for any signs of T.K. With the size of the edifice, it was probably a lost cause, but he scanned his surroundings anyway. While he didn't see T.K., he did notice Mother Mildred Tides, Reverend Tides's wife, enter from a side door flanked by two attendants. She sat up front in a corner chair with other hat-wearing women who appeared to be church mothers. He saw two tall, handsome young men, who he knew to be Reverend Tides's sons, walk in as well. One stopped at the front row of the center section and the other made his way to the pulpit, pausing to kneel and pray before taking his seat.

"How late do they stay in service here?"

Mason looked at Elaine and struggled to keep his aggravation from showing on his face. He wasn't as successful with keeping it out of his voice. "This is my first time being in service here too, Elaine. Your guess is as good as mine."

She looked back at him like he had some nerve getting facetious with her. "Seems like you would have found that out before agreeing to come. What if this is one of those four-hour Sunday morning service churches? I have work to do. Writing deadlines to meet. I can't be here all morning and all afternoon. It don't take all day to praise the Lord."

Mason sighed, willing his unraveling nerves to remain under control. "T.K. is never in church that late, Elaine. I don't think that's something that we have to concern ourselves with. Just sit back and relax. It's almost time for service to get started."

"Yeah. *If* they start on time."

Mason bit his bottom lip to keep from saying the words that were bombarding his mind. What was her problem today? Elaine wasn't usually a grouch like this. Maybe if she ate more, she wouldn't be so grumpy. His mama had always taught him and his brothers to eat well before going to school and before going to work. She said hungry people always had foul attitudes. Until now, Mason had questioned the validity of her declaration, but Elaine was living proof.

It wasn't as if services at Temple of God's Word ever kicked off on time. And what was the hurry anyway? Elaine had plenty of time to get some writing done today. It wasn't like she had anywhere to be. Mason tossed a glare in her direction. She was really getting on his nerves.

"Let us stand and give our God a worthy praise," Minister Jackson Tides said, taking the podium.

It was only then that Mason began to unwind.

"Let's let the Father in heaven know that He is welcome in this place," Jackson urged in a commanding voice while his eyes scanned the crowd. "Cast your cares, pitch your problems, hurl your heavy burdens. . . . Toss everything that threatens to steal your joy at the feet of the Almighty King." While he spoke, he held the cordless microphone in his right hand and gestured vigorously with his left, as though he was using all his might to throw his problems at Jesus' feet.

Amidst the rising sounds of music from the keyboard, organ, drums, and guitar, the crowd of thousands that had assembled into New Hope Church began a verbal worship, accompanied by clapping, waving; some even leaping as the Holy Spirit wasted no time saturating the sanctuary.

And just like that, Mason felt himself being drawn into the presence of holiness. He felt balls of tension—tension that he didn't even realize he had in his neck and shoulders—loosen. At the end of his meeting with Reverend Tides, the pastor had used those same words: *Cast your cares*. Mason had heard them before, but had never given them any real thought and basically didn't even know what they meant. Up until his talk with Reverend Tides, they'd just been words that church people used, but the patient preacher had talked to him; given him a crash course on what it meant to truly release it all to God. It had been hard to reach that point during the meeting, but as he stood in praise with the body of New Hope, Mason felt as though he had spiritual cheerleaders egging him on; daring him to give God all he had.

"Praising Him will be the beginning of your healing," Reverend Tides had told him. "Satan is going to do all he can, even use anybody that he can, to try and dissuade you from praising your way through. But you've got to do it anyway."

No truer words had ever been spoken. Getting to church today and finding the strength to worship had been anything but easy. Realizing now that it wasn't just a battle that he'd won against Elaine, but a war for which he could claim victory over Satan, Mason felt overjoyed with emotions. He found himself really wanting to work his way to the center aisle and froggie tap his way the full distance to the front of the church.

And he did.

Chapter 18

Angel's Story

She used the sweatband on her wrist to wipe away perspiration that had begun pooling on her forehead. "See, this is why I feel so guilty when I exercise with you," Angel told Elaine. "I know that if I weren't here slowing you down, you'd be on your way back by now."

"Girl, please," Elaine said, waving her hand at her for added effect. "You're not slowing me down. I kinda feel like power walking instead of running today anyway."

Angel looked at her friend. Elaine was breathing harder than normal today, like the brisk walking was as much a challenge to her as it was for Angel. Angel wasn't fooled though. She knew it was all an act—albeit, a good act—for her benefit. Angel knew that Elaine wanted her to believe that she was getting the benefits of a full workout so Angel wouldn't keep harping on holding her back. She appreciated the empathy.

Elaine added, "And if you really look at it the way it is, you're the one who's doing me a favor. I called you and asked you to come walk with me today, anyway; remember?"

"Yeah, I remember," Angel said. "But I still know this isn't the intensity of your regular routine."

"Will you stop it? I'm fine," Elaine panted. "I read in one of my many sports magazines that you don't burn a whole lot more calories running than you do when you power walk anyway. The main reason I took up running was because I was told that it was excellent exercise for people who wanted to lose their stomachs or flabby thighs." Elaine gave her belly a few quick pats. "I still have a little pouch, but it's not as bad as it was. I'm hoping I'll lose it all soon. I'm working really hard."

Angel laughed as much as her shortened breath would allow. "Girl, all you got left to lose is your mind, and I'm 'bout to think you've already gotten a jumpstart on that too. There's not a pouch anywhere in your midsection. Are you crazy or something? You're about to be *too* small now. What does your daily diet consist of?"

"I eat," Elaine defended. "And I'm a long way from being too small. I was looking at my butt the other day and wanted to slap my grandmama. Of all the things to pass along to me, she had to give me the trunk of a Buick."

"Elaine, what kind of mirror do you have in your house? If you think your butt is big, then it must be one of those fun-house mirrors that distorts your image and makes you look shorter and fatter than you actually are."

"You haven't seen me naked, Angel. I promise you, there's still work to do."

Angel shook her head as though she were talking to a hopeless case. "Mason has seen you naked. I don't think for a minute that you've heard him complaining."

As soon as she said the words, Angel wished she could take them back. She, of all people, should have known better than to say something so stupid. Elaine had probably confided in her more than she had with anyone else, and Angel was well aware of their situation. She was just about to apologize for her thoughtlessness when Elaine spoke up, not sounding at all offended.

"Think again. When we were talking the other night, he walked up to me, looked me right in the face, and asked me what was going on with my weight. Said I needed to do something about it."

Angel almost stumbled over her own feet. "Mason said that?" She couldn't believe he'd be so tacky, let alone cruel. And he had some nerve!

What room did he have to complain? From the looks of things, every pound Elaine had lost over the past year, Mason had found. "Are you sure you heard him right, Elaine?"

"Oh, I'm *very* sure. And then yesterday, he was staring at me like he wanted to say something more, but I stared him down. I was daring him to say something I didn't like. I wasn't in no mood for him to say nothing about my weight, and if he had, it was gonna be on and poppin'. Whether we were at church or not."

They rounded a crucial corner in the Windward subdivision that Angel had nicknamed Suicide Hill. It was the point at which the community came to a dead end, but the final house was on elevated ground. After reaching the mailbox that was situated at roadside of the hilltop, there was nothing to do but turn around and start the trek back. But it was a lot harder than it sounded. The hill climb started three houses back and getting to the peak of it was no easy task. Not for Angel anyway.

There had been days when Angel had seen Elaine run the length and height of it, then stand at the top, jogging in place while she waited for her slower counterpart to catch up. But today, all in the name of love and friendship, Elaine's face showed Oscar-worthy strain as she struggled to the top alongside Angel. When they got there, it was Elaine who stopped, propped her hands against her knees, and took a breather.

"Girl, you need to stop." Angel giggled and wheezed at the same time. She couldn't deny that she was grateful for the chance to catch her breath, but Elaine was taking the performance too far. "You know good and well that you're not tired or out of breath." She patted Elaine on the back as she spoke.

Standing to her full height, Elaine lifted her shirt to wipe sweat from her chin that was falling to the pavement in slow drops. She pulled her bottled water from her fanny pack and gulped down several swallows, leaving it almost empty. When she was done, she snapped the cap back into place and said, "I'm not the Bionic Woman, Angel. You act like this workout is a cakewalk for me. It's not." She paused to catch another breath. "If it were easy, I would have lengthened it a long time ago to add more challenge."

"It might not be easy, but it's not as hard as you're trying to make it seem. I've done this exercise with you plenty of times. I've seen you get through it barely needing to drink from your bottle of water. Today, we still have two miles to go before we're back at Braxton Park, and you have less water left than me. I know you're just trying to make me feel good."

Elaine grinned and began the much easier walk downhill. "Is it working?"

Breaking into a laugh, Angel said, "Like a charm."

The laugh felt good. The air felt good. The tension-free company felt good. In her house and within the confines of her marriage, not much had felt good to Angel lately. She tried not to think about it because thinking about it only depressed her. She couldn't believe the giant backward steps her and Colin's relationship had taken in the past few weeks.

"You said that Mason stared at you on the church grounds yesterday. What happened? Did he make you so mad that the two of you went back home without coming inside? You all weren't at church yesterday." Angel was grateful for the sudden breeze that cooled her skin.

"Oh." Elaine snapped her fingers, indicating a recollection.

"That's what I had in mind to talk to you about when I called you this morning and asked you to come walk with me."

Angel looked at her friend for two reasons. One, they were walking far slower than they normally did during these exercise sessions, and two, she thought she saw a smile tugging at Elaine's lips. She hadn't seen any sign of joy on

Elaine's face in a long time. Not when the subject matter was Mason. Could they have possibly finally done . . . *it*?

"We went to a different church yesterday. I thought you knew. I heard Mason talking to Colin on the phone, telling him where we'd be."

Angel took a swig from her bottle before answering. She hoped her expression wouldn't give her away. She wasn't ready for the world to know that communication in her household had all but vanished. "No; I didn't know that. I guess Colin forgot to mention it. Where'd you go?"

"New Hope Church in Stone Mountain."

Angel thought hard. "New Hope Church? You mean, T.K.'s church?"

"Yeah, that's the one. But if T.K. was there, we never got the chance to see him."

"How did you all end up there? That's a good drive from Alpharetta."

"Tell me about it. Mason told me that he ran into the pastor and was invited to come and worship. So he chose yesterday to take him up on it."

"Reverend Tides?" Angel had seen the preacher on a few occasions. She and Colin had even gone to the church a couple of times when New Hope had special services that didn't conflict with the schedule at Temple of God's Word, but she'd never spoken to Reverend Tides directly. "Mason ran into Reverend Tides?"

"That's the same thing I asked," Elaine said with a chuckle. "And to tell you the truth, I didn't believe him when he first told me. I just figured that he concluded that I'd be more likely to agree to go visit with him if he said he had a personal invitation directly from the pastor."

"So, how was service?" Angel wondered if Elaine's experience there was as great as the ones she and Colin had.

Elaine's excitement rose. "Girl, it was something else! We should all get together and go there one day when Reverend Owens is preaching out of town or something. You'd love it."

Smiling, Angel disclosed, "I've been there before. And you're right, the services at New Hope are outstanding. If Colin and I had known about New Hope before we joined Temple of God's Word, I'm sure things would have been different. But when we settled in and began searching for a church home, it just seemed natural to follow Ms. Essie."

"And Temple of God's Word is a great church," Elaine put in.

"Oh, yes. It is. Temple of God's Word is wonderful."

"No doubt about it."

"Right. It's great." And it really was, but Angel suddenly felt as if she and Elaine were trying to convince each other. Both their tones sounded defensive, like they thought they'd betrayed Pastor Owens by praising another ministry.

"New Hope Church is just . . ." Elaine seemed to search for the right word.

"Different. It's different," Angel said.

"Yeah, different. The praise and worship was like on a higher level. I'd never seen anything like it."

Angel couldn't agree more. "From start to finish."

"Definitely." Elaine nodded. "And get this. Girl, I saw my husband dance for the first time in my life."

"Dance? As in outward worship? As in shouting . . . like the holy dance? Mason?" Angel didn't want to sound as if she thought mountains would move before Mason would, but the most emotion she'd ever seen him show in church was to raise his hands. And most times when he did that, it was because Pastor Owens had instructed the congregation to do so, and Mason was complying along with everyone else.

"Can you believe it?" Elaine asked.

Angel stopped walking for a moment. "I would have loved to have been a fly on the wall to see that for myself. That's wonderful, Elaine. I know you shouted right along with him."

They started walking again, a move initiated by Angel. Elaine seemed satisfied just standing there. She was strangely out of character today.

"Actually, I didn't," Elaine replied. "I was so staggered that I didn't really know what to do."

"Staggered?" Angel almost laughed at Elaine's choice of words, but she could understand why. She would have been pretty stunned too.

"Yeah. I mean, in the first place, when he suddenly started edging past everybody to get to the aisle, I thought he was going to the bathroom or something. Second of all, I'd never seen him at that level of praise before, and third, church had just started."

She stressed the last part like that was the biggest shock of all.

"You mean, praise and worship was just getting underway?" Angel needed a deeper understanding.

"No, I'm saying church had *just started*. The praise and worship leaders hadn't even started singing their first song. Reverend Tides—the son, not the father—had just taken the mic, and he was sort of exhorting the congregation, you know."

"Yeah." Angel nodded like she was there and had seen the whole thing.

"Girl, he'd barely said ten words, and Mason was out in the floor dancing."

"Was the music even playing yet?"

"Just kind of softly. Like I said, church was just getting started. But when Mason took to the aisles and people started noticing, the music cued up, and it was like a brush fire that jumped from one side of the church to the other. Before I knew it, people were dancing all over the church, and I eventually lost sight of Mason in the crowd."

Angel laughed. "I just can't imagine Mason catching the Spirit and dancing like that."

Elaine laughed too. "Angel, you should have seen him getting it out there on the church floor. I thought Mason had a little bit more rhythm than that. The music had one beat and his feet had another. He looked like he had drunk a can of Red Bull for the first time and just couldn't help himself."

They'd stopped again, and Angel was doubled over with laughter as she imagined the Spirit moving through Mason and his inability to control his own reactions.

Elaine continued. "My husband looked like a tap dancer on an overdose of crack."

When the laughter finally ceased, Angel looked at Elaine and asked the question that was burning her tongue. "So is everything okay now? I mean, are the two of you back to normal? Did you . . . you know . . . once you got back home?"

The prelude to Elaine's answer was a heavy sigh, and Angel knew the answer wouldn't be a good one.

"No, but let's back up a bit. I never even saw Mason after he scooted out of the row we were sitting together on. When all the praising finally stopped and service continued, I think he took a seat somewhere nearer the front and decided he'd just stay there. I didn't see him again until after the dismissal. It was only then that I knew he wasn't joking about Reverend Tides—the father, not the son—inviting him to church."

Angel's eyes grew. "Did you get to meet him?"

"Him and his wife." Elaine said it like she was proud. "And when we approached him, he addressed Mason by name, so not only had they met like Mason said, but the preacher remembered him like they had a real relationship or something.

Mother Tides invited us to dinner, but we came on back home and ate."

Angel felt a twinge of disappointment. The story lacked the exciting ending that she'd conjured in her mind. "So, you just came home and ate. That's it?" Maybe she wanted to hear about somebody else's love life because she hadn't had much of one of her own lately.

Elaine nodded and shrugged like she didn't understand it either. "The ride home was real quiet, like Mason had a lot on his mind. He never even talked about the spiritual experience he had. It was almost like he was there in the car with me, but not there at the same time. We had regular conversation when we got home, and we ate dinner together. But when it was time to go to bed, he climbed on the sofa as usual."

Angel quickened her pace to keep up with Elaine, who had suddenly begun taking faster strides. Their arms were pumping again, and the momentum for the exercise had returned. But Angel had the feeling that Elaine's depression was returning as well.

"It's gonna get better, Elaine. Let's pray that God's move on Mason yesterday was the start."

"Yeah. God moved him down the aisle of the church, but He didn't move him back in the bedroom." Elaine's tone had turned bitter.

"One step at a time, girlfriend." Angel hoped that her chipper tone sounded authentic. She really did want things in the Demps household to get better. But one thing that Angel knew for certain was that having a husband in the bedroom still didn't equate to happiness.

Chapter 19

T.K.'s Story

He sat at his desk and tapped the hardwood surface rhythmically with the bottom of an empty plastic water bottle. It was the tenth sixteen-ounce bottle he'd drained down his throat since reporting to work seven hours earlier. It had been a part of an unconscious, unsuccessful attempt to drown a mixture of emotions that threatened to prevent him from performing his duties as an educator. All it had really done was sent him to the teachers' lounge for frequent bathroom breaks.

The school didn't have windows that he could look out of, so T.K. just stared at the wall closest to him. It was plastered with posters of some of the best track and basketball superstars that the United States had ever produced. Colorful, life-sized action shots of Jesse Owens, Wilma Rudolph, Bruce Jenner, Mary Decker, Carl Lewis,

Joan Benoit, Edwin Moses, Florence Griffith Joyner, Evelyn Ashford, Valerie Brisco-Hooks, and Gail Devers, covered one side of the wall, while glossy images of Julius Ervin, Magic Johnson, Kareem Abdul-Jabbar, Michael Jordan, Dominique Wilkins, Patrick Ewing, Jason Kidd, Shaquille O'Neal, Charles Barkley, David Robinson, and Tim Duncan wallpapered the other.

"How can she be even thinking about marrying anybody but me?" T.K. asked the question out loud, like one of his sports heroes had the answer that even God hadn't been kind enough to provide.

Nothing about the past several days had made sense. First, Jennifer suddenly became cold and distant. Then she completely cut him off, not answering or returning his phone calls. And if all of that wasn't strange enough, a call from Jerrod on Saturday evening all but paralyzed T.K. He could barely move as Jerrod spoke frantic words that were as foreign to T.K.'s ears as broken Greek.

"And she gonna stand right there in my face and tell me that she's marrying *Devon Washington.*" Jerrod had said his father's name like it was clabbered milk. "Coach D, she had the nerves to tell me that she was doing this mess for me. Talkin' 'bout it's the best thing for us. She said

Devon told her that he wanted to make us a real family. Said the best thing he could do for me was to make it legal and be my daddy." A swear word slipped from Jerrod's lips; a word T.K. had never known him to say before. Then, without missing a beat, the boy added. "I can tell that fool what the best thing is that he can do for me. I can tell both of them what they can do for me."

That was when T.K. stepped in to defend two people that he didn't think deserved his support or Jerrod's respect. He only defended them because it seemed like the Christian thing to do. God commanded that people honor their parents, but T.K. wondered if Jerrod should get a VIP pass for what he'd been through.

"You can't talk about your parents like that, Jerrod. I won't let you. No matter what they did." Even saying the words left a bad taste in T.K.'s mouth. His defense of them was far from genuine, but he stuck to it anyway. "I know that you're hurt, man, and I understand that. But you still need to watch what you say. They're still your parents, whether you like them right now or not."

That ticked Jerrod off even more. Before T.K. could say anything else, he heard the dial tone; a result of Jerrod hanging up the phone on him.

The combination of his concern for Jerrod's state of mind plus his confusion at Jennifer's actions had prompted T.K. to do something he hadn't done in ages: spend a Sunday morning at home doing nothing instead of going to church. With the demons he was wrestling, New Hope Church was probably the place T.K. needed to be most. Instead, he'd chosen to sit at home and wallow in his own pity, asking himself questions that he couldn't answer if he wanted to.

What was going on with Jennifer? How could a girl who felt so good for him turn out to be such the opposite? Just how long had she been seeing her ex? Was it really as sudden as it all seemed? What was going to happen to Jerrod now? Would Devon be the kind of father that the boy needed? How much had he changed since he denounced his girlfriend and unborn child all those years ago? Was Devon a God-fearing man who would be the household head that Christ ordained?

While T.K. didn't have the answers to all of the questions that bombarded him, one thing he knew for sure was that the future of his life, as he'd planned it, had totally unraveled. And he had no control over it. Jennifer was a grown woman, and if she could be so manipulative that she would use him then dump him like yesterday's garbage, then he was better off without her anyway. But Jerrod was different. Jerrod didn't have a choice in this matter, and after talking to him Saturday night, worried about his well-being more than ever. Although Jerrod wouldn't answer his repeated calls when T.K. attempted to reconnect with him after their phone conversation abruptly ended, T.K. found solace in the hope that he would be able to talk to Jerrod face-to-face after classes ended today. There was no track practice on Mondays, but Jerrod always stayed around and shot a few hoops with him in the gym or just kept T.K. company while he packed away his things in preparation to head home.

But not today. Jerrod wasn't among the children that piled off of the school bus this morning, and that just heightened T.K.'s anxiety. His phone calls to Braxton Park had gone unanswered. T.K. didn't expect Jennifer to answer because he figured she'd be at work. He wouldn't have wanted her to answer had she been there. Talking to Jennifer wasn't high on his list right now. What he did hope was that Jerrod would answer, even if answering would verify his suspicion that the boy had chosen to play hooky today. At least if Jerrod were at home,

T.K. would know that he wasn't roaming the streets doing anything stupid. T.K. figured that Jerrod wouldn't answer the phone if he saw his name or number show up on the caller I.D., so he devised a plan; implemented the star-six-seven code so that his identification would not be disclosed. But even doing that rendered futile. Still, he thought he'd give the cell phone one last try.

"Jerrod, this is Coach D." His voice was stern. "I know you're getting my messages, and I'm about sick and tired of being nice about this whole thing. I'm not asking you to call me anymore. I'm *telling* you to call me. This ain't just about you, you know. I thought you were my partner; my right hand man. You think you're the only one who ain't happy about this mess? I can't believe you'd leave me hanging like this. You're being a spineless, selfish brat. How you gonna be mad at your mama? You're just like her. Ain't thinking about nobody but your own selfish self. Who cares about T.K., right? Just do what's good for you, and forget about everybody else. Is that your household rule or something?"

T.K. closed his eyes and took several shallow breaths, then some deep ones. His heart was pounding so hard that he felt it in his throat. Frustration had gotten the best of him, and he wished he could press a button that would erase everything he'd said and start over. But if such a button existed, T.K. wasn't technologically savvy enough to know which it was.

"I . . . I'm sorry, Jerrod. I didn't mean that. God knows I didn't. I'm sorry." A long moment of silence passed, and T.K. knew his message would be cut off soon if he didn't wrap things up quickly. "I'm hurting, kid, and I know you are too. We need each other, man. I know you love your mama. I love her too." Another pause. "And I mean that. I don't just love Jen, I'm *in love* with her. I never told you that, but I do. I love her and it's gonna take a minute to get over that even though I know she's with some other dude now." Another pause. Longer this time. "I was gonna ask you for her hand, Jerrod. Already bought the ring and everything. Can you believe it?"

T.K. released a soft laugh. It was more at his own naïveté than anything else. He couldn't believe he'd been played for such a fool. "I thought I was gonna be the one she pledged her lifelong love to. I thought I was gonna be the one to complete the family. Thought it would be me who was gonna be the one you . . ." T.K. took a breath. "The one you called Daddy." His voice cracked, and it was barely audible when he ended his message with, "I just need to know you're okay. Please, Jerrod. Call me."

Snapping his phone closed, T.K. dropped it
on a stack of incomplete paperwork that sat in
the middle of his desk, then pressed his forehead
against his clenched fists. When his phone rang
just seconds later, T.K. squared his shoulders
and straightened the slump from his back. His
eyes darted to the telephone, praying that Jerrod's number would be illuminating on the
screen.

"Jen?" he whispered with a scowl, pulling the
phone closer to his eyes like he thought he'd misread the numbers on the display.

What was she doing calling him? What could
she possibly have to say to him? Was she finally
calling to tell him that she was back with her
son's father? Jerrod was the one to disclose the
catastrophic news. T.K. had yet to speak to Jennifer. She'd not given him the common courtesy
of telling him that she'd ended their relationship. Any woman who could be that cruel didn't
deserve to speak to anything other than his voice
mail.

When T.K. dropped the phone back onto the
desk, a nagging throb began to drum in the back
of his head. This was just too much drama to
him. Drama that he thought he'd left behind
when he finally got over Deena's deception back
in his days at Georgia State University.

"The church boy loses again," he muttered at the irony of it all.

Deena needed somebody to fulfill her physical needs. Quench her sensual thirsts. Somebody who talked about strong Christian values, but didn't live by them. As disappointed as T.K. had been with her, he had to give Deena some grace. At least she wasn't saved. At least she didn't proclaim to be a born again Christian. What Deena did was sinful, but what more could he really expect from a sinner? Sin was what sinners did. Jennifer was supposed to be different. She was everything that Deena wasn't. Or at least she was supposed to be. Saved, virtuous, trustworthy, blah . . . blah . . . blah.

The size thirteen Air Jordan that T.K. wore on his right foot kicked the leg of his desk in annoyance. He was well aware of the fact that all Christian relationships didn't last, but having Christ at the head of it should have at least made the breakup amicable. This thing with Jennifer was about the dumbest he'd ever experienced. Everything was fine one day and then the next . . . bam! Everything went up into smoke. A whole year of his life *wasted*. T.K. wasn't even sure what Jennifer's motives were.

"Who knows? Maybe they were the same as Deena's," he reasoned aloud.

Maybe her flesh couldn't stand the wait either, and she found the man that doused the flames when she was a teenager and signed him on to fill the position again. The thought of it sickened T.K., but he didn't know what else to think. Everything had happened too fast for there not to have been extended and extensive contact between Jennifer and Devon before Jerrod was made aware. Surely she didn't reconnect with and decide to marry this guy within just a few short days. She couldn't be that crazy. Not so crazy that she'd trust a guy who left her pregnant and eventually, a homeless, single teenaged mother.

Thoughts continued to bombard T.K.'s mind as he heard the beeping of his phone, indicating that a message had been left. He used the thumbs of both of his hands to place pressure on his temples, hoping to ease the headache. All the while, he wondered if he was just going to add insult to injury if he listened to whatever it was that Jennifer had said.

He released his head and began using his right hand to apply pressure against the individual fingers of his left, causing his joints to make popping sounds while he contemplated his next move.

Should he listen to the message or shouldn't he?

After running out of fingers on his left hand, T.K. switched. The joints on the fingers of his right hand crackled in the otherwise quiet classroom.

Did he want to hear what Jennifer had to say or didn't he?

Curiosity won over his better judgment. T.K. pressed the code to listen and held his breath.

"Hi . . . hi, T.K. It's me. Jennifer." She sounded flustered and out of breath. "I know we haven't talked lately and I . . . I . . . I know that's my fault."

"Dang skippy, it's your fault," T.K. grumbled. "Get to the point and get off my phone."

"I'll explain everything later," she said.

"Oh yeah? I'd like to see you try," T.K. responded to the recorded message.

"But right now, I need your help."

"Need my help?" T.K. sneered, and his voice was filled with insult. How dare she even shape her mouth to ask him for anything? He picked up the phone and scanned the room, wondering which wall would be the best to sling it against. He'd enjoy watching it burst into a million pieces. If Jennifer thought he'd assist her with anything, he must look a whole lot dumber than he ever imagined. If she wanted help of any kind, she was calling the wrong man. She needed to be calling the one she chose over him.

"Jerrod is missing."

Her statement was followed by a burst of frantic tears, and it froze T.K.'s arm in place. "What?" he asked, putting the phone to his ear for clearer hearing. "Missing? What do you mean, Jerrod's missing? Where is he?"

"He's gone, T.K.," she wailed on cue as if she were responding to his interrogation. "I don't know where he is. He won't answer my calls. He won't return my messages. I haven't seen him since Saturday afternoon." Jennifer paused, and T.K. could hear her trying to gather herself. "We had an argument about . . . well, I'll fill you in on all of that when you call. But it got ugly. Real ugly. And he left on his bike . . . in the rain. I thought he needed to put some distance between us and cool off. I thought he'd come back before his curfew time, but he didn't." That was a prelude to another tearful outburst and Jennifer's next few words were almost lost in her emotions. "I haven't seen him since. I know it's a lot to ask. Especially under the circumstances. But I don't know anywhere else to turn, T.K. Please . . . please call me."

The line went dead, and T.K.'s fingers went numb. It was worse than he'd thought. Far worse. Yet and still, talking to Jennifer wasn't something that he wanted to do right now. Knowing that her little stunt had sent a recovering gangster-wannabe back into the same streets that had almost been the source of his demise once before, angered T.K. even more. Instead of returning her call, he got up from his chair and crammed his belongings into the leather shoulder bag that he used for transporting classwork home. He hoped to get the opportunity to check the tests that his Physical Education students had taken today, but doing so had been moved way down on his priority list now.

"Lord, help me find this boy," he whispered into the air as he slung the door open to his classroom and raced down the empty hallway. The water he'd been drinking all day was once again weighing on his bladder, but T.K. couldn't stop right now. He had more important matters to tend to. "Help me find him before it's too late."

Chapter 20

Jerrod's Story

Connecting with the Dobermans last year had proven to be the single biggest example of poor judgment that he'd ever made; but something good came out of it. Jerrod had found temporary shelter.

When the smoke cleared, only two members of the school-based gang survived without being burned in the process. Jerrod was one, and the boy who sat across from him on the living room floor of the studio apartment in Midtown Atlanta was the other.

Jerrod didn't know many teenagers who had their own place. Especially not one as young as Toby Simon. But at sixteen, his former classmate lived independently of his parents. Toby's family was well-to-do. His daddy was a popular gynecologist to Atlanta's elite entertainers, and his mother was a partner in one of the city's most esteemed law firms. She was the face of the company, appearing in their television commercials and everything. But even with a doctor daddy and a lawyer mama, Toby's family wasn't the Huxtables by any stretch of the imagination.

Shortly after the trial that sent Freddie and the other Dobermans to prison, Oscar and Josephine Simon discovered that their son was struggling with homosexuality. They uncovered Toby's secret when they read a string of e-mails from his computer. He'd forgotten to shut down the system that morning before leaving for school. The unearthing nearly made Dr. Simon need a physician of his own, and if Toby's grandmother hadn't been at the house when he got home from school that afternoon, Attorney Simon probably would have needed her own lawyer.

It was a shock to his schoolmates too, once the news leaked into Alpharetta High. No one would have ever known. Toby never *acted* gay. Still didn't. Other than the fact that he didn't care much for sports, and he kept a spotless house, Toby didn't seem to be much different than any of the other guys that Jerrod knew.

The studio apartment came compliments of Toby's parents. Dr. and Mrs. Simon had a reputation to be concerned with. They weren't only pillars in their community, but also important people in their church. No way could they have a queer child living in their house. So they pushed Toby out of the nest, cushioning his fall by supplying him with a roof over his head.

Jerrod and Toby hadn't been in contact since last summer. Jerrod had run into him at the movies one day, and it was then that Toby informed Jerrod that he wouldn't be returning to school for their sophomore year. He said it was just too hard to be around his peers. While none of them made fun of him to his face, they'd all started treating him differently once they found out. There were other guys at the school who were openly gay, but Toby said he didn't want to be seen as "one of them." He just wanted to be a regular boy, viewed and treated like everybody else. But once his secret was unveiled, all possibilities of that were destroyed. Because his parents were such high-profile professionals, the news had seeped well beyond Alpharetta. In Toby's words: "Everybody knows."

So, at sixteen, Toby Simon was a high school dropout, working as a cashier at a local Publix grocery store. Although his parents paid his rent and utilities, he was responsible for his own cell phone, groceries, clothing, cable, and Internet services.

Calling Toby was a long shot, but desperate times called for desperate measures. When Jerrod stormed out of his house on Saturday, he had pedaled his bike for at least two miles before he realized that he didn't have anywhere to go. His first thought was to turn around and go back to Braxton Park. When he started helping Angel with packing away Ms. Essie's belongings, he'd been given a key to the old lady's house. Jerrod figured that if he were careful, he could probably camp out there for a day or two before anybody would notice. But the spare key was inside his mother's house and going back there wasn't even an option.

Once he completely buried his first consideration, Jerrod immediately thought of T.K. If he called T.K. and told him what had just gone down with Jennifer and Devon, there was no way that his coach wouldn't agree with him wholeheartedly. Once Jerrod got T.K. all riled, he had then planned to ask him if he could come and crash with him in Stone Mountain for a while. But Jerrod never got the opportunity to ask. He couldn't believe T.K. had taken Jennifer and Devon's side, defending them like what they were doing was right.

Serious consideration went to calling Tashina O'Neal. She was older; a former lead cheerleader at Alpharetta High who had graduated last year. Now a Georgia Perimeter College freshman, Tashina lived in her own apartment not far from the school she attended. She was the girl Jerrod lost his virginity to in order to qualify to become a full-fledged Doberman. They'd never been a real couple, but he knew she still had a soft spot for him, and with his alternatives running out, Jerrod was tempted to take advantage of that. He hadn't seen her since she left Alpharetta High, but prior to her graduation, they'd hooked up a couple of times for instant replays of his initiation activities. Calling her wouldn't only provide him with temporary shelter, but a little excitement on the side; the kind of excitement that he hadn't had in over a year.

Jerrod battled with the attractive notion for a long while, but a nagging voice in the back of his head—one that sounded very much like Essie's—threatened the wrath of God if he went that direction. Fear, along with Jerrod's conscience, eventually directed him down another path.

Calling Toby had been an act of desperation. Nightfall was just a few hours away, and if Jerrod didn't find somewhere to go soon, he would have been facing a night outdoors, sleeping in clothing that had been soaked by the constant drizzle. When he got to Toby's number in the address book of his cell phone, Jerrod said a little prayer before dialing it. Whether it was a prayer answered or just plain old luck, Jerrod didn't know. But Toby answered and told him that if he could get to his house in Midtown, he could stay there until he figured out what he was going to do next. A few hours later, after taking MARTA, Atlanta's public transportation, Jerrod was standing at Toby's door with nothing but his bicycle and the wet clothes on his back. Thankfully, they were virtually the same size, and he was able to borrow some of Toby's.

"You decided what you gonna do yet?" Toby asked after they'd exchanged pleasantries upon his arrival home from work. He took off his shoes at the door, as was his custom, then picked up the remote control to turn down the volume of the television before throwing a chocolate-covered M&M into the air and catching it in his mouth. "You can't stay here forever, you know."

Jerrod fastened the top button of the pajama set that Toby had loaned him. "I done overstayed my welcome already?" It was only Monday night. He'd figured that he wouldn't be able to stay at Toby's place indefinitely, but he didn't think he'd have to be moving on this soon.

"Naw, dude. Nothin' like that. I'm just sayin'. I know your mom's got to be worried sick about you by now. Have you at least called her?"

"No, and I ain't gonna call her either." Jerrod held out his hand. It was a silent request for Toby to share his sweets.

"There's a whole case of them in the kitchen cabinet under the sink," Toby said, pointing in the direction. "Good thing about working at the grocery store is that I'll never go hungry."

Jerrod snickered as he scuffled to his feet and took the short walk to get his own bag. He ended up getting two before crossing the threshold that separated the kitchen and dining area from the living room that doubled at night as a bedroom. Jerrod sat back down in the same corner floor space that would soon serve as his bed for the third night in a row. Blankets were piled beneath him to provide some cushion. The one sofa that was situated against the adjacent wall was for Toby.

Jerrod tore open the first bag of candy, tossed his head back, and poured several pieces into his mouth. "I can't believe Mama did this mess." It wasn't easy to say with his jaws full of bite-sized treats.

Toby shrugged his shoulders. "At least your parents want you. Your daddy might've been trifling all your life, but at least he wants you now. That's more than I can say about my dad. Mama too, for that matter."

Jerrod looked around the small apartment. To him, it didn't look like Toby had such a bad deal. As a matter of fact, he'd trade places with him any day. If he had a place like this, far away from whatever life Jennifer and Devon were about to build, it would be like heaven on earth.

"That's why I joined the Dobermans, you know."

Toby's words brought Jerrod's eyes back to the opposite wall of the apartment. "What's why you joined the Dobermans?"

Toby got up from the floor and sat in a bean-bag chair that was nearby. His eyes darted from the late night comedy on television to Jerrod. "I wanted to become a Doberman so I could feel like I belonged."

Jerrod folded his legs Indian style. "Belonged to what?"

"Anything, man," Toby said. "I just never felt like I belonged anywhere. I just didn't fit in. I always felt awkward around girls, and boys intimidated me. At church, I always felt like I was being preached at, and at home I got ignored. I just didn't fit nowhere."

Jerrod squirmed a bit, hoping he wasn't about to cross the line. "Is that why you turned . . . *gay*?" He whispered the last word like it was some sort of secret password.

Toby laughed out loud, rolled over to the side, and then tumbled onto the floor. He held his stomach like the spontaneous eruption from his belly was causing him to cramp.

Confused, Jerrod stared at his friend until he finally calmed down. "What's so doggone funny?"

"You; that's what," Toby answered, breathless from his fit of laughter. He eventually crawled back onto the beanbag. "Man, don't nobody *turn* gay. You're either gay or you're not."

"Oh." Jerrod had more questions, but wondered if he should ask.

"I've always been gay. Even before I knew I was gay, I was gay. I was born this way," Toby explained. When Jerrod didn't offer a response, he lifted an eyebrow, cocked his head to the side and added, "I know a lot of church people that don't believe that. My parents totally disagree. They think sexuality is a choice. I say otherwise, 'cause I believe if I had a choice, I'd choose to be what's considered normal, so people will treat me normal."

Jerrod just couldn't even imagine being attracted to another boy. Sure, he'd met guys who he thought were nice looking. Handsome, even. Take Colin, for instance. Colin was one of the best looking men Jerrod knew. Clean cut, tall, lean muscular build, strong jaw line, nice smile. But when Jerrod looked at him, all he saw was another good looking brother. And if a pretty girl would walk in the room—like Angel, for instance—Colin would disappear. *Poof!* Just like that, Colin would be as good as gone. No way would Jerrod rather look at Colin than at Angel. No way.

Toby continued. "Your mama 'nem are church people, right? I bet she told you that people can't be born gay, didn't she?"

Shaking his head from side to side, Jerrod said, "Actually, no. My mama ain't never talked about whether somebody could be born gay or not. The subject never came up between us. And we ain't been going to church all that long. Just really started the morning after Ms. Essie died."

"Ms. Essie?" Toby looked more than a little confused.

"Yeah. You don't know her, but she used to live next door to me and my mama out in Braxton Park." Jerrod wanted to tell Toby that Essie was the one who made the anonymous call that got the Dobermans arrested, but he decided not to. "Ms. Essie died a year ago, but she's the one who got Mama going to church."

"Has your pastor ever preached about gay people?" Toby asked, seeming to really be interested in the points of view of others.

Jerrod thought real hard. "Not that I can re-member. But once when I went to church with Coach D, I heard his pastor say that he never argued with people when they said they were born that way. He says we're all born sinners, so he believes that it's possible." Toby looked fasci-nated, so Jerrod kept talking. "Reverend Tides said it very well might be that alcoholics are born to drink, thieves are born to steal, murderers are born to kill, and gay people are born to . . . well, be gay." Jerrod hoped he wasn't being insulting.

"Really?" Toby didn't sound offended. "That's the first time I've ever heard anybody say a preacher said something like that. So you're say-ing that Coach D's pastor is okay with the gay lifestyle?"

"Naw, man, I ain't saying that. You ain't let me finish. Reverend Tides didn't stop right there. What he said, when he explained the whole thing, was that Jesus made a command that said that in order to go to heaven, everybody had to be born again."

"Born again?"

"Yeah. Like a rebirth. But not a natural one, a spiritual one. So even if it's true, and gay people really are born gay, if you allow Christ in your life, you are then *born again*, and what you were born as in the beginning, don't make no difference one way or the other, 'cause when you get saved, Jesus cleanses all that junk from you, and you become a new person. So, if you were born an alcoholic, you ain't no alcoholic no more. If you were born a thief, you ain't no thief no more."

"And if you were born gay, you ain't gonna be gay no more?" Toby offered.

"Not after you've been born again."

The room was quiet for an extended period of time. The silence was broken by Toby's chuckle. Once again, Jerrod had missed the humor.

"What's so funny?"

"You, that's what."

"I said something funny?"

"Naw, dog. You ain't said nothing funny, but it's funny that you sounded just like a preacher when you was talking."

Jerrod frowned for more than one reason. "Two things you can't call me," he said, just before playfully throwing a piece of candy across the room. "A preacher and a dog. Deal?"

Toby picked the M&M from his lap and popped it in his mouth. "Whatever you say, man. Now, when are you gonna call your mama?"

Another frown appeared on Jerrod's face. This one lasted much longer. "Man, I told you I wasn't calling her. She was blowing my phone up all day yesterday, and today's calls started rolling in at seven o'clock this morning. Probably as soon as she got up for work. Woke me up out of my good sleep. I finally turned the whole thing off around noon and put it away. I can't deal with her right now."

Toby crumpled an empty candy bag in his fist and tossed it in a nearby wastebasket like a basketball. For a kid who didn't like sports, he had skills. "You should call her."

"Are you trying to get rid of me, Toby?"

"Look, J. You can stay here as long as you want to. I enjoy the company. Good to have somebody to just shoot the breeze with around here. But are you sure you want to keep hanging around me? People might start to think you're . . ." Toby finished the sentence by holding out his right hand, palm faced downward, and rocking it left and right in quick motions. It was a signal that the kids in school used when referring to homosexuals.

Jerrod sucked his teeth. "Man, please. I ain't worried 'bout what nobody say 'bout me. And I'll bet you a million dollars, they won't say it to my face. Don't nobody want to mess with me right about now. All I need is a reason."

"Cool. Then stay," Toby said. "But you shouldn't make your mama worry about you.

No matter how mad you are at her. You ain't got to talk to her. Text message her. Call the house when you know she's at work and just leave a message. But it ain't right for you to make her worry like that."

"If you was me, would you call your mama?" Jerrod challenged.

"No. But I'd call the answering machine."

Jerrod lay back on his blankets and stared at the ceiling. "I'll think about it."

Chapter 21

Angel's Story

Something strange was going on. What it was, she wasn't quite sure. But her womanly instincts told her that her marriage was in even more trouble than she knew. Angel looked at the clock on the wall, staring at the second hand as it ticked its way from the six to the twelve. Those thirty seconds alone felt like a lifetime.

Eleven P.M.

What in the world is going on?

A part of her wished for a phone call from any one of the hospitals in metropolitan Atlanta. If a voice on the other end of the line told her that her husband had been in a horrible accident and was brought in with his life hanging in the balance, at least then she'd know that Colin didn't have a choice in the matter. If he were in the ER, with tubes running down his throat and doctors pounding on his chest, at least then she'd know that the only reason he wasn't at home was because he couldn't be. *Couldn't* . . . not wouldn't. There was a difference.

But something inside of Angel told her that it wasn't an accident that was keeping Colin away. It wasn't even work.

There was something else. S*omeone* else. Angel gasped at the sudden thought.

Colin had never been this late coming home. She had called the office twice and got no answer. Called his cell phone three or four times. More like five or six. She'd lost count. Each time, she got the same message: "I'm sorry you've missed me. Please leave a name, number, and brief message, and I promise to get back with you at my earliest convenience."

Promises, promises. There was no way that Colin hadn't had the opportunity to call her back. Not after all these hours. What could he be doing that a *convenient* time to return a call hadn't yet presented itself? Angel's heart thudded in her chest. She'd seen enough *Oprah* and listened to enough Michael Baisden to know that when men made sudden unexplained changes in their routines, something wasn't right.

Usually she'd be in bed by now, but Colin's absence had kept her wide awake. The house had never been so spotless. Since putting Austin to bed, Angel had washed the dishes, wiped down the stove, mopped the kitchen floor, vacuumed the carpet in the master bedroom, waxed the wood flooring in the living room, dusted the coffee and end tables, scrubbed their whirlpool bathtub, and sponged down their shower stall. Now she was separating loads of clothes in preparation of laundering them.

Each time that Angel had listened to Elaine moan about her marital grief, she thought to herself that nothing could be worse. What could be more demoralizing than having a husband who walked around the house, displaying the conduct of a celibate monk?

"*This*, that's what," Angel sputtered, throwing down the pants she'd worn during yesterday's run, on a stack of dark-colored clothing. Venting about it made her feel better, even if there was no one around to listen. "Having a husband who's never at home is far, far worse. At least Elaine knows where her husband is. He might not be giving her the kind of attention she wants, but at least she knows no other woman is getting his affections either. I'll take her problem any day over *this*." She flung one of Austin's onesies onto the pile with the whites.

"Where are you, Colin?" Angel yelled into house. She immediately covered her mouth with a shirt she'd pulled from the hamper. Austin was asleep in his room down the hall. The last thing she wanted to do was wake him. She pulled the shirt away and looked at it. The smell that teased her nostrils was foreign. It was definitely a woman's fragrance, but it wasn't hers. Angel took another whiff.

"Whose is this and how did it get in his shirt?" she pondered. Her heartbeat quickened even more when her eyes found a second clue. A stain. A *red* stain.

It couldn't be.

But it was.

Lipstick. And not the color of any that she wore. When it came to makeup, Angel stuck to neutral colors: bronzes, golds and browns. She never wore red makeup of any kind, but there was no mistaking that somebody with red lipstick had been with her husband. And whoever *she* was; she'd left her mark behind on his collar, where she'd apparently rested her painted lips against the left side of his neck.

Chapter 22

Jennifer's Story

She'd been separated from her family for so long that she sometimes forgot she had one. As far as Jennifer knew, both her parents were still living, but she was fifteen, pregnant, and scared out of her wits the last time she saw either of them. David and Phyllis Mays were in the middle of a messy divorce wherein they fought endlessly about their daughter. Not like normal, loving parents would though. David demanded that Phyllis have physical custody, and Phyllis insisted the same of David.

By default, Jennifer's dad won when he walked out without giving notice to his wife or his only child. His move forced Phyllis to accept guardianship. But when Phyllis handed her daughter an ultimatum: abort the baby or get out, Jennifer opted for homelessness. She couldn't kill her baby. She needed someone to love and someone who would love her back. The child growing in her belly was her last chance at finding either.

Ultimately, the frightened teenager was accepted into a group home where she was given prenatal care and a warm place to stay. For three years, she lived there with other unwed teen mothers from all walks of life. Despite their differences in race, social backgrounds, and family upbringing, all of them had at least one thing in common: parents that had disowned them, or no parents at all. Either way, they were on their own. Little girls who'd lost their innocence and their childhood to poor choices and unfortunate circumstances. Forced to be women way before their time.

At eighteen, each girl had to leave the nest. Ready or not.

Through hard work and determination, Jennifer made it. Worked her way from certain failure to become a college graduate with a good job who lived in a nice neighborhood. God had been good to her even when she had no real concept of who He was.

But in all of the favor she'd been granted in her life, Jennifer couldn't understand how she'd come full circle. She still had the college degree, the nice home, and the good job. But the one thing she loved most in the world—her son—had once again slipped through her fingers. All the transformation that had taken him from gang activity to good grades, from being a child she feared to a child she admired; all of it was filtering down the drain.

"Where did I go wrong?" she whispered into the darkness. "I'm only trying to do what's best for him. Can't he see that?"

Jennifer hadn't moved from the living room couch in hours. It was still afternoon when Jerrod stormed from the house in a rage after she'd tried to properly introduce him to Devon.

"Hi, Jerrod. I'm your dad. Good to meet you, son." Those were the words Devon had said as he stretched out his arms to embrace Jerrod.

Jennifer had told Devon to be patient; to take everything one step at a time. Told him to let her do the talking and set the tone. But no. He had to walk into the house with his own agenda. If she had known that Devon would try to hug Jerrod or show any physical affection at all, she would have warned him differently. She knew her son better than anyone else. No way was he going to fall into Devon's arms like he'd waited his whole life to meet him. Jerrod had lived through the struggles with Jennifer. He knew the whole story of how Devon cruelly abandoned them when he found out that she was pregnant. He had gone without because his father had chosen the easy way out. Jerrod probably wouldn't have even shaken Devon's hand, let alone hugged him.

"Who you calling son?" Jerrod had snarled as he asked the question, and he looked Devon up and down like he was prepared for a head-to-head match if it came down to it. "I ain't none of your son. I ain't nobody to you, and you ain't nobody to me. *Believe* that."

And it went downhill from there.

"Watch your mouth, boy."

Jennifer was horrified at Devon's commanding tone of voice. Didn't he know that he was going to have to walk on eggs with Jerrod for a while? Jerrod was being disrespectful, yes, but Devon hadn't yet done anything to deserve the boy's esteem. He couldn't appear out of nowhere and expect to take on the daddy role just like that. This wasn't a fairytale movie, and it wasn't a fictional novel. This was real life. And real life just didn't work that way.

"Devon . . ." Jennifer thought she'd step in and save the day.

"I ain't yo' boy either." Jerrod was the exact height of his father, and he stepped to Devon as if to dare him to repeat his words.

"Jerrod . . ." Jennifer wasn't sure which of them needed rescuing most.

"Don't worry, Jenny," Devon spoke her name, but he kept his eyes on Jerrod. "Everything is gonna be just fine. Leave everything to me, baby. I got this. This boy ain't been raised worth nuthin'. No wonder he ended up in gangs and foolishness. He ain't had no daddy around to show him how to wear his britches, but that's about to change. We fixin' to be family now, and I'ma make sure he stay straight. He 'bout to be a star, and I ain't gonna let him mess that up."

Jennifer wasn't certain what made Jerrod bolt from the house without so much as a good-bye. All she knew was that her son looked at her as though she'd spit in his face, and then he was gone. Jennifer hadn't seen him since.

"What was he thinking?" Jennifer pounded her thigh with her fist. She couldn't believe Devon didn't put more thought and preparation into his entrance. When she confronted him after Jerrod's departure, Devon promised her that the fresh air that the rain provided would do Jerrod some good, and that he would be back before she knew it.

That was nearly two and a half days ago, and Jennifer couldn't rid herself of the sinking feeling that she had lost the only blood family that she'd had left. First her grandmother, to death. Then her dad, to divorce. Then her mom, to abandonment. Now Jerrod, to who knows what. Maybe another gang. Maybe drugs. Maybe jail. In his state of mind, there was no telling where he'd end up.

Over the past year, when she had problems with Jerrod, the one person Jennifer could always depend on was T.K.

T.K. The sudden thought of him sent warm tears spilling down her cheeks. She curled her legs beneath her body and leaned her head against the back of the sofa. She missed T.K.'s arms. Longed to hear him tell her that everything was going to be okay. Longed to hear him say, "Let's pray about it. Then we won't make a move until God says so."

That was Jennifer's last thought before she grabbed the crumpled blanket from the arm of the sofa, wrapped herself in it and drifted off to sleep.

"Lord have mercy, child, what you done gone and did?"

"Hmm?" Jennifer stirred at the voice, but she pulled the blanket closer around her neck and once again, found slumber.

"Ah-uh. You gon' wake yourself right on up. I ain't got but a minute to talk to you, so you best make the most of it. Wake up, girl."

Two nudges against her legs and Jennifer's eyes flew open. Her breaths came quick, and for a second, she could hear her own heart pounding in her ears. Jennifer lay completely still for a short span. Listening. Looking. But when she saw nothing but darkness, little by little, she relaxed. Chuckling softly at her own sleep-induced experience, she closed her eyes again.

"I ain't gon' tell you no more to wake up now."

This time Jennifer shot up into a seated position. There was no question that she wasn't alone in her home. "Huh? Who's that?" She reached for something she could use to defend herself, but all that she felt were the decorative pillows on the sofa. They were too soft for anything except to smother someone with. That would take too long and be too much work. If she could dash to the kitchen for a butcher knife . . .

The echo of heartwarming laughter made Jennifer feel oddly at ease, but the familiar sound of it terrorized her equally as much.

"Calm down, child. It's just me."

Jennifer blinked in rapid succession and looked in the direction of the voice that came from a place on the sofa not two feet away. The room was pitch black. "Ms. . . ." She felt stupid even saying it. "Essie?"

"Ain't you got a lamp over there somewhere? If you turn it on, you wouldn't have to ask."

With a trembling hand, Jennifer fumbled for the switch on the tall floor lamp that was only an arm's length away. And when she switched it on and saw a living, breathing Essie Mae Richardson, sitting on the sofa beaming from ear to ear, Jennifer emitted a dog-like yelp and jumped to her feet. She cowered into the nearest corner, wanting to scream more, but was unable to find her voice.

Her horror was met with another unruffled chuckle from Essie. The grey-haired woman smoothed out her white dress and said, "It's all right, Jennifer. You ain't got to be scared." She patted the surface of the sofa beside her. "Come back and sit down. It's okay."

Jennifer didn't know what to do or think. Her widened eyes remained fixed on a woman who looked just like the one she'd helped to bury a year ago. This couldn't be happening. Essie couldn't really be sitting in her living room. Jennifer had been one of the five people who'd gathered in Essie's bedroom along with the paramedics on the night the woman slipped into a peaceful coma. She'd been standing there at 3:57 A.M. when the medics declared her dead. Jennifer had suffered through the crowded funeral and listened to Pastor Owens eulogize Essie; sat at the gravesite right alongside other neighbors and friends and watched the mortuary service lower her casket into the ground. She'd kept Austin many-a-day while Angel cleared out the belongings that Essie had left behind in her home. It just wasn't possible that the same woman was sitting on her living room couch looking as happy and healthy as ever.

"Girl, stop pinching yourself and come on over here and sit down. I ain't got all night to be fooling with you."

Jennifer hadn't even noticed that her thumb and index finger were working hard, squeezing the flesh of her own thigh, trying to see if it was all a dream.

"Have I ever done anything to hurt you, Jennifer?" the woman asked, still patting the space beside her for Jennifer to occupy.

"N . . . No." Jennifer could barely hear her own response.

"And I ain't 'bout to hurt you now," Essie assured her. "Come on and sit down so Ms. Essie can talk to you for a spell."

A spell. That's what Jennifer felt she was under as she inched toward the sofa, choosing to sit on the space closest to the armrest. It seemed to be a safe enough distance from the living dead woman who was talking to her.

Essie readjusted her position on the sofa so that she faced Jennifer. "Now I can't deny that I ain't the happiest camper right now. For one, I had to leave my Ben to come and see 'bout you."

Jennifer wondered what all Essie knew. She tried to look as clueless as she could. "See about me? Why?"

Essie shook her head as if Jennifer's dramatic act of innocence was the worst she'd ever seen. "Don't play games with me, girl. Like I said in the beginning, I ain't got but a little while to help you fix this mess you done got yourself in." She looked around the room. "He ain't came back home, has he?"

With downcast eyes, Jennifer shook her head from side to side and blinked back tears. There was no need in putting on false pretenses and she knew it. She couldn't fool Essie in life, and apparently, she couldn't fool her in death either. Jennifer's fear was evaporating now. She still didn't understand how Essie could be sitting beside her and be in the grave at the same time, but she was glad to have her there. She needed her. "He doesn't understand that what I'm doing is for him . . . for *us*."

"And how you reckon that marrying that boy is helping Jerrod?"

"Devon is his daddy." Jennifer's tone was frank.

"Child, you and me both know that Jerrod ain't never had no daddy. Devon might have planted the seed, but it don't take no real skills to do that. Being a daddy is a whole lot deeper that seed planting. He wasn't never around to fertilize him, cultivate him, or help him grow up strong. You been the closest thing to a daddy that that child has ever had. At least, 'til T.K. And now, thanks to you, that's in jeopardy too."

Jennifer looked away. Was there anything that Essie didn't know? "I . . . I, uh—"

"Been stupid," Essie said. "That's what you been. You been just plain stupid." A year in the cemetery buried under six feet of dirt hadn't changed her one bit.

Jennifer squirmed in her seat, wanting to say something in her own defense. But it was no use. Nobody understood that she'd made the changes in her life so that she could be positioned to receive the answer to her prayers. All she wanted was a husband for herself and a father for Jerrod. Was that so bad? Devon was offering both those things, and Jennifer just didn't see why everybody was against her on this. What could be better than Jerrod's actual father fitting the bill?

"Baby, let me tell you something," Essie said, leaning forward with an expression on her face that said that all of Jennifer's thoughts had been read loud and clear. "In the Word of God, there was a woman that acted just like you. Her name was Sarah. She was Abraham's wife and had just about everything she wanted 'cept a baby. The Lord had promised her a baby, but she just couldn't wait on Him to do it in His own time. So what she went and done?" Essie paused, giving Jennifer time to answer the question.

"Uh . . . um . . ." Jennifer rolled her eyes to the ceiling as she thought. She was certain she'd heard this story before, but the combination of the unexpected question and having a dead woman pose it to her, threw her off. Her overloaded mind couldn't compute the answer quickly enough.

"Lord have mercy," Essie moaned. "Is Reverend Owens still the pastor over there? Is he teaching y'all anything nowadays?" When Jennifer continued her oblivious pondering, Essie released a burdened sigh and continued. "Never mind, child. Don't have no aneurism trying to think of the answer. Just sit back and listen."

Jennifer scooted back in her seat, embarrassed by her biblical ignorance.

"Sarah went and picked out one of her hand-maids, and like a fool, gave that gal over to her husband. Told Abraham to sleep with the hired help and have a baby wit' her. Like that was gon' be the same thing as him having the baby wit' his wife. Like God needed her help to make His will come to pass." Essie curled her lips and gave her head a slow shake, like Sarah had to be the big-gest dummy in biblical history.

"So Abraham done just what she told him to do. Laid up wit' Miss Hagar and had a baby. And just 'cause it was done out of God's will, that boy couldn't be blessed the way the Lord intended to bless Abraham's seed. He had a plan for Sarah and Abraham to have a child out of their own loins, and 'til they did it like God said do it, they couldn't receive the blessing. And you know what?"

Jennifer didn't want to disappoint Essie again. "Sarah had a baby?" Her uncertainty resonated in her voice.

Essie laughed and clapped her hands at the same time, apparently pleased with her student's answer. "Amen. Sho' 'nuff did. When she got out of the way and allowed the Lord to have *His* way, everything worked it out just like He planned for it to happen in the beginning 'fore she stepped in and messed things up." Essie's face turned serious. "Jennifer, you got to get out of the way, honey. You 'bout to destroy everything that God planned for your life and Jerrod's. The Good Lord don't need your help, sugar. He knows what He's doing. 'Fore I left to go join Ben," she pointed upward as she spoke, "I taught you real good 'bout God's perfect timing. I told you that He had a time and a season for everything in our lives. But we got to be willing to wait on Him."

Jennifer searched Essie's face in preparation to plead her case. "But Ms. Essie, I'm thirty—"

"And Sarah was *ninety*," Essie cut in. "Age don't mean nothing to God. He knew what you wanted 'fore you even asked for it, chile. But just 'cause you asked don't mean He got to answer right away. Psalm 27:14 tells us to wait on the Lord. Sometimes God tests our patience to see if we really ready for the blessing that we asking for. And honey, you 'bout to fail big time. You so busy trying to play God that you destroying your son's life, and you on the verge of destroying yours too, by trying to put something together that wasn't never meant to be."

Jennifer stared at Essie. What was she trying to say? "Are you saying that me and Devon weren't meant to be?"

"What in the world ever made you think you *were* meant to be?"

Jennifer had to make her understand. "Isn't he the obvious choice?"

"How so?" Essie challenged.

"We have a child together."

"A child that he abandoned."

"That was fifteen years ago, Ms. Essie."

"Fifteen years and not a peep from him 'til now. Don't that tell you something, baby?"

"Yes," Jennifer nodded. "Better late than never."

Essie popped up from the sofa with the ease of a teenager. She walked the length of Jennifer's living room floor, and then returned to her original seat. "Think with your brain, girl," she said. "My time is running out, and I need you to get this and get this fast."

Shrugging, Jennifer asked, "Get what?"

"Father, help me," Essie whispered the prayer through a heavy breath and with eyes turned toward the ceiling. She brought her sights back to Jennifer. "Where that boy been all this time?"

Jennifer suddenly felt dim-witted. She hadn't even asked Devon of his whereabouts over the past fifteen years. "I don't know," she said, hating to admit it. "I guess he's been in South Carolina where he grew up."

"You *guess*?" Essie looked at her like she'd lost her mind. "You 'bout to marry some scoundrel who you *guess* been living somewhere?"

The mounting feeling of stupidity didn't suit Jennifer. She squirmed again. "He's only been back in my life for a few days, Ms. Essie. We haven't had time to talk about all that."

"But you done talked about marrying him. What kind of foolishness is that?"

"Ms. Essie—"

"Listen to me, Jennifer Mays, and you listen good. How did that boy find his way back to you?"

The last few days had been a blur. Devon's reappearance into her life had happened so fast that she had trouble putting the pieces together. "I . . . I don't know, really. He just called me up one day, out of the blue. He'd been looking for me for a while, and he finally found me."

"Anybody believe that can stand on their eyelids."

Jennifer ignored the sarcasm. "I don't have a reason not to believe him, Ms. Essie. I may not know all the details, but I know it was an answer to my prayer because I'd been talking to God about my situation. Telling Him that I wanted a husband, and Jerrod needed a dad. Then Devon called and—"

"And you just assumed that he was the husband and father that you'd prayed for," Essie interjected.

"Come on, Ms. Essie. It's too much to be coincidental. You have to admit that."

"Oh, it ain't no coincidence. You got that right. But I need you to think deeper, honey, 'cause the devil knows you were praying too. And he knows how to try to trick you into believing that this boy is your blessing, when he ain't."

Jennifer's eyes widened.

"Timing, baby, timing," Essie stressed. "Look at the timing. See, God's got perfect timing, but the devil knows how to make things look timely too. He knows how to counterfeit just about anything. He's an evil little trickster and you got to be watchful."

Jennifer was even more confused than before. Her heart thumped in an off-beat fashion. She didn't know what Essie was about to say, but she knew it was something she didn't want to hear.

"What happened right 'fore that boy contacted you?" Essie asked.

"Uh . . ."

"*This* happened, that's what." From nowhere, Essie pulled out a copy of the local section of last weekend's edition of the *Atlanta Weekly Chronicles* newspaper. On the front page of it was a photo of a smiling Jerrod and T.K. A photo they'd taken at Benihana on the day T.K. made the announcement of Jerrod's phenomenal speed on the track. The same day Jennifer thought that she'd be getting a proposal.

When Jennifer failed to make an immediate connection between the article and Essie's accusation, the woman spoke again.

"That boy don't love you no more today than he did near 'bout sixteen years ago, Jennifer, don't you see that? He didn't seek you out 'cause *his heart couldn't deal no more with being apart from you."*

Jennifer winced. Those were almost the exact words that Devon told her when they met for their first reconnection date. He said that he'd been looking for her for years because his heart was bleeding after she'd been ripped from it. He blamed his parents, saying that they were the real reasons he couldn't be in her and Jerrod's life. But Devon claimed that since the age of twenty-one, when he moved out of his parents' home, he'd been searching for his long lost love and the child she'd had. Devon told her that he'd arbitrarily come to Atlanta, seeking a better job opportunity, and God allowed him to spot her name as he randomly opened the telephone book one day to look up the number for a job lead he'd been given.

"Lies, all lies," Essie insisted like she'd heard those thoughts too. "This here is what brought

that boy back in your life." She tapped the newspaper. "He seen this and seen dollar signs. That
boy been in Atlanta for years. This same newspaper, as well as the *Atlanta Journal-Constitution*,
had plenty of stories in them when Jerrod was
testifying at the trial of them boys who raped
that teacher. You think Devon didn't know y'all
were here? You think he didn't know that the
Jerrod *Devon* Mays, son of Jennifer Mays, who
was mentioned in all them articles was his boy?
Yeah, he knew." Essie placed the paper on the
coffee table and slid it closer to Jennifer as if she
needed a better view.

"You ain't told that boy one thing about Jerrod's track record," Essie continued. "Am I
right?"

Jennifer nodded her head slowly.

"Well then, how he know?"

"He doesn't," Jennifer defended. "Like you
said, I never told him. So this can't be the reason—"

"Oh, he knows," Essie assured her. "When he
was talking to Jerrod the other day, he said he
was gonna make sure Jerrod stayed on track.
Said he was 'bout to be a star. Remember that?"

Jennifer's mouth dropped open. She was
right. He did say that.

"I sho' am right." The thought-reader struck again. "Right as rain. Devon came back to you 'cause he knows that Jerrod's gonna be a famous track star. He's gonna make millions from endorsements and interviews. Devon knows now that what he gave up fifteen years ago was not only his child, but his blessing. It's dollar signs, not valentines, that brought him back to you, baby. He don't care nothing about you, and he don't care nothing about his son either. Not really. But he knows that the only way that he can reap the benefits of what Jerrod is about to bring to the table is to pretend that he loves you and wants to make an honest family out of y'all. And if he can convince you of that before Jerrod starts making the money, then he know he's in and it won't look like a scam. But believe you me, that's exactly what it is."

All Jennifer could do was stare at the article with swelling tears and mounting regret. She wanted to second-guess Essie, accuse the old woman of not knowing what she was talking about, but deep down, she knew that every word of it was true. Devon was still the same smooth talker that he was as a teenager. She wiped away trickles of tears from her cheeks, ashamed of her own self. Ashamed that she wasn't able to see through Devon's mask. Ashamed that she'd so quickly left T.K., the one she truly loved, to follow a lie. Ashamed to know that her own selfish folly was the reason for her son's disappearance.

She sobbed. "What am I gonna do now? I've just messed everything up."

"Yes, you have," Essie agreed. "But one of the good things about God is that when you serve Him, you serve the One who can do anything but fail." She chuckled and then added, "I used to hear the church folks say that God is the only somebody who can unscramble scrambled eggs. That means that ain't nothing too hard for Him."

Between sniffles, Jennifer said, "I don't know if Jerrod will ever forgive me. Let alone T.K." Her heart sank a little further at the thought of T.K. "He must hate me right now."

"Child, didn't you just hear me say that God can unscramble scrambled eggs?" Essie clapped her hands again, rocking back and forth with glee. "If the Lord can put a black man in the White House, He can do anything. Who would have ever thunk it?" She stood to her feet again and used her hands to smooth out her dress. "If you pray and put your trust in Jesus, everything will be fine. Pray and wait. Remember those two things." Essie sounded like she had no doubt in her mind. "Now, stand up and give me a hug. I gotta go."

Jennifer rose to her feet and didn't hesitate to accept Essie's embrace, holding her as tight as she could. More tears fell. "Ms. Essie, I've missed you so much. Please don't go. Can't you stay a little longer?"

"No, child." Essie pulled away and kissed Jennifer on the forehead. "Ms Essie's got two men waiting on her. Jesus and Ben. And as much as I love all y'all, I don't want to stay away from them no longer than I have to." She wiped Jennifer's cheeks with the palms of her hands. "Now, I need you to do something for me, okay?"

Jennifer nodded, noting how smooth Essie's hands felt. Too smooth for a woman of her advanced years. They felt like hands that had never known work.

"First of all, you ain't got to tell Jerrod that you saw me. He feels my presence all the time, and I'm always wit' him, but my assignment don't include a visit with him. But I want you to give him a hug for me anyway; okay?"

Jennifer nodded. She only hoped she'd get the chance to hug her son again.

Essie pointed. "What I need for you to do is to get that there blanket to Elaine."

Following the direction of Essie's finger, Jennifer noticed the blanket that Essie had finished knitting just a few days before she passed away.

When Jennifer groped in the dark and pulled the cover over her before going to sleep, she hadn't realized that she was covering herself with the same pink and blue blanket that Jerrod had brought home from Essie's house.

"Get that to Elaine, now; you hear?" Essie reiterated. "I'm on a mission to visit all the daughters the Lord gave me, but in order for me to fulfill it, I need you to do that for me."

"Yes, ma'am."

Essie pointed toward the sofa. "Now, you lay on back down and finish getting your sleep. You got a whole lot of work to do tomorrow, and your first order of business is to get that devil that you let back in your life, out."

Jennifer sat down, but still held on to Essie's hand. "But what about Jerrod and T.K.? I don't know where Jerrod is, and T.K. didn't even return my call when I told him that my son was missing. What am I supposed to do about them?" "Pray and wait," Essie reminded her. "Pray and wait."

Chapter 23

Colin's Story

Nearly half an hour had passed since he pulled his Pathfinder in the driveway of his home. Colin couldn't believe his own gall—arriving home this late. Riddled with guilt and regret, he buried his face in his hands for the second time.

It was supposed to be just a quick meeting over coffee at Starbucks. How it turned into dinner . . . and then dessert . . . and then a movie . . . at *her* house, he didn't know. How in the world would he explain this to Angel? It was nearly two in the morning. What could he possibly say to her that wouldn't make things sound even worse than they actually were?

"I fell asleep on the couch and she didn't wake me up," he rehearsed.

It was the truth, but Colin knew Angel wouldn't believe him. In the first place, how would he explain going to his assistant's house for dinner when his wife, no doubt, had dinner waiting for him at home? No. . . . Forget all that. He'd never even get that far. First he'd have to come up with one good reason—just *one*—that he had for taking in a movie at Nona's instead of coming home after work like any decent, married husband and father would. No. . . . Scratch that too. Before he could begin to sell that one on Angel, he'd have to make her understand that he'd only agreed to have coffee with Nona to catch her up on the details of some of the client files he'd been working on.

"I'm a dead man," Colin whispered, banging his forehead against the steering wheel.

There was no way he was going to succeed in convincing his wife that his walking into their house at 2:00 A.M. was all an innocent mistake. He was barely able to convince himself. There were details about it all that even Colin couldn't explain away. Like when Nona asked about them discussing the files over coffee, why didn't he just refuse and insist, instead, that they set aside a specific time tomorrow to do it? He could have worked through his lunch hour to get it done, if necessary. Wasn't like he hadn't worked through lunch before.

And after coffee, when Nona invited him back to her house for potluck, saying that she had a bunch of leftover food from the big meal she'd cooked over the weekend, why in the world did he accept?

"We're family now, remember?" she'd said. "Come on over and let your big sister feed you."

Big sister. Yeah, right. Colin almost laughed at the thought of him using that one. If he tried to use the it's-no-big-deal-she'sjust-like-kinfolks angle in his explanation to his wife, it would be like putting a down payment on his funeral. Maybe he wouldn't die physically, but it would be the death of his marriage for sure.

Colin massaged his throbbing temples. He and Angel had had their disagreements in the past; especially in recent days. But this? This was different. He'd never come home at such a blasphemous hour before and certainly not without calling Angel at some point and giving her an update on his whereabouts. Innocent or not, how was he going to explain himself? And if everything were so innocent, why did he feel like a wanted fugitive, looking over his shoulder, expecting at any moment to be captured and punished to the full extent of the law?

"Oh, God, help me," Colin whispered through a heavy exhale. He could feel tightness building in his neck and shoulders. Tension. Guilty tension.

Reality was beginning to break through Colin's makeshift cloud of virtue like the Arizona sun. He knew why he felt like dirt. Why he felt like filth. Why he felt like the scum of the earth. It was because although there had been no sexual misconduct in his eight-hour fellowship with Nona, nothing about it was proper. The heaviest burden of guilt, the one that was bringing pain to Colin's upper body, was the fact that although he hadn't gone to bed with Nona, he'd slept with her.

"I didn't mean to," he said aloud, defending himself to the invisible accuser who occupied the car with him. "It's not like it was planned."

By most people's characterization, the brief two-person slumber party would be seen as anything but inappropriate. It was as simple as Colin falling asleep on the sofa halfway through the movie. He hadn't even felt himself getting sleepy. When his eyes came open shortly after 1:00 A.M., it took a while for him to become coherent. The first few moments were spent trying to define his unfamiliar surroundings and figure out how he'd gotten there. It was then that Colin noticed pressure being applied against the left side of his body. When he looked through the dim light provided only by the flickering television screen, he was able to identify the lump of flesh beside him as Nona. At some point during the evening, she'd followed his lead; fallen asleep and was using his shoulder as a pillow. Colin nearly scared her to death when he frantically jumped from the sofa, fumbling for the shoes he'd abandoned when he made himself all too comfortable.

"Why didn't you just come home?" he scolded. But there was no sense in second-guessing himself now. It was too late. "Besides, I didn't do anything wrong," he spoke into the darkness, once again, pleading his case to the unseen. "I went to sleep and she went to sleep. That's all it was. It wasn't *us* going to sleep. We didn't sleep together."

Pause.

"I mean, we did, but not like that. We just happened to be on the sofa together, and both of us fell asleep. It could have happened to anybody."

Pause.

"I'm a dead man," Colin moaned, again burying his face in his hands.

When he would get into mischief as a child growing up in his parents' home, Colin's mom would often say, "I might not know everything, and your daddy might not know everything, but there are two beings in this world that you won't ever be able to fool: God and yourself."

And she was right.

For days, God had been whispering to Colin, telling him to draw some boundaries in his relationship with Nona. She may have been old enough and friendly enough to be his big sister, but she was also young enough and attractive enough to be his other woman. Colin knew he'd crossed the line when he began dumping the details of his marital discord in Nona's ears. But it felt good to have someone listen to him. Empathize with him. Value him. Appreciate him. He'd gotten too comfortable with the person who was supposed to only be his office assistant, and he'd allowed her to get too comfortable with him.

That became clearly evident when she embraced him instead of just saying good-bye after they shared lunch on Saturday, the day he took Austin in to work with him. Although he'd planned to only work a couple of hours and leave early, Colin ended up staying long enough to accompany Nona for lunch at The Brookwood Grill. When they parted ways, Nona not only took the time to hug Austin, but she did the same to Colin, placing a quick kiss on his neck before releasing him. It momentarily took him aback. Caught him by surprise. Left a lingering feeling of awkwardness. But Nona never indicated that the act of affection was anything other than chaste, making it fairly easy for Colin to dismiss it as such. But after tonight's little sleepover, the two incidents combined made him feel like the cheating husband that he knew he wasn't.

Two-thirty.

Another half hour had passed. Colin knew that no matter how many seconds ticked away on the clock, the task ahead wasn't going to go away, and it wasn't going to get any easier. He was just glad that the house was completely dark. It meant that Angel was in bed and most likely asleep. If he could get through the night without having to deal with this, maybe daylight would provide a brighter outlook.

Colin's body felt like a block of hardened cement as he opened the door to his vehicle and peeled himself away from the leather interior. The pleasant night air provided no comfort during his trek to the front door. Even with the door key already positioned in his hand, Colin fumbled with getting it into the lock to open the door. Once inside, the quiet of his house enveloped him. A mixture of hovering aromas gave way to the fact that dinner had, at an earlier hour, been prepared for him. Colin's heart sank lower.

In the shadows of the living room, he began his normal ritual; the one he did on days when he came home like a decent husband would. Colin peeled off his suit jacket and hung it on the coat stand near the door. Then, with movements slowed by mounting remorse, he stepped from his shoes and pushed them in the corner beside the base of the coat stand.

Turning to his left, he saw a faint glimmer of light peek underneath the door down the hallway. It was Austin's night-light. Colin couldn't believe he'd once again allowed his son to go a full day without spending any quality time with him. He'd let his frustration with Angel spill over into his relationship with his child. Colin's shoulders slumped in shame.

He couldn't wake up Austin as he'd done a few nights ago. If he did, it would wake up Angel too, and theirs was an argument that he just didn't have the energy or willpower to participate in tonight. He wasn't ready. Before talking to Angel, he needed to do some thinking. Some planning. Some praying. But Colin dared not go to bed without at least peeping in on his son. He'd kiss the boy goodnight, then make up for his absence tomorrow.

Feeling for the light switch in the darkness, Colin found it and flipped it upward. He let out a startled yowl and almost lost his balance when the brightened room revealed that he wasn't alone. "Angel," he gasped, trying to steady himself with a hand to the wall, and his racing heartbeat with a hand to his chest.

Angel stood beside the sofa in their spotless living room, looking like she'd been posted there for hours. Waiting for his arrival. Her jaws trembled. Her lips were fixed. Her hair was tousled. Her puffy eyes indicated that tears—lots of them—had been recently shed. In her hand, she clutched one of Colin's dress shirts.

Colin looked away from her disturbed and distorted face. He couldn't bear to look at her and know that he'd been the cause of her obvious anguish. Instead, he dropped his eyes to wood flooring whose shine told him it had been recently polished. He didn't know what to say.

"It's almost three in the morning, Colin Stephens," she growled through clenched teeth. Then in a slow, calculated tone, one that made every word seem like a sentence of its own, she asked, "Where . . . have . . . you . . . been?"

Colin's mouth opened and closed twice, but no words escaped.

"Answer me, Colin! Where have you been?"

Her uncharacteristic scream pierced his ears and his heart. Colin's hopes of avoiding this battle until tomorrow were dashed. Ready or not, it was on.

Chapter 24

T.K.'s Story

Road rage was as common in metropolitan Atlanta as skyscrapers were in New York City. Good thing his first class wasn't until 9:40 A.M.

T.K.'s fingers drummed against the steering wheel of his Corvette. It was an early model classic with more than 200,000 miles to its credit. But, the recently bathed white exterior and the polished black leather seats that he'd had reupholstered two years ago looked showroom new. T.K. only drove it occasionally these days, in hopes of preserving it for at least another few years.

"C'mon, dude. If you're gonna drive this slow, you might as well walk," he yelled to no avail at the driver in the car in front of him. T.K. was quickly losing the battle to remain calm as he worked his way through rush hour traffic. "There's room for at least three cars to get between you and the guy in front of you. Why are you riding on your brakes? If you're afraid to drive, take the doggone bus! The least you could do is get over in the slow lane with the other turtles."

The traffic that flowed in the lanes on either side of T.K. prevented him from going around the overly cautious road menace. Every time that T.K. thought he had an opening to whip from behind the sluggish driver, someone behind him would beat him to the punch.

"My grandma drives faster than you, man!" he belted in frustration. "And she's dead!"

Time wasn't working in his favor. On a good day, the drive from T.K.'s Alpharetta home to his destination in Midtown would be just over thirty minutes. Today, it had already taken him that long to get just over half as far.

Most days, the heaviest part of rush hour didn't begin until around seven in the morning; when the bulk of the early morning commuters took to the highway. When T.K. received the six o'clock call from Jerrod, he'd immediately kicked off his covers and jumped out of bed. It took him about half an hour to shave, shower, and get dressed, but he still didn't expect to run into this kind of bumper-to-bumper havoc.

"Lord, *please* help me get from behind this man."

It was more like an exacerbated groan than an earnest prayer, but no sooner had the words left T.K.'s mouth than the driver put on his signal to merge into the lane to the left of them. It took a few moments, and the car came dangerously close to being rammed from behind by a fast-approaching vehicle, but the "man"—who turned out to be a middle-aged female wearing a base-ball cap—cleared the way for T.K. to increase his speed.

"Women drivers," he muttered before shifting gears and applying pressure to the gas pedal.

Midtown wasn't an area that T.K. often fre-quented. He wasn't as savvy with maneuvering around its neighborhoods as he was with other parts of the city, but what he didn't know, his Garmin GPS Navigator did. T.K. breathed a sigh of relief when he parked in the lot of the small complex. The clock on his dashboard said that he wasn't as late as he thought he'd be.

Seven-twenty. Still time enough to scoop up Jerrod and get back to Alpharetta before his stu-dents could declare him MIA.

Climbing out of the vehicle, T.K. took a second to scope out his surroundings. It wasn't the best neighborhood, but it wasn't the worst either.

He felt certain that the Platinum Stargazer alloy rims of his cherished sports car would be safe until he returned. T.K. had no plans to be in the apartment for long, but for added security, he tucked his portable GPS in his glove compartment, then engaged his locks and his alarm system.

The community was so quiet that he could hear the grains of debris crunching beneath his shoes as he took the short stroll to the door that displayed the number that Jerrod had given him. T.K.'s fist was still mid-air, preparing to knock, when the door opened.

"Hey, Coach D. What's up?"

T.K. removed the sunglasses from his eyes and broke into a smile. He hadn't seen much of Toby since the trial. "What's going on, stranger?" he replied, pulling his former student in for a quick embrace. "Good to see you."

"Good to see you too." Toby's grin was so tight it looked permanent. He stepped aside and pointed toward the sofa. "Come on in, Coach. Not much space in here, but there's enough for you to sit down."

T.K. looked around the cozy space as he took Toby up on his invitation. It was a small place, indeed. But it was clean and inviting. "So what have you been up to?" T.K. knew the backstory of Toby's withdrawal from school. Jerrod had filled him in a long time ago. He thought it was a shame that the boy's parents had basically washed their hands of their son because of his admission. Surely there was a law against putting a sixteen-year-old up in his own apartment, forcing him to function like a grown man. But T.K. decided not to bring up any of that. "I hear you're a working man now."

Toby's new smile didn't appear to be as genuine as the one before it. "Yeah. A man's gotta do what a man's gotta do." He shrugged. "I work the three to eleven shift at Publix. Not a Fortune 500 job, but it pays the bills that I have to cover."

T.K. took another moment to scout out the place. It reminded him a little of his off-campus apartment during his college days. Toby misread his quiet exploration, apparently thinking that T.K. was in search of the boy he came to pick up. "Oh . . . J's in the bathroom," he explained. "He's a cool guy, and he's been great company, but boy is he messy. He's in there cleaning out the sink. I told him to rinse out the face bowl after he brushes his teeth, but he never does. So I got him in there cleaning all that dried toothpaste from out of my sink."

T.K. laughed. "Yeah, he can be a pig if you don't stay in behind him."

"Tell me about it." Toby walked toward the kitchen. "You want something to drink, Coach? I got water, apple juice, Kool-Aid and Coca-Cola."

"Coke is good."

Toby returned with a glass of water in one hand and a can of soda in the other. He handed T.K. the can. "Here you go."

"Thanks." Bracing himself for a possible spill, T.K. popped the tab. The carbonated drink fizzed in his mouth before going down his throat. "Toby, I want you to know that I appreciate you taking Jerrod in like this. You didn't have to do that."

"No problem," Toby replied. "Me and J . . . well, we been through a lot together. There was a time when it felt like it was just me and him against the world."

T.K. nodded. "I know."

"Plus, he didn't start acting all funny when he found out I was—" Toby stopped, like he wasn't sure how much his former educator knew. Like he was afraid that if T.K. found out like this, that he'd all of a sudden start treating him differently too.

T.K. nodded again. "I know." Toby gave a half-smile. He was clearly relieved.

"Hey, Coach D." Jerrod emerged from the bathroom, drying his hands on a paper towel.

T.K. stood. He was so happy to see Jerrod that he was tempted to run to him, grab him around his waist in a big bear hug, lift him off the floor, and spin him around a time or two. There was no way that Jerrod could know how much he'd worried over his disappearance. T.K. restrained himself; only embracing the boy briefly. "Don't ever do anything like this again." His voice was low, but firm. T.K. released the boy and looked him in the eyes. "I mean that, Jerrod. You hear me?"

"Yeah . . . yes, sir." Jerrod's eyes dropped to the carpet. His demeanor was that of a child ten years younger.

His remorse was genuine and endearing, and T.K. couldn't help but smile before looking over Jerrod's shoulder at Toby. The boy was quietly watching the exchange while sipping from his glass. "Toby, I hate to dip in and out so fast, but I've got a class to teach this morning and—"

"Yeah, I know. It's cool." Toby raised his glass like he was toasting as he spoke.

T.K. loosened his hold on Jerrod and walked closer to Toby. "Listen, son, I wouldn't be who I am if I didn't try to encourage you to get back in school." Toby opened his mouth to speak, but T.K. raised his hand to stop him. "I know it got rough for you after the trial and after your parents found out about you, and I understand that. But living here puts you in a whole new school district. You really have no excuse for not getting your diploma, Toby."

"If they found out at Alpharetta High, they'll find out here," Toby said. "It'll just be a matter of time."

Time. The word reminded T.K. that he was running out of it and needed to leave. This would be a subject that he'd have to take Toby to the mat on at a later date. Somehow, he had to convince him that running away from his troubles wasn't the answer. If he ran now, he'd be running for the rest of his life. Toby's sexual struggle was a demon that he needed to face head-on. But not by himself, or he'd lose every time. He couldn't keep hiding out like this. He needed God's help. There was so much more that T.K. realized he needed to say, but today wasn't the day to say it. T.K. knew where the teen lived now, and he knew his work hours. He surmised that he'd come back on another day and talk more. Timing was everything. That was a lesson that T.K. learned from Essie Mae Richardson in the short time that he knew her.

"Got all your things?" he asked Jerrod, tapping him on the shoulder.

"What things? Except for my bike, these clothes I got on were all I had when I got here. I been having to wear Toby's stuff."

T.K. turned back to Toby and ducked his head in gratitude. "Thanks again. You taking Jerrod in like that really means a lot. I owe you one. I mean that."

A smile and a nod was Toby's reply. He followed T.K. and Jerrod as they walked to the door of his apartment. Just as Jerrod opened it, Toby said, "Hey, Coach D?"

T.K. turned. "Yes?"

"You say you owe me one. Can I cash in now?" I couldn't help but wonder what he'd gotten himself into. He paused to think. Toby was a teenager, having to live off of a cashier's salary. Sure, his parents paid for most of his bills, but was certain that there were extra things that he wanted. Just like any boy his age, Toby, no doubt, wanted to have something that reminded him that he was still a kid despite having to live independently of his parents. "Sure," T.K. said, fully prepared to reach into his pocket and pull out a few spending dollars to give the boy. "How much do you need?"

Toby let out a short laugh, shook his head, and then shoved his hands in the pockets of his baggy jeans. "I don't need no money, Coach D. I mean,

Jerrod did eat me out of house and home, but if there's one thing I got plenty of in this house, it's food."

"Oh." T.K. felt a bit foolish for his premature assumption. "What is it that you want?"

Toby's eyes shot to the floor, and he shifted his feet with a twinge of uneasiness. "Uh, I was just wondering. Me and J was talking last night, and well, he was telling me that sometimes he goes to church with you. And uh . . . he was telling me about how much he liked your preacher man and everything."

T.K. hadn't heard anyone refer to a pastor as a preacher man in ages, but he kept his thoughts quiet so Toby could finish.

"I was just wondering if, you know . . . if maybe I could come with you some time on the Sundays when J's gonna be there. You know. So I'll know somebody besides you on the day that I go. I mean, I know I live kind of out of the way and all. And if you can't come get me then, you know, I understand. I was just thinking and—"

"I'd be happy to come pick you up, son," T.K. said, looking from Toby to Jerrod, and then back at Toby. He was surprised to hear that the boys had been discussing matters surrounding church, but he saw God's hand all in it. This would be the open window for him to minister to

Toby further. Knowingly or unknowingly, Jerrod had apparently already gotten the ball rolling.

"I'm in the phone book. Anytime you want to come, just let me know, and I'll just get Jerrod to come with me on that day too so you'll feel more comfortable." T.K. hoped he was telling the truth in light of Jennifer's decision to start a new life with Devon. He knew it wasn't going to be easy, but he couldn't let Jennifer's renewed relationship with her former ex change things between him and Jerrod. He didn't have a say-so in what Jennifer did with her own life, but he'd die before he sat idly by and allowed her to ruin Jerrod's. "Anytime you want to go, you call me, Toby," he added with renewed confidence.

Toby's smile said that he was pleased with T.K.'s response. "Okay. I will." The door of the apartment closed quietly behind them, and T.K.'s longer legs led the way as he and Jerrod made the walk to his waiting car; bicycle in tow. They crammed the bike into the trunk as best it would fit, and T.K. used a mechanism that he pulled from a toolbox to secure the trunk. No words were spoken between them until the car doors were shut, their seat-belts were secured, new directions had been programmed into the GPS system, and T.K. was driving out of the small complex.

"You mad at me, ain't you?" Jerrod asked over the GPS's order to turn left.

Anger was nowhere in the mix of emotions that T.K. was experiencing as he navigated back toward Alpharetta. "I'm disappointed that you'd run off like that and not tell nobody, but no, I'm not mad at you."

Jerrod sank into his seat. "I just didn't know what else to do."

T.K. tossed a glance at him and then focused again on the road ahead. "You could have called me."

"I did. Remember? You took their side."

"I didn't take anybody's side, and if you hadn't hung up in my face, you might have realized that. And you didn't tell me that you had run off from home either. All you did was tell me about Jen and . . ." T.K.'s tongue wouldn't even form the name, "*him*," he concluded, frowning at the thought of it.

He could feel Jerrod's eyes boring into his skin during the interim silence. "Can I see it?" The boy's voice was low and quiet.

T.K. glanced at him. "See what?"

"The ring. You said that you had bought Ma a ring and was gonna ask me for her hand. Can I see the ring, or were you just saying that to get me to call you?"

"Have I ever lied to you?"

"No, sir."

T.K. thought about the beautiful piece of jewelry that he purchased weeks earlier. A flawless one-carat, oval-shaped solitaire diamond encased in a band made of white gold. Beautiful. Just like Jennifer. "It's at my house. I'll let you see it later," he told Jerrod.

"I would have said yes," Jerrod said, keeping his eyes fixed on the windshield. Then, as though he thought T.K. may not have been clear on what he meant, he added, "I would've been glad to have you marry Ma; would've been glad to call you Daddy."

T.K. had to swallow hard to keep his emotions in check. They drove in silence for most of the remaining ride. When T.K. turned in the direction to head toward Alpharetta High, Jerrod protested.

"I don't want to go to school. Not today."

With raised eyebrows, T.K. asked, "Why not?"

"I just don't. I ain't feelin' it today, Coach D. Please don't make me go."

T.K. didn't regard not feelin' it as a good reason to miss school. Especially since the boy had already missed classes yesterday. "I want to keep an eye on you, Jerrod. I can't take a chance on you running off again."

"Then take me to your house."

"I can't watch you at my house. I'll be at school, remember?"

"You don't trust me?"

The car weaved a bit when T.K. took his eyes off the road to shoot a grimace in Jerrod's direction. "Have you given me any reasons to lately?"

Jerrod sank deeper into the seat, but shot into an upright position a moment later. "Let me earn your trust back, Coach. If you take me to your place, I promise to God that I won't leave. I'll wait right there 'til you get home. If I run off, you ain't never got to trust me again."

T.K. knew Jerrod was being sincere, but there was more that they needed to consider. "What about your mother, Jerrod? She needs to know where you are. She's been worried sick about you. The only reason she didn't get the police involved is because I called and told her that I'd take care of everything."

Jerrod's face lit up. "You talked to her? You and Ma are talking again?"

It broke T.K.'s heart to disappoint him. "I left a message at the house yesterday when I knew she wouldn't be at home."

"Oh." He sounded dejected as he readjusted himself in the seat and faced the windshield again. "Well, you can tell her that I'm with you if you want to. I just don't want to go home right now."

T.K. conceded and turned toward Braxton Park. He was getting dangerously close to being late for his first class. "Your mom should be at work right now, so we'll swing by your house so you can pack a few things. I'll find a way to convince her to let you stay with me for a few days."

"Okay." A smile graced Jerrod's face for the first time since he got into T.K.'s car.

T.K.'s eyes searched the neighborhood as he pulled onto Braxton Way. A part of him hoped to find Jennifer's car parked in the yard. He hoped she had been too upset to go to work. It would give him a chance to see her. To talk to her. To talk some sense into her. But the driveway was vacant.

"What's that?" Jerrod pointed at what looked like a mound of cloth in the street about a hundred feet from his home.

T.K. squinted. The downhill slope prevented him from having a clear view. "Probably just something that fell off the back of somebody's truck or something."

The men climbed from the car and headed toward the front steps of Jennifer's home. While Jerrod fished his keys from his pocket, T.K. found himself looking again in the direction of the thing in the road. The more he looked, the less it appeared to be an inanimate object. In fact, he was almost sure that he saw it move.

"Wait up, Jerrod," he said, taking a few cautious steps toward the fixation.

"It's moving, Coach," Jerrod observed, following close behind. "Somebody hit a dog or something."

T.K. could feel the gradual increase of his heartbeat. Something wasn't right. "That's not some*thing*, Jerrod," he suddenly said, coming to a stop still fifty feet away. "That's some*body*."

Jerrod stepped from behind him and took off running toward the mound of crumpled flesh. T.K. wanted to shout at him to use caution, but instead, he found himself following suit.

"It's Ms. Elaine, Coach!" Jerrod yelled as he knelt down beside her. "It's Ms. Elaine!"

Chapter 25

Elaine's Story

She didn't exactly know where the melodic sounds were coming from, but it was definitely nearby. Elaine turned her head and could hear her own quiet murmurs, but she couldn't understand the words that were attempting to come out of her own mouth. Yet, the lyrics continued.

"Steal away, steal away, steal away, steal away to Jesus, steal away, steal away, I ain't got long to stay here."

Again Elaine tried to speak, but couldn't. She was thirsty, hungry, tired, and hurting. If she could get the attention of whoever was near her, perhaps she could get some relief from her pain and discomfort. Using all the energy she could muster, Elaine pushed out the loudest groan possible.

The singing stopped and was replaced by a voice. "'Bout time you woke up, child. I been sitting here near 'bout all day long, waiting for you to come to."

Elaine struggled to open her eyes, but the weight of her eyelids was too heavy. Only darkness surrounded her. "Wa . . . Wa . . . ter." The word was barely audible, but at least, now she could hear herself speaking. "Water."

"I got you, I got you," the woman said.

Elaine could hear the sound of water pouring in a glass, and it was the most beautiful sound she'd ever heard. Her throat felt like it hadn't been irrigated in ages. It felt like someone had laced it with baby powder, and then shoved in cotton balls to top it off. Footsteps approached her bed, and Elaine knew that relief was only a moment away. She felt the head of her bed raise, and then a strong, but soft hand cradled the back of her neck, lifting her head forward. When she felt the glass touch her lips, Elaine parted them and tried to take in as much of the liquid as she could. The cold liquid felt blissful.

"Got enough, or you want more?" the Good Samaritan asked.

Elaine hated to be a bother, and her mother had raised her on the rule of never accepting anything from people she didn't know—especially food. But until she could do for herself, Elaine decided that she had no choice but to depend on the kindness of strangers. "M . . . M . . . More."

"Child, you sho' 'nuff was thirsty," the lady said once the contents of the second glassful was drained.

Something about those words and the chuckle that followed sounded oddly familiar to Elaine's ears.

"Got more if you want it," the woman offered.

Elaine really did want more, but she responded with a whispered, "No, thanks," then listened to the sound of scuffling feet as the lady walked away. "Wh . . . Where am I?" Elaine was afraid that if she stopped talking, the kind stranger would leave, and she was too afraid to be left alone right now. Too many unanswered questions. Too many cloudy, mangled, snapshot-type memories.

It sounded like the woman had taken a seat somewhere to the right of her. "Dumb people end up in one of three places, sugar," she said, taking Elaine by surprise. "The cemetery, the jailhouse, or the hospital. Now I ain't saying that everybody in them places is dumb, 'cause they ain't. Not by any means. I'm just saying that them are the places where dumb folks end up. And you been mighty dumb lately, so you in the hospital right now. They brought you in this morning."

"The hos . . . pital?" Elaine was too healthy for the need of a hospital.

"Uh-huh. Pale as a ghost. Sick as a dog. Skinny as a stick. Dumb as a box of rocks. Laying up in a hospital bed."

Suddenly, Elaine felt that being left alone wasn't such a bad option. The only problem was that if she suddenly banned the woman from her presence, she might not get her other questions answered. "Who are you?" She laced the question with as much attitude as she could, but she was just too weak to incorporate the raised voice, the neck roll, and all of the other accessories that would be needed to do the job just right.

"Oh, that's right," the lady said. "On top of all that, you 'bout blind as a bat too, ain't you?" She had a good laugh at Elaine's expense. "Let me see what I can do to help you out."

Elaine could hear the woman stand from her chair. If she'd had the strength, when the lady got close enough, she would grab her around the neck and see who would get the last laugh then.

"Let's see here." The woman's hands covered both Elaine's eyes. Her touch had a soothing, almost medicated type effect, like how Halls cough drops felt to a sore throat.

It felt good, but Elaine was still fuming from all the earlier comments regarding her stupidity. She appreciated the water and all that had been done to help her, but she didn't know who this woman thought she was. Elaine hadn't allowed anyone to speak to her in such a tone since . . .

"Ms. Essie!" Elaine yelled, eyes wide with disbelief when the hands that covered them had been removed. She couldn't believe the figure that stood at her bedside. Elaine's depleted strength wouldn't allow for her to bolt from the bed and run through the concrete wall of the room, leaving a gaping hole in the shape of the outline of her body like she'd seen cartoon characters on television do when she was a child.

But her voice had returned, and if she could talk; she could scream. And she did. For what seemed like an eternity, she closed her eyes, braced her head against her pillow, gripped the railings on the sides of her bed, and screamed to the top of her lungs. When she was all yelled out, she opened her eyes to see Essie doubled over with laugher.

"Child, cut that foolishness out," she said through a sigh as she calmly made her way back to the chair. "Common sense ought to tell you that if I'm here, then something's going on that ain't natural. This is God's doing, girl. Them doctors can't hear you."

"Am I dreaming? What's happening here?" It was then that she took note of her covering. It was the blanket. Her eyes were fixed on the pink and blue weaving that rested on top of her hospital sheets. How did that get here? What on earth was going on? Elaine reached beneath the covers, trying to feel her way through to the cotton fabric of the hospital gown that covered her nakedness.

"Lord have mercy." Essie sighed. "There you go with all that pinching yourself and going on. Just like Jennifer did. Stop it 'fore you break something. Ain't no meat there no way. Last thing you need to do is pinch yourself so hard that the skin breaks and a bone come sticking through."

Elaine felt as though she was genuinely losing her mind. Everything about her current situation felt surreal. All of the wild details blended together to make an even-layered dish of sense and nonsense. She'd never felt so out of it, yet so fully aware at the same time. "What's going on here, Ms. Essie? You can't be here. You just can't. It's not possible."

"With God, all things are possible," the old lady replied, pointing toward the ceiling. "Now, I'm gonna need you to stop trying to figure all this out and listen to what I got to say. I ain't got long to say it, and you ain't got long to listen. So, for the next few minutes, I need you to lay quiet and let me do the talking. Deal?"

Elaine nodded. What other options did she have? Agreeing with Essie just seemed like the right thing to do. It seemed like the *only* thing to do. Elaine's initial fear had evaporated all of the water that she'd drunk. Swallowing was nearly impossible now. There was no moisture left on her tongue or in her throat.

Like she had some sixth sense, Essie walked back to the cart where the pitcher of water and glasses stood. She filled one of the glasses and walked back to Elaine, handing it to her. This time, Elaine was able to hold her own glass. When she reached for it, she realized that she had a needle inserted in the back of her right hand and another one going into a vein of the opposite arm. Elaine's eyes trailed the length of the tubes and they led her to bags of liquid that were hanging on metal poles that stood behind her bed.

"Scary sight, ain't it?" Essie said, pulling Elaine's attention back to her.

Elaine thought hard. The last thing she could recall was sticking the key to the front door of her home into her shoe and jogging up the street to begin her morning run. How did something that she did every day lead to this?

"Too much exercise and not enough eating will send anybody to the hospital," Essie said, answering Elaine's unspoken question. "What's gotten into you, child? I mean, you always did run. That's what you were doing the first day I ever spoke to you." Essie smiled like the memory was a fond one. "Wanting to be healthy is one thing, but you been eating like a squirrel lately. You been exercising more and more and eating less and less. Look at you." She pulled the covers off of Elaine's body, then pulled up the hem of the gown so that her slimmer thighs and legs were in full view. "This don't make no kind of sense, Elaine. You went from being a beautiful, healthy woman to a dried-up bag of bones."

Elaine reached to try to cover herself, but Essie's voice stopped her.

"What you trying to hide it for? You *worked* for this. It ain't like you been sick or forced to live in some third world country. You actually put on clothes and shoes every morning to go out and work to have this kind of body. What's wrong with you, child? You trying to kill yourself?"

Every question that Essie hammered out sounded accusing. Elaine didn't want to answer, and she wasn't going to. Besides, Essie had asked her to just be quiet and listen; so that alone gave her permission to remain silent.

"Don't try to get smart with me, girl," Essie warned.

Clearly, the thoughts in Elaine's head were somehow being transmitted to Essie's ears. The old lady always did have an oddly keen sense of hearing, but this . . . this was just too weird.

"Answer me," Essie insisted. "What are you trying to do?"

This was a battle that Elaine knew she couldn't win. She had always had a mulish streak, but her stubbornness had never been any match for Essie's persistence. "I'm not trying to kill myself, Ms. Essie. I just want to do whatever I can to make myself attractive."

"Attractive to who? Dogs? They the only ones who want bones."

Elaine smiled. "You're just saying that to try and make me feel good, Ms. Essie. I'm not skinny and you know it."

A frown began forming between Essie's eyebrows and soon covered her entire face. "You think boney is a compliment?"

"I think *weight-loss* is a compliment, yes. I'm not skinny and I'm not boney. I just want . . . *need* to lose a few more pounds; that's all."

"For what? You can't weigh over a hundred twenty-five soaking wet. You look worse than them skinny, flat-chested girls on that show 'bout women trying to be big-time models. Half of them look hungry, and the other half look like they need to eat. Society might call it pretty, but it ain't. Not for them, and it sho' ain't pretty for you. You ain't even built to be like that. God gave you them hips for a reason, child. They ain't no curse, they're a blessing. You always been beautiful, Elaine, and you ain't never been fat. Who got you thinking like this? You used to be so much more confident than this. What done got into you?"

Elaine could feel tears stinging the backs of her eyeballs. Why was Essie torturing her like this? Surely, she already knew the details. That Mason hadn't touched her in over a year. That she slept alone in the bedroom, while her husband snuggled nightly with the sofa. That she was losing the weight as a desperate last attempt at making her husband desire her again. God had probably told Essie all of that before He sent her down, or whatever had transpired to bring this dead woman back to life and into Elaine's hospital room.

Essie's heart must have softened at the sight of the stream that trickled down Elaine's cheeks, because she returned Elaine's covers back to their rightful place, then lowered the bedrail and sat on the side of the mattress. Elaine thought that Essie was going to start one of her lectures, but the old lady said nothing. All Essie did was cover Elaine's right hand with her left and sat in silence. Her hand was as soft as butter, and her brown eyes radiated kindness as they locked on Elaine and remained there. Without verbalizing, Essie seemed to be telling Elaine that everything was going to be all right. That she was there to listen and to help. That she wasn't leaving until she knew Elaine was okay.

"Ever since the morning after, things have been a mess, Ms. Essie." Elaine used her free hand to dry her cheeks.

"The morning after?"

"The morning after you died."

"Oh. I see." Essie squeezed Elaine's hand and smiled. "It ain't really dying when you got Jesus, you know. It's living. As a matter of fact, it's life eternal. Imagine beautiful weather every day. Peace and happiness every day." Essie stood from the bed and twirled around like a ballerina. "No more sickness. No hurts. No pains." She spread out her arms, and her eyes took on a far away gaze. "Everywhere you look, it ain't nothing but *good* people. Ain't no killin' and stealin', ain't no cussin' and fussin'. Just good people lovin' God and lovin' each other. Angels singin', music playin', people worshippin'. No loneliness, no sorrow, no judgin'." Essie looked back at Elaine and chuckled as she approached the bed again. "No wonder my Ben left me so early to go there. I can't blame him one bit."

The words struck a chord in Elaine, forcing her to face a reality that she'd never before admitted to herself or anyone else. "Then maybe I did wanna die." New tears threatened her eyes. "I think I did. I mean, I didn't know that I was trying to kill myself, but maybe I was. I'm just so tired of being judged. Tired of being in pain. Tired of being rejected. If I die and go to heaven, then I won't have to worry about any of those things."

"Child, if you kill yourself, going to heaven is the thing that you ain't gonna have to worry about doin'."

Elaine pressed her thumb and her middle finger in the corners of her eyes. She just couldn't win for losing. Living or dead, she was doomed to hell.

"Talk to me 'bout you and Mason." Essie straightened out the blanket that she'd knit-

ted with her own hands. "What's been going on
'tween the two of you?"

"Nothing, Ms. Essie; that's what's been going on between us. Absolutely nothing." Elaine
became annoyed at the thought of it. "I might
as well be dead. As far as Mason is concerned, I
am."

"That's not true, baby. He's just—"

"Yes, it is!" Elaine was fed up with people
making excuses for her husband. "I know I
messed up, Ms. Essie. I know I did. And I admit
that I deserved to be punished. One month, sure.
Two months, maybe. Three months, understandable. But a whole year? A whole year of
sleeping in separate rooms? A whole year of no
touching, no kissing, no lovemaking? Mason
might as well have divorced me. I can't tell you
how many days I've wished he had."

"Hush your mouth, girl."

"I mean it, Ms. Essie." Elaine wiped more
tears. "I would have felt lonely and abandoned
for a while, but so what? I feel that way anyway.
I would have wallowed in pity and soaked in
guilt for a while, but so what? I do that anyway.
I would have missed having him lying beside
me at night, but so what? I'm sleeping by myself
anyway. If he had left me, at least by now I might
have been able to get over him. Maybe I could

have been able to pick up the pieces and move on with my life."

Essie's hand was back on top of Elaine's. "I know it's hard, honey, but sometimes things aren't as black and white as they seem. You're not the only one in torment. Mason's hurting too."

"Hurting? Are you kidding me?"

"You don't think he's hurting from all this?" Essie searched Elaine's face. "There ain't no way for a marriage to go through the changes that yours has without both people being hurt."

"I know I hurt him, Ms. Essie, but—"

Essie held up her hand. "Time for you to stop talking and just listen again."

Elaine released a heavy sigh and sank deeper into her pillows.

"I ain't talking 'bout what happened back then. God forgave you for that a long time ago. He ain't punishing you, and Mason ain't trying to punish you either, sugar."

That was the same message that Angel tried to relay to her. Elaine found it hard to accept then, and she found it hard to accept now. "Then what is it about?"

"You and Mason need to talk, Elaine. Ain't nothing ever gonna be solved if y'all don't sit down and talk it out. Pray and talk. That's what y'all need to do. You 'round here killing yourself, running for miles, half-eating, making yourself vomit . . ."

Elaine's eyes widened. She didn't think anyone knew. Essie kept talking like she hadn't even noticed Elaine's reaction.

"You doin' all this 'cause y'all ain't talked. If you talk to Mason, you'll find out that he prefers you the other way. With some meat on your bones."

"I doubt it, Ms. Essie. He didn't touch me when I was that way either."

"But it ain't had nothing to do with your size." Essie stood from the bed and paced for a moment. "When he was looking at you funny the other day, when he said you needed to do something about your weight, he was trying to tell you that you were losing too much; not that you were fat."

Using her hands for stability, Elaine tried to pull herself up. "What?"

"You would know that if you talked to him."

Mason thought she was too thin? She never would have guessed. Had she known that, she would have handled things a whole lot different. Why wouldn't he just say that if that's what he thought? Why did she have to be the one to talk? Why couldn't it be Mason's responsibility to get the ball rolling? "What about him?" Elaine blurted. "Why can't he come talk to me? When did starting a conversation become my responsibility?"

"Child, women been the ones doing the most talking in marriages since the beginning of time. God made us to be better communicators. More expressive. More open. Men don't talk as much as us. They show everything through . . . well, they're more physical creatures."

Elaine let out a grunt and rolled her eyes. That sure didn't sound like Mason. He hadn't made a move to be physical with her in forever.

"And I can't believe you been sitting by for a year without confronting your husband 'bout this."

"I promised that I would give him time. That I'd be understanding and patient."

Essie propped her hands on her hips. "Did you promise him you'd be a fool too?"

Elaine leaned back against her pillows again. Nobody understood her plight.

"Sugar, you listen to me and you listen good," Essie said, approaching the bedside once more. "This ain't about pointing fingers, 'cause if the marriage falls apart, it ain't gonna matter whose fault it was. Besides, if the whole truth be told, ain't neither one of y'all doin' what you s'posed to be doing. Ain't y'all learned nothing from experience?"

Confusion etched its way onto Elaine's face. What kind of experience was Essie hinting at? Elaine had never been in this position before. There was no history to draw from.

"It might be a different situation, but it's being brought on by the same problem," Essie said, challenging Elaine's thoughts. "Both of y'all acting just like you did back yonder when you fooled around and messed wit' that other boy."

Elaine turned her face toward the window in protest. She didn't need to be reminded of her past sins.

"Think about it," Essie said, apparently disregarding Elaine's nonverbal attempt to shut out her words. For added effect, she walked around to the other side of the bed so that she was in Elaine's view once again. "Back then, Mason was dealing with issues and so were you. Remember?"

She did, but Elaine chose not to answer.

"Everybody knew 'bout your problems 'cept Mason, and everybody knew 'bout his problems 'cept you," Essie pointed out. " 'Fore you knew anything, Mason was trying to soothe his pain by buying expensive cars and hanging out with the wrong friends, and you was scratching your itches with some other man's fingernails."

Elaine frowned. She wasn't particularly fond of Essie's choice of analogy.

"All of that could've been avoided if the two of you had just *talked* to each other and told each other what you were dealing with. Do you see what I'm getting at, child?"

Elaine remained silent.

"A few minutes ago, you was telling me about the morning after. But something else happened the morning after too. God extended another chance to you and Mason. Your marriage was all but over, but God used my going away to put y'all back together." Essie glanced toward the ceiling, like she was getting her words directly from heaven. "When I was here, it had got to where you would lean on me. You'd talk to me. Tell me 'bout your hurts and pains." A smile stretched her lips. "I needed to go so you could lean on *him*. Mason. Your husband. And you did. He became your rock, and he comforted you on the days you was hurting real bad. I had to go so you could see how much that boy loves you. He proved it by sticking by you in spite of what had happened. For his own reasons, Mason was distant from you for a certain time during your marriage, and that was the excuse you used to run out and bring truth to that old seven-year-itch theory, but he was there for you when you needed someone the most."

Elaine released a soft sigh. "You're right." She had to give credit where credit was due. "Mason was very much there for me. From the time you took your last breath, he was right by my side. Talking to me. Praying for me. Sometimes crying with me. We even rededicated our lives back to God on the same Sunday."

"I know. See?" Essie exclaimed. "That's exactly what I'm talkin' 'bout."

"But Ms. Essie, that's no more than any good friend would do. I could have gotten Angel to do any of those things for me." Elaine noticed the sparkle in Essie's eyes at the sound of Angel's name, but she wanted to keep the subject on her and Mason. Besides, she wasn't finished making her point. "Mason and I weren't the only two to come to Christ that Sunday. Jennifer walked to the altar right along with us. Don't get me wrong. I thank God that Mason was there for me as a friend, but I already had friends. What I really *needed* him to be was my husband. He wasn't my husband on those days when I yearned to be held, caressed, kissed, made love to." Elaine wiped away a new tear. "He wasn't there for me as a husband then, and he hasn't been there as a husband at any time since."

Essie looked at her watch like she was pressed for time. "I wish I could just tell you everything you need to know 'bout Mason, sugar, but that ain't the way God wanted it to go. He sent me here to point you in the right direction. After that, it's all up to you."

If that was supposed to be some kind of hint, Elaine wasn't sure that she was getting it. She shook her head from side to side, needing more information, but wondering if Essie had enough time to supply it.

"The right direction is to talk to him," Essie urged. "Don't just sit by talkin' 'bout you promised to be patient. You *have* been patient, Elaine. Can't nobody accuse you of not keeping that promise. But now, it's time to talk. Just like there were deeper reasons why he was distant back then, there are reasons now. And if he ain't got the guts to come to you and talk about it, then you go to him."

Elaine stared at the blanket that covered her lap, wondering how she could bring up the subject of her need for intimacy to Mason without upsetting him. She didn't know how she could do it without him seeing it as a broken promise.

"*Pray*," Essie stressed. "Then talk."

Elaine lay in silence. Pondering.

"No excuses, baby." Essie bent forward and kissed Elaine's forehead. "Now, you get yourself some sleep so when you wake up, you can have a fresh mind."

Elaine looked up at Essie, blinking her eyes and wondering why she was all of a sudden becoming fatigued. "Thank you, Ms. Essie."

"If you really want to thank me, you'll do one thing for me."

Elaine yawned. "Talk to Mason?"

Essie chuckled. "That too. But I was talkin' 'bout something different." She tapped the blanket. "Jennifer put this over you when she came by to visit on her lunch break. I need you to give it to Angel the first chance you get."

Fingering the knitted yarn, Elaine said, "You're not gonna be here when I wake up, are you?"

"I'm always here, sugar," Essie reassured. "I'm always here."

Chapter 26

Jerrod's Story

He sat up on the side of the bed and stretched. Forty-five. He made a mental note of the number he'd set on the Sleep Number bed. It had been perfect. And the nap had been just what the doctor ordered. Jerrod hadn't realized how uncomfortable the makeshift bed had been that he'd slept on for the past three nights. It felt like nails in comparison.

Yawning, Jerrod looked at the clock on his cell phone and stretched his eyes in amazement. He must have been more tired than he realized. It was nearly three o'clock. Time never went this quickly when he was in classes. At school, every hour that passed felt like two. Except when it came to his after-school track practices. That was the only time of the day that didn't seem like a chore. Jerrod enjoyed making good grades, but he had to work hard for every one of them. Running, on the other hand, came easy. Like second nature. If practice was on his Tuesday schedule, he probably would have gone to school today in spite of everything.

Today had been an adventure all by itself. The first few hours of the day had handed Jerrod enough excitement to last a while. He'd called 911 like his coach instructed when they discovered Elaine on the side of the street. From the looks of things, she was just getting started on her morning run, but collapsed before she even reached the mouth of Braxton Park.

It took only minutes for the ambulance to arrive at the Braxton Park subdivision. Seeing the medics climb from the truck and begin working on Elaine brought back year-old memories for Jerrod. Unpleasant memories. Memories that he knew he'd never be able to permanently bury. His heart pounded in his chest as the men did their job. The medics who had been sent to revive Essie that night had failed. Thankfully, Elaine's EMTs had been much more successful. They had her stabilized before loading her into the emergency vehicle and rushing off, sirens blaring.

Jerrod had been given five minutes to run into the house to pack a suitcase. T.K. chose to remain in the car. Jerrod didn't blame him. He figured that T.K. didn't even feel comfortable coming in the house now that Jennifer had replaced him with another man. More like half a man. One fourth of a man would be more accurate, although it too was a bit generous. Thinking about Devon and the havoc he'd wreaked on the Mays household only infuriated Jerrod; so he forced the thoughts from his head by continuing to recount the happenings of the day.

Jerrod loved T.K.'s Corvette. Something about the hum of the engine was exhilarating. When T.K. navigated out of the subdivision, Jerrod thought that they were headed to his teacher's Stone Mountain home. Instead, they wound up at Northside Hospital, where they sat in the waiting room to hear updates on Elaine's condition. En route, T.K. used his cell to call Mason, and then Angel, to relay the news. His call to Mason made common sense. After all, he was Elaine's husband. But Jerrod figured that T.K. had called Angel because he knew if he told her, the word would also get to Jennifer. Jerrod drew that conclusion when T.K. made it a point to tell Angel that Jerrod was with him when he found Elaine. No doubt, all of the people in Jennifer's inner circle knew that Jerrod had run away. T.K. was leaving a trail of popcorn for Jennifer to pursue. If she wanted to see her son, she'd have to follow the path that would lead her to the man whose heart she'd broken. T.K. was forcing her to face him whether she wanted to or not. "Smoooooth, Coach," Jerrod sang softly, mentally tipping his hat to T.K. As far as he was concerned, his mother owed T.K. that much. "How she just gon' bring some other dude in the picture without even telling a brotha?" he mumbled. The reality of it was still hard to accept.

Had they hung around the hospital long enough, she probably would have gotten her chance. Jerrod was sure that Jennifer dropped everything when she got the news of her friend's illness. Elaine looked pretty bad when the medics first placed her in the ambulance, but when Mason came out and told them that the doctor had given Elaine a favorable prognosis, T.K. and Jerrod left so T.K. could salvage the rest of his workday.

After driving Jerrod to his house and walking the teen inside, T.K. told him to make himself at home, and then he headed to Alpharetta High. Jerrod enjoyed having the full run of the house. His first order of business was to raid the refrigerator since he hadn't had time to eat breakfast before T.K. picked him up. The fridge was stocked with goodies, and Jerrod grabbed several slices of turkey breast deli meat, which he folded and piled between a hamburger bun slathered with mayonnaise and mustard. He washed down the loaded sandwich and a bag of chips with two cans of fruit punch while he sat in front of the television and watched *The View*. It would definitely remain his secret that he'd gotten hooked on the women's talk show in just one day of watching it at Toby's.

By the time the show ended, Jerrod could barely keep his eyes open. He peeled off his shirt, tennis shoes, and blue jeans and tossed them on top of his suitcase before becoming one with the bed in the room where T.K. had told him he'd be staying.

Now, some hours later, Jerrod reluctantly kicked the covers from his legs, and then sat on the side of his mattress. Scoping out the room, he guessed that it was about fifty percent larger than his bedroom at home. T.K.'s four-bedroom home could just about swallow the two-bedroom domicile that Jerrod shared with his mother. This room was what every kid dreamed about. Plenty of space, its own connected bathroom, a wall-mounted television, and a study desk in the corner that included a flat-screen Gateway computer. He could get used to this, but with his mother's decision to marry Devon, Jerrod knew that this could be nothing more than a fantasy.

Putting back on the clothes he'd abandoned earlier, Jerrod walked out of the room and made his way to the kitchen. The least he could do was prepare dinner for T.K. That would help him feel that he was earning his keep.

Jerrod had seen some ground beef in the refrigerator during his earlier raid. The one meal that he knew how to cook well was spaghetti. Finding all of the needed ingredients, he washed his hands in the kitchen sink and began his task. Jennifer had taught him how to make homemade sauce, but a can of Prego in the cabinet allowed him to save some time. The teenager felt like a regular chef G. Garvin as he twisted the black peppercorn grinder over the skillet that held the heating sauce. He cooked up a pound of ground beef, drained the excess grease from the pan, then set it aside while he tossed fresh chopped onions, basil leaves, oregano, parsley flakes, and Italian seasoning in with the simmering sauce.

Jerrod pulled some garlic bread sticks from the refrigerator and placed them in the oven. While they baked, he added the cooked ground beef to the sauce mix; then stood back to view his masterpiece in the making. In no time, the kitchen smelled like a Sicilian restaurant.

"Hey, kid. What's this? You're cooking?"

The voice didn't startle Jerrod. He'd heard the garage door open and close and knew that T.K. would be entering the house soon. Jerrod turned to face him and grinned. "Hope you like Italian."

T.K. peeked into the oven and took a whiff. "If it tastes as good as it smells, I *love* it." Fifteen minutes later, they were sitting at the dining room table enjoying the meal. It was so tasty that Jerrod wanted to pat himself on the back after T.K. had taken his turn.

"This is really good." The coach's words were muffled behind the napkin that he used to wipe his mouth. "You've been holding out on me, Jerrod. You're about as skilled in the kitchen as you are on the track."

Jerrod wished it were true. "Not really. This is pretty much all I know how to make. This, hotdogs, and hamburgers. That's about it."

"Just enough to live off of, huh?" T.K. laughed.

"Uh-huh."

"I still appreciate it. I usually have to come home and cook after working all day. This makes today a whole lot easier."

Jerrod was glad that he had lightened T.K.'s load. "Just my way of saying thanks for letting me come and crash with you for a while."

T.K. was quiet while he drank a few swallows of his fruit punch. He wiped his mouth before speaking. "Your mom called me today."

Somehow Jerrod knew that he was going to say that. That small space of silence had felt a bit strained. He wasn't ready to go back home, and he hoped that T.K. wasn't going to force him to. Not yet. "What did she want?"

"I'm not sure, actually." T.K. leaned back in his chair and patted his stomach like he was full. "She called twice. The first time, she left a message. That was during one of my classes. She was at the hospital with Mason at that time. Said Elaine was still sleeping. Then she said she'd call me back once she knew I was finished with my classes for the day."

"So when she called back, you actually talked to her? She didn't leave another message?" While Jerrod wasn't ready to move his things back to Braxton Park, he was eager to hear what his mother had to say. He missed her. Even worried about her. But not enough to balance his disappointment.

"She called as soon as I got in my car and was pulling out of the school parking lot," T.K. revealed. "The first thing she did was ask about you. Then she thanked me for finding you and allowing you to bunk with me until everything could be sorted out."

Jerrod was surprised that Jennifer wasn't angry that he'd run away to begin with. "So she was okay with me being here?"

T.K. nodded. "She seemed to be. We didn't talk too much because she said that she didn't want to talk over the phone. She wants to come over and talk to you in person."

"Just her?" Jerrod wanted to be sure that he wasn't about to be surprised by another appearance by Devon.

"Just her," T.K. assured. "She said she owed an explanation for everything that had happened over the past few days. She wants to come by this evening after she gets off from work and has had the chance to go by the hospital again to check on Elaine."

Jerrod fidgeted. He wasn't sure he wanted to hear what his mother had to say. "So what did you say? Did you tell her she could come by?"

After draining the rest of his fruit punch, T.K. replied, "I told her that I needed to speak with you first. I wanted to be sure that you were ready and willing to have a face-to-face meeting with her. A meeting won't do any good if all parties involved aren't open-minded and prepared to be rational."

T.K. had lost Jerrod at: *I told her that I needed to speak to you first.* It meant everything to him

that his coach had considered him and his feelings. As the adult, he could have easily just given
Jennifer permission. T.K. could have handled it
like Jennifer and Devon did. Jerrod was in no
way prepared to meet his biological father, but
he hadn't been given a choice in the matter. This
time he had.

"So is it okay with you?" T.K. asked. "I told
your mom that I'd call her back and let her
know."

"What if I say no?"

T.K.'s shrug made it seem that the answer
was a no-brainer. "Then I'll call her and tell her
that you aren't ready yet, and we'll have to do it
another time."

"If she comes over and talks tonight, does that
mean I'll have to go back home tonight?"

Twirling the last of his spaghetti around his
fork, T.K. said, "Not unless you want to. I already
told her that you'd be staying here at least until
Sunday, and she didn't fight me on it. I mentioned the fact that you had a friend who wanted
to go to church with me on Sunday, but he would
only go if you were there; so you might as well
stay here until then."

That was all that Jerrod needed to know. He
could breathe much easier now. "Okay. Then she
can come over and talk. As long as it's just her,
and I won't have to go back home with her."

"Okay." T.K. nodded. "I'll give her a call a little later and make certain that she's clear on the terms." He got up from the table and placed his empty plate in the sink. "Sit here. I'll be back."

Jerrod watched as T.K. rounded the corner, disappearing from his view. While he waited for his teacher's return, Jerrod finished the last of his meal, then wiped his mouth with his napkin. T.K. walked back into the dining room just as Jerrod was polishing off the last of his punch. As he placed the empty can on the table, T.K. slid a small box on the table in front of him.

"Is this the ring?" Jerrod knew the answer before he asked the question.

"Yeah." T.K.'s whisper was wrapped in regret.

The red velvet box was so striking that Jerrod just knew the ring would be too. And he was right. Jerrod had to catch his breath when the solitaire captured the overhead light and sent a blinding sparkle into his eyes. It was somewhat simple, but stunning at the same time. Seeing the jewelry reminded Jerrod of what could have been. What should have been. What *would* have been had it not been for his mom. He faulted her the most. Devon might have been the big winner, but he wouldn't have if Jennifer hadn't let him in the game. Jerrod couldn't be mad at him without feeling anger toward his mother as well.

"Nice, huh?" T.K. said, breaking the silence.

Jerrod blinked back liquid distress. "Yeah." His unstable smile must have given away his inner anguish. The chair beside him pulled away from the table and T.K. sat in it.

"You know this won't change things between me and you, right? I mean, just because I'm not gonna be dating Jen anymore, doesn't mean that you and I can't still be tight. You know that, right?"

Jerrod nodded his answer. Speaking was out of the question right now. He needed to channel all of his energies to winning the fight against his tears.

"Come on, Jerrod." T.K. nudged him with his knee. "Don't do this. I mean, I'm glad that you wanted this to happen for me and Jen, but it's hard enough to deal with my own disappointment. I don't need to walk around with the added guilt of feeling like I let you down."

After a deep inhale, Jerrod said, "What you got to feel guilty about? You ain't the one who let me down. This ain't your fault. You loved Ma. You bought the ring. She's the one who messed it up." Jerrod slumped in his chair and stared at the ceiling. "I can't believe she did this."

T.K. pulled the ring from the jewelry box and held it in his hand. "Me either, kid. But you know what? I've spent enough hours asking myself where I went wrong and asking God why He allowed it to happen. I thought I'd found the one this time, but I was wrong. Jen has made her choice, and somehow I have to respect it. And you know what? So do you."

Jerrod sat up straight and stared at T.K. "How? How am I supposed to respect that? How am I supposed to respect him? That man ain't never did nothing for me, Coach. How he just gonna come pop out of the blue and expect me to call him Daddy?" Jerrod's chin quivered and he lost the battle with his tears. "Everything was going so good. The morning after Ms. Essie died, it felt like the world was coming to an end. Then somehow, with your help, I was able to get it together. I don't know what I would've done if you hadn't been there for me."

"And I'll always be here, Jerrod. That's what I need you to know and believe. I will always be here for you. No matter what."

Jerrod used his shirt tail as a handkerchief. "It ain't the same. What if he don't let me spend no time with you? What if he won't let me go to church with you? What if he moves us away somewhere to some other city or some other state, and I don't never get the chance to see you no more?"

T.K. stiffened like that last scenario hadn't entered his mind until now.

"I don't think I can do it, Coach D," Jerrod mumbled. "I ain't gonna be able to take living with him if you can't be a part of my life too." His tears had limited his sight, but Jerrod could feel T.K.'s strong hands as they planted firmly on his shoulders.

"Then we're gonna pray," T.K. said. "We're going to pray together that God will work everything out. He has to work it out, kid. Because to tell the truth, I won't be able to live with that either."

Chapter 27

Mason's Story

Four hours ago, he'd pulled the chair close to the bed so that he could hold his sleeping wife's hand while she battled for consciousness. In those four hours, he hadn't left the chair once. Mason had lost count of the number of people that had stopped in since Elaine's early morning admittance. If visitation was an indication of alliance, Elaine sure had her share of friends.

Those that couldn't come because of obligations or distance had kept the local florists busy. The windowsill of Elaine's private room looked like an extension of the Atlanta Botanical Garden. Roses, sunflowers, carnations, dandelions, violets, irises, green ferns . . . they were all accounted for. Mason's cell phone had been ringing frequently too. Even his mother—a woman who'd never said two nice words about Elaine in all the years they'd been married—sounded genuine when Mason called to update her on Elaine's status. More glowing words had never been heard than the ones Georgia Mae Demps had said about her daughter-in-law today. She'd used unfamiliar phrases like "perfect wife for you" and "couldn't have happened to a nicer person." One time, she even said, "If I need to pack a suitcase and come to Atlanta, just let me know. There are always flights out of Dallas to Atlanta, and I don't mind coming and helping out while Elaine is recuperating; bless her sweet heart."

Bless her sweet heart? That time, Mason had to pull the cell phone from his ear just to double-check to see if he'd dialed the right number. If Elaine had died on the side of the road on Braxton Way, Mason imagined that there wasn't a living, breathing soul anywhere who would have outshone his mother at the funeral. Either Georgia Mae was putting on a Tony Award winning performance with her kind words, or God was in the process of working a turn-water-into-wine kind of miracle on her. Mason prayed it was the latter.

The hospital room was quiet now; a welcomed sound. But the revolving door of earlier visitors replayed in Mason's head. T.K., Jerrod; there were even visits from some of the local staff writers from a couple of the magazines to

which Elaine contributed articles and short stories. Then there was Reverend Owens, flanked
by a few of the members of Temple of God's
Word, who sat with Mason for a while. Reverend
Owens lingered around even after the church
members had dispersed. He'd helped himself to
most of the grapes in one of the fruit baskets that
had been delivered, then dozed off in one of the
empty chairs.

Mason was surprised when Reverend and
Mrs. Tides walked in the door. They had been
the last visitors to stop in. Mason had called
Reverend Tides to let him know that he wouldn't
make their counseling session tonight due to
Elaine's illness, but he never expected the prom-
inent pastor to make a personal appearance. And
when the Tideses walked in, they did so with a
purpose. Mrs. Tides carried a small, burgundy,
leather bound Bible in her hand, and Reverend
Tides had a personal size bottle of anointed oil
wrapped in his closed fist. Before engaging in
any long, casual conversations, they each stood
on either side of Elaine's bed and held her hands
in theirs. In lowered voices, they sang a worship
song; then Mrs. Tides read a passage of scripture
before Reverend Tides dabbed the top of Elaine's
hair with oil and placed a gentle hand on her
bandaged forehead. The prayer that followed

was spoken in a soft tone, but the Holy Spirit's presence in the room was so powerful that Mason felt the hairs on his arms come to attention.

But as moving as the moment was, it was equally as awkward. Reverend Owens was still there at the time, and he'd greeted Reverend and Mrs. Tides with what appeared to be genuine warmth. However, Reverend Owens was obviously thwarted that Mason had apparently called on another pastor—one whose church he wasn't a member of—to come and pray for his wife's healing. Mason felt the need to defend himself. To tell Reverend Owens that he hadn't asked Reverend Tides to come, let alone pray. The leader of New Hope had made those decisions on his own. Besides, Reverend Owens had been there a good hour before the Tideses arrived. If he'd wanted to pray, he certainly had plenty of opportunity to do so. Mason couldn't help but feel a bit bad at the thought that Reverend Owens felt slighted, but he wasn't about to turn down any prayers in order to nurse his pastor's unwarranted bruised ego.

There had been other visitors too. Angel had stopped in early that morning. Colin came by on his lunch break and was thoughtful enough to bring lunch for Mason too. Until he caught the aroma of the Zaxby's meal, Mason hadn't realized how hungry he was. They ate lunch together in the room where Elaine lay sleeping. They talked a little and even shared a few much-needed laughs, but it didn't take a rocket scientist to decipher that something was weighing on Colin's mind. When Angel came by, she'd seemed preoccupied at times too. Mason got the feeling that something unsettling was going on between Colin and Angel. What had disturbed the nest of the quintessential lovebirds, he didn't know. Mason was too concerned with Elaine's well-being to pry, but he was sure that his assumption wasn't wrong.

For the last four hours, it had been just the two of them: Mason and Elaine. Occasionally, they were interrupted by a pretty, blond-haired, overweight nurse named Felicity, whose smile never faded as she answered all of Mason's calls to the nurse's station. The meds in those bags hanging behind Elaine's bed were apparently quite potent. Never before had Mason seen anyone have such a restless sleep. Elaine's tossing and turning started shortly after Reverend Tides left the room. Often times, the excess movement was accompanied by mumbling; like she had a whole conversation going on inside of her wounded head. Her episodes were frightening at times; so much so that Mason had made frequent use of the call button.

"I know you're concerned, Mr. Demps," Felicity said when she'd been called in for the fourth time, "and that's totally understandable. But I assure you that there's nothing abnormal about your wife's behavior. In fact, this is a good sign." While she spoke, the nurse took Elaine's vitals and checked the contents of the bags of fluid being fed into the patient. "Mrs. Demps was severely dehydrated and malnourished when she was brought in, and her concussion was pretty severe. The doctor predicted that it would probably be a good twenty-four hours before the fluids and meds took full effect, and maybe a bit longer before she would become fully alert." The nurse charted something on her clipboard, then looked at Mason, who sat only a few feet from where she stood. Felicity smiled like a toothpaste model. "At the rate she's going right now, I wouldn't be surprised if she wakes up before nightfall."

She turned and began walking toward the door, adding, "Look at it this way, Mr. Demps. As long as she's moving around and making noises it means she's alive. I know Dr. Zbornak already told you how close she came to death. Bulimia, in and of itself, is a serious thing. Coupling it with the rigorous exercise you've told us that your wife was doing on a regular basis is a recipe for disaster." Felicity turned back to face Mason just before leaving him alone with his wife. "She's a miracle, Mr. Demps. Maybe she's talking to God. After all, she sure does have a reason to be thanking Him."

The nurse's parting words gave Mason renewed faith. Not that he feared his wife would die. Dr. Zbornak had assured him that she'd be fine, but all of the unsettling behavior he'd watched her display made Mason wonder if she'd be the same Elaine he knew and loved when she awakened. He worried that maybe the impact that her head made with the pavement—the impact that left a sizeable contusion on her forehead—had done more damage than the doctor had been able to detect during his examination. Elaine looked so frail lying there. Mason shook his head, still not understanding his wife's maddening need to lose so much weight. He never would have guessed that she was bulimic, and if the tests the doctors had run hadn't proved it, Mason would have disputed them without a second thought.

Bulimia. "I must be the worst husband in the world," he whispered to himself, lowering his head in regret. "I stood by and watched you half-kill yourself and didn't say a word. I might not have known you were bulimic, but I knew something was up and didn't confront you about it. I don't care how headstrong you can be, it was my duty to say something." Mason brought the back of Elaine's hand to his mouth and grazed it with his lips, careful not to disturb the needle that was inserted there; held securely by a strip of surgical tape. "I should have put my foot down and been a man about it."

A man. Mason felt like anything but. He knew why he hadn't been more adamant about intercepting Elaine's so-called health kick. Mason hadn't felt worthy to make any kinds of demands regarding what his wife should or should not do with her body. A body he hadn't touched in months. A body he knew she wanted him to touch. A body he knew she *needed* him to touch.

But Mason knew he couldn't deliver. And if he couldn't meet his wife's basic needs, he had no grounds to take his place as head of household. That was the way he thought then—and God help him—it was the way he thought now. Even with the counseling, the renewed faith, and the increased dedication to God, Mason knew he'd always feel inadequate as long as he was unable to fulfill all of his duties as a husband.

Mason looked toward the partially closed blinds. He had been at the hospital for almost eight hours. The day was winding down now, and it wouldn't be long before the sun would disappear completely. If Felicity was right, his quiet time with Elaine would end soon. If he were going to say anything to his wife; talk to her like Reverend Tides had told him to do during their first session, he needed to do it now.

"I'm so sorry, babe," Mason whispered, standing from his chair. He continued to hold her right hand in his left, but used his right hand to brush his fingers across her cheek. Her skin felt warm. And soft. It had been a long time since he'd touched her face. A heavy sigh preceded his next words. "I should have talked to you a long time ago and explained myself. You deserved to know what was going on inside of me."

Elaine was moving and mumbling again, and Mason hushed to see if he could make out any of what she was trying to say. Just like the times before, nothing was coherent. If she were indeed fighting to awaken from her injury-induced sleep, Mason figured that he'd better start talking faster. He'd feel much better saying what he had to say if he were certain that she couldn't really hear him. It was the way of a coward, but it was the only way he could bring himself to do it. He sank back down in his seat.

"I just want you to know that this sleeping on the sofa thing . . . it stopped being about you a long time ago." Mason used his free hand to wipe beads of perspiration from his hairline. Even without her ability to comprehend what he was saying, the words were painful to form. "I know you think I'm doing it because I'm still upset about what you did, and to tell the truth, I do still have days when that whole thing still messes with my head. But that ain't the main reason why I've been sleeping apart from you."

Mason released Elaine's hand and stood up again. He paced the floor behind the chair; his heart racing like a thoroughbred. He hated to think of how difficult of an admission this would be if Elaine had been awake; eyes wide open with her ears hanging on to his every word. Mason turned his face to the wall, closed his eyes, and tried to pray for help. This was a lot harder than he imagined it would be. He took another breath, rubbed his sweaty palms against his pants legs, and then spoke again.

"Something's happened to me, Elaine." Mason couldn't even bring himself to look at his wife as he continued. Even knowing she couldn't hear him didn't erase the utter embarrassment. "I'm not sure when it happened or why, but I've . . . I've"—he swallowed the bitterness of the words—"I've lost the ability to . . . you know . . . *function* like a real man." Mason shoved his hands in his pockets and stared at the hospital floor. The waxed and buffed tiling looked so shiny that he was afraid it would reflect his image. An image he didn't want to see. Mason brought his eyes back to the cream-colored wall.

"That's how I met Reverend Tides," he admitted. "Remember when I told you I'd run into him, and he invited me to his church? Well, the real way that I came about seeing him was because I went to him for counseling, trying to find some answers; trying to find out why I can no longer . . . *perform*." It wasn't easy to come up with words that didn't sound as terrible and as permanent as the proper scientific terminology. Saying the words *I've got ED* or *I'm impotent* just wasn't an option for Mason. He inhaled and said, "Reverend Tides prayed with me, and he believes that although I've said that I forgive you, I really haven't. Not the way God commands that we forgive. There are parts of this whole thing that I haven't been able to let go for some reason, and the poison from harboring it is killing me. Parts of me anyway."

Mason removed his hands from his pockets, brought them together and blew into them as though they were frigid and needed to thaw. Cold . . . hot . . . cold . . . hot; he had lost the sensation of both. All Mason truly felt was disgrace.

"I want to forgive you, Elaine. I really do," he continued. "If we're gonna make this marriage work, I know I'm gonna have to. We've been together for a long time now. I know how healthy your . . . *appetite* is, and I know you won't be able to stay in a celibate marriage for much longer. It's only by the grace of God that you've lasted this long. I can't tell you how much I thank Him *and* you for hanging in there. But I ain't stupid. I know that if I don't man up, you're gonna leave me soon." Mason was blindsided by the fluid that rose in his eyes. He wiped away the uninvited moisture with his hands. "I don't want to lose you, babe. Despite everything we've been through, I love you. And I want this marriage to work."

The shame of a new admission arose, and Mason released another heavy sigh. "All this while, I've known that you believed that I was still sleeping on the couch because of what happened last year, and I knowingly allowed you to keep thinking that. As long as you thought I was still punishing you, you'd see it as something you deserved, and you wouldn't question me or pressure me to do anything different. Because you promised you would give me all the time I needed. And I knew you'd keep that promise." Mason closed his eyes and a tear trickled out of the left one. "I figured that I'd just let you keep thinking that until I got my manhood back. I thought this invisible OUT OF ORDER sign that was hanging on me was just a temporary setback. I didn't think it would last a whole month, let alone a whole year. And if I could make you think I was still upset about what you did, then you'd never know that I lost *it* to begin with. You know?" Mason's shoulders slumped.

"It was a selfish, terrible, despicable thing to do, babe, and I ain't got no excuse for it. All I can say is I'm sorry. I knew you were being tortured by my alienation, but I let you go on believing that it was all your fault because I didn't want to face you. I just couldn't bring myself to tell you that I wasn't able to satisfy you anymore." Mason wiped his face again and sniffed before continuing. "Reverend Tides ministered to me and told me how wrong I was. Told me that God wasn't pleased, and I'd never find deliverance in the middle of living a lie. He told me I had to be honest with you. Then he said that once I've done that, I have to start putting my faith and my words into action. In other words, I have to swallow my pride and move back into the bedroom with you."

Mason shook his head. "This is hard enough. Talking to you even though you can't hear me is hard enough. Lying next to you, looking at your beautiful form, inhaling your natural fragrance . . . Lord knows I don't know how I'm gonna be able to do that knowing that there's nothing I can do with anything I see or smell or . . . touch. And if you look back at me and need some loving, I won't even be able to give it to you."

Mason shuddered at the thought, then used the hem of his oversized Sean John shirt to dry his face. "I told Reverend Tides that you probably won't even want me in bed with you. How many healthy, vibrant, sexy women want to have a cold, limp, dead fish lying next to them? None. That's how many. None."

Kicking the base of the wall, Mason then spun on the balls of his tennis shoes and walked briskly to the other side of the room. He lifted the blinds and stared out the window for a brief moment; not looking for or at anything in particular. Then he buried his nose in an African violet plant that one of Elaine's writing associates had brought when she visited earlier. Mason inhaled as deeply as he could, hoping that the fragrance would clear his head of some of the agony that rested there.

At the sound of the room door pushing open, he turned; glad that he'd taken the time to dry his tears beforehand. "Hey, Angel." Mason hoped he didn't sound flustered. "What are you doing here?"

"What do you mean? I told you I was coming back this evening, remember?" she said.

Mason blinked. "Oh. Yeah. That's right, you did." He couldn't believe he had forgotten.

Angel's eyes studied him for a moment, then they shifted to the bed and her entire demeanor brightened. "Elaine! Hey, sweetie; how are you?"

Mason's eye widened as they darted toward the bed. He barely felt it when Angel slapped him on the arm in reproof.

"Mason, I can't believe you didn't call me and tell me she was awake." Angel made a beeline for the bed.

"I . . . uh . . . I . . . uh . . . I . . ." Mason's breath came quick as he watched Angel bend down and gather Elaine in her arms as best she could. She held her and told her how much she'd been praying and how glad she was to see her awake. The whole while, Elaine's eyes were locked on Mason, and all he could think was, *How long has she been awake? How much did she hear?*

Chapter 28

Colin's Story

Last night, for the first time in his four-year marriage, conflict had forced him to sleep separately from his wife. Not only had Colin not slept in the same bed with Angel, he hadn't even slept in the same house with her. And not only had he not slept in the same house with her; he hadn't slept at all. Most of the night—or what was left of it—had been spent pacing the floor, calling Angel's cell phone, and praying that this disastrous ordeal wouldn't destroy their union. When Colin wasn't pacing, phoning, or praying, he was lying in bed staring up at the ceiling, asking himself what on earth had he done. The blaring of his alarm clock at 6:00 A.M. was more than unnecessary. He wasn't even close to being asleep, but his body ached with fatigue. A just punishment for walking in the house only three hours earlier.

Colin immediately retreated to his office upon arrival to Wachovia Bank, and the first thing he did was send Nona an e-mail with strict instructions that he was not to be disturbed for any reason. Nona's e-mail reply to him went unanswered.

> Okay, Mr. Stephens; I'll be sure to take messages and let callers know that it may be tomorrow before you can get back to them.
>
> Is everything all right? I hope this doesn't have anything to do with last night. Once again, I do apologize for not waking you. I'm crossing my fingers that you didn't get into any trouble with Mrs. Stephens. Whenever you're ready to talk, your big sister is here.

It angered Colin that Nona didn't know any better than to use their corporate system to send an e-mail with such a strong personal undertone. If it were ever read by anyone, it could easily be misconstrued. Put off by her carelessness alone, Colin deleted the message without the courtesy of a reply. Maybe he was treating her unjustly. Maybe Nona deserved an answer. But deserving or not, she wasn't going to get it. Not today anyway. Colin couldn't think of anything that he wanted to do less than talk to his *big sister* about the issue that may have permanently torn apart his family. Talking to her was what had gotten him in trouble to begin with. He wasn't exactly blaming her, but Nona was the last person Colin wanted to see or speak to.

He'd only left his office twice today: to visit Elaine in the hospital during his lunch hour, and then at five when he shut down his computer for the day. Both times, he managed to avoid direct contact with his assistant.

Worry had kept Colin alert enough to get through his shift, but worry had also left much undone. At half past four, when he packed his briefcase and turned off his office lights, there were still phone calls that needed to be made, e-mails that needed to be answered, and paperwork that needed to be completed. But none of that was more important than finding and talking to Angel. Colin shook his head every time he thought about his idiocy.

When he walked in the house in the wee hours of the morning and found his wife waiting up for him, Colin didn't know what to think. He didn't know what to say. Angel was seething, and she had every right. Even the late, great Johnnie Cochran couldn't have created a defense for Colin that his wife would have bought. A man walking in the house at three in the morning only meant one thing as far as Angel was concerned. She'd used words to describe him that he'd never heard her say before. She called him unfaithful, an adulterer, a liar; even a lowdown, cheating dog. Every verbal assault was excruciating. A lashing with a bullwhip couldn't have been more painful.

As wrong as Colin knew he had been for spending the unnecessary time with Nona, he was honest when he told Angel that having an illicit affair with his assistant had never even been a consideration. When she shoved his stained shirt in his face, Colin's mind was racing so fast that he couldn't even come up with a viable defense for the lipstick on his collar or the exotic perfume smell in the fabric. And his reason for walking in the house at such a dastardly hour—though true— sounded ridiculous even to his own ears. *I just fell asleep by mistake* was about the most ridiculous thing he'd ever heard, so he sure couldn't expect Angel to accept it.

Colin made a valiant effort to explain his side of the story, but Angel wasn't even coming close to hearing it. He wasn't given a fair trial. His wife wasn't only the prosecuting attorney; she also served as both judge and jury. Every objection he tried to implement was overruled; every defense he voiced was met with contempt. She had already deliberated his case and handed down his guilty verdict before he even walked in the door. Her suitcase was already packed, and though Colin didn't notice it when he first arrived, their son had already been brought out of his bedroom and was sleeping on the sofa beside where Angel stood. Her uncharacteristic yelling awakened Austin, putting him in the middle of a war zone that he was far too young to have been exposed to. And when Angel stormed out the door with the suitcase in one hand, she had their wailing son perched on the opposing hip. That was the last he'd seen of either of them. The punishment felt like a life sentence.

Now, as he exited the interstate and merged onto the access road that would lead him to home, Colin sought heaven for an appeal. He needed a retrial and he needed it fast. Every hour that passed without Angel knowing the full truth was an hour that wasn't working in his favor. He had to find her; get her to listen to him. Colin had to redeem himself. If she'd just give him ten minutes—even five would do—Colin knew he could say the words that would put his marriage back on the right track.

He looked toward Essie's home upon turning into Braxton Way and felt the urge to stop. Colin parked his car on the side of the road in front of the house. He got out of the car and walked the length of Essie's property; strolling down one side of the yard and back up the other side. This was the most time he'd spend on the land since the morning after Essie died; when he came with neighbors and friends to hold a candlelight memorial in honor of her life.

"Hey. I thought that was your truck that I saw through my bay windows."

Colin was standing near the edge of Essie's lawn, staring blankly at the strip of empty land across the street when he heard Jennifer's call. He turned to see her standing on her porch wearing a white Baby Phat T-shirt, green knee-length shorts, her hair pulled in a ponytail with bangs covering her forehead, and no shoes. She looked like little more than a teenager.

"Iota Phi Lambda in the house," she said with a laugh. Then she put the tips of her index fingers together to form an upside down "V" and struck a camera-ready pose.

It was the first time he had ever heard her mention being in a sorority. Thus the green and white ensemble, Colin assumed.

He grinned in approval. She looked nice, but probably not as nice as his companionship-starved eyes made her look. "I see," he replied. He cleared his throat and reeled in his thoughts.

"I didn't scare you by parking so close to your house, did I?"

"No, you didn't scare me. I knew it was your vehicle. I was just wondering whether it was you or Angel that was driving it."

"Well, it's me." Colin shifted his feet, wondering if Jennifer knew what had happened between him and his wife.

"Are you coming to pick up Austin-Boston? Angel left him with me as soon as I got home from work today. She was over there at the house when I arrived, and she said she'd be back soon. She knows I have an appointment this evening. When I saw you, I figured her visit with Elaine at the hospital was running later than expected, and she asked you to stop by and pick up the baby."

Colin relaxed. Not only because Jennifer obviously didn't know about his marital discord, but because God had already answered a portion of his prayers by giving him the opportunity to see his son. He should have known that the hospital was where Angel would be. She and Elaine had gotten quite close over the past year. "Yeah, I'm here to pick him up." It wasn't a lie. That may not have been what he'd originally come for, but it was what he was there for now. "Is he asleep?"

"I fed him a little while ago," Jennifer said as she nodded her head. "He ate real well, so I knew it wouldn't take long before he was out like a light. I'll go wake him up and get him ready."

Colin looked toward Essie's house and suddenly had an uncanny urge to go inside. "Hey, Jennifer?" She turned to face him. "Do you have a key to the house? I haven't been inside in a while. While you get Austin ready, I'd like to take a look around."

"Yeah, I have one," she answered. "It's really Jerrod's." Colin noticed the way her eyes saddened when she said her son's name, but she stuck out a brave chin when she added, "Let me run and get it. I'll be right back."

It only took her a minute to return. At first, Colin wasn't going to say anything about Jerrod, but when he reached to receive the key from Jennifer's hand, he couldn't resist. "How's Jerrod doing? T.K. told me that he found him. Is he back home yet?"

Jennifer didn't seem to mind his prying. "Not yet. I haven't had the chance to speak to him, but T.K. says he's doing okay. He'll be staying in Stone Mountain until Sunday evening."

"He couldn't be in better hands." Colin's words were genuine, and Jennifer nodded like she agreed wholeheartedly.

"I know. I'm not worried about him. Not as long as he's with T.K."

Colin hesitated. He knew that with his next words, he was taking a risk. But he said them anyway. "Listen, Jennifer. Don't take this the wrong way, okay? I know you're a grown woman who is fully capable of making her own decisions, but I really wish you'd rethink this whole thing with T.K." When her face didn't cringe into an angry scowl, Colin figured it was safe to continue. "I can't even begin to tell you how hurt he was, and still is, about the way you ended things. T.K. is an exceptional man, and he really cares about you. I don't know how you feel about this other dude, but I know how you feel about T.K. Donaldson. I've seen the two of you together, and I know what's in your heart for him. Feel free to correct me if I'm wrong, but I don't believe for a minute that this other guy is any match for T.K." Colin sighed. "Okay, maybe I'm being biased. I mean, T.K. is my friend, and I've never even met Jerrod's father, but like I said . . . correct me if I'm wrong." Colin watched a wet trail quietly make its way down each of Jennifer's cheeks before she whisked them away. "I'm sorry," he said. "I didn't mean to—"

"Don't apologize, Colin." Jennifer wiped her face again.

"You're right. I don't know what I was thinking or how I could have treated T.K. so badly. I
messed up real bad, and I wish I could take it all
back, but I can't."

Colin knew that feeling all too well. He propped
his right foot on the bottom step that led to her
porch. "You may not be able to take it back, but
you can at least try to reach out to him."

"I did."

"And what? He won't talk to you?" Colin knew
that feeling all too well too.

Jennifer shook her head in protest. "No, that's
not it. That's my appointment. I have to drive
over to Stone Mountain in a couple of hours to
talk to them."

"Well, that's a good thing, right?"

"I don't know." Jennifer shrugged her shoulders, then folded her arms in front of her. "T.K.
thinks that I'm only coming to apologize to Jerrod about the sloppy way I sprung everything on
him about his dad and me."

"And you're not?" Colin's interest was piqued.

"Yes. But that's not all I want to talk to him
about." A light breeze brushed past them. Jennifer combed her fingers through her bangs to
correct what had been ruffled; then refolded her
arms. "I want to tell them both how stupid I was
and what a big fool I made of myself. I want to

tell them that I want things back the way they were. With *both* of them."

Colin's eyebrows rose. "You want to get back with T.K.? You mean it's over between you and this other cat . . . for good?"

A frown furrowed Jennifer's brow, and her eyes dropped to her bare feet. "I ended everything with him today. There wasn't really anything to end," she continued. "Nothing genuine, at least. He never loved me, and I never loved him either. When I took an honest look at my heart, I knew it never belonged to him. I was just taken in by what he was offering, not even questioning why he was offering it."

"What was he offering?" Colin couldn't imagine that Jerrod's father could offer Jennifer anything that T.K. couldn't match and supersede.

"A family." Jennifer's arms dropped by her side. "I want a *real* family so bad that I was willing to risk everything. But when it came down to it, Devon didn't want a family, he was only interested in the benefits that making us a family would bring. He had dollar signs in his eyes."

Colin was confused. "You got money?" His blurted words didn't quite sound right, and he was just about to offer clarity when Jennifer burst into laughter.

"No. I didn't mean it like that. What I meant is that Devon saw fame and fortune in Jerrod's future. He was just making an early investment because he knew that if he showed up at my doorstep later on, after all these years, I would have seen right through the façade. If he staked his claim now, then he'd already be in the picture to reap the inevitable benefits."

"You mean the benefits of Jerrod's track skills?" It all made sense to Colin now.

"Yeah. He knows that colleges are already waiting on Jerrod, and the news features on television and in the newspaper told him that Jerrod's competing for the Olympics was just a matter of time. He's been living in Atlanta for years, but never even made his presence known until he found out what his son had the potential to become. Devon was really using us." She shook her head. "He's always been a user; just in it to get what he wants, and then he moves on. I guess it was wishful thinking that made me believe he'd changed from the person he was when we were teenagers."

Colin could hear the regret in her voice. "How'd you find out?"

Jennifer paused and looked toward Essie's house before responding. "God revealed it to me. It's a long story, but I'm just glad that He opened my eyes before it was too late. Even if T.K. doesn't take me back—which I wouldn't blame him if he didn't—I'm glad I found out the truth before I made the biggest mistake of my life."

Colin nodded silently. He could write the book on biggest mistakes. He looked skyward at the faint sound of a thunder roll. "Let me go ahead and do this real quick. I want to get Austin-Boston out of your hair so you can get to your meeting tonight without getting caught in the rain. Just give me about ten minutes."

"Okay. I'll have him ready." She assumed a bent knee position on the porch so that she was closer to Colin's level and whispered, "Alarm code is 1130." She returned to her full height and smiled. "Mr. Ben's birthday was November thirtieth."

Colin waited until Jennifer was inside her house before he headed next door. Once inside Essie's home, he deactivated the alarm system and placed the door key on top of the floor model television set. He shoved his hands in the pockets of his slacks and looked around the spacious area. The shelves once cluttered with whatnots and photographs were empty, but the living room was still in place. Sealed and labeled boxes lined the floor in an orderly fashion, waiting to be transported to storage.

The house was quiet, but Colin could almost feel Essie's presence. He walked to the far corner of the living room and touched the pinewood casing of the grandfather clock that had come to define the elderly woman who'd once lived there. Essie always talked about God's perfect timing; often citing Ecclesiastes, third chapter as a biblical reference to support her belief. She said that God never made mistakes and that He knew everybody's predicaments before they ever got into them. Essie declared that there wasn't any problem too hard for God to solve; people just needed to have the patience to wait on Him to move in His own time. Now, more than ever, Colin hoped that she was right.

The kitchen looked almost untouched. Colin stood in the middle of it and viewed the big wooden spoon and fork that still hung over the stove, the stocked spice rack that was posted on the wall above the electric can opener, and the blue oven mitt and matching pot holder that lay on top of the microwave oven. The sink had two dishes inside: a cereal bowl and a spoon. Odd since no one had lived there in over a year.

Colin made his way back to the living room, having no idea why he'd come into the house or what he was looking for. He took slow steps toward the bedroom, feeling as if he were about to invade Essie's privacy as he gave the door a cautious nudge. The hinges made a long, faint, creaking sound, and it almost seemed like the door opened all on its own. Colin's push had been gentle, but the door opened fully; coming to a halt only when it hit the doorstop.

Colin didn't walk into the space right away. From the doorway, he noted the country theme of the room. The same straw hat that hung on the wall above the headboard when Essie was alive was still in place. The large wooden rocking chair still sat in the corner near the head of the bed. Essie's sewing machine remained to the immediate right, nestled between the door that led to the master bathroom, and the one that led to the closet. Colin took a few steps inside. The bed had been disturbed. The patchwork quilt had been pulled away from the rest of the covers. That's when it dawned on him. This had to be where Angel had fled. She and Austin had slept here.

Approaching the bed, Colin reached out and touched the pillow where he knew Angel's head had lain. He'd bet anything that if he sniffed the fabric he'd be able to smell her hair products. Colin brought the pillowcase to his nostrils and inhaled. There it was. Just like he knew it would be.

Placing the pillow back where he found it, he took a seat on the mattress and buried his face in his hands. He was burdened with a mountain of regrets that he wished he could undo. "Lord, please forgive me for any wrongdoings; whether they were sins of commission or sins of omission. Forgive me for any ungodly thoughts that may have crept into my head and for any level of disrespect that I may have displayed toward my wife and son; intentional or not. Please soften Angel's heart to forgive me, and help me to be patient with her. Whatever she's going through that had caused her recent distance, you knew about it even before she began facing it. I ask that you do a work in both of us so that we can come together and talk rationally as man and wife. Help us to put you first and allow you to work out these unfamiliar issues that we're facing. Put us on the right track so that we will please you in all that we do."

Colin paused. He hadn't planned on praying, but the words were pouring out like water from a fountain—the kind of fountain wherein children pitched pennies and made wishes that couldn't possibly come true without the help of a miracle. "And Lord, please help me not blame Nona." All day long, Colin had been having peculiar feelings about his assistant, and he didn't know why. He didn't want it to be brewing hatred prompted by his desire to point the accusing finger at her. It wasn't her fault. Not completely anyway. "I'm sorry for not listening to your voice when you were clearly instructing me to place distance there; telling me that the relationship was leading to trouble. Lord, I take full responsibility for the consequences of my disobedience, but I ask that you have mercy, and grant me pardon for my hardheadedness. Let my insubordination not destroy my marriage and my family. Bring harmony to my home, and allow your peace that surpasses all understanding to rest and rule."

The prayer was emotionally draining. Colin took a breath and concluded with, "It is in Jesus' name that I ask all these things. And by faith, I thank you in advance for what you're going to do . . . in your own time. Amen."

When Colin opened his eyes, his sight locked onto a shoebox sized container that was sitting on the floor beside the bed, in front of the nightstand. It was a colorful box, and he didn't know how he'd not seen it earlier. When he attempted to pick it up by the handle on the lid, the top lifted off instead. Colin's first instinct was to replace the cover. Whatever was inside wasn't any of his business. But the collection of photos and papers inside provided to be too tempting for him to ignore. He picked up the box and placed it on his lap. As he began thumbing through the contents, the first thing he noticed was the folded letter that Essie told Angel she read every night before going to bed. It was the last letter that her husband, Ben, had written her before he was killed in World War II. They'd found the letter clasped in Essie's hand on the night that she died.

"That was some kind of love," Colin whispered as he bypassed the letter and looked further. .

The box was a treasure chest of mementos: more letters from Ben, outdated postage stamps, a silver cross necklace, the deed to Essie's house, a man's gold band that Colin assumed was Ben's wedding ring, and several photos. A worn black and white photo of three girls grabbed his attention. The threesome appeared to be in their early teens and wore long dresses and hairdos that made them look like a wannabe version of The Supremes.

The words: *Essie Mae, Lillie Pearl, and Annie Belle. Mama made our dresses and we thought we were too cute even for the camera,* were written on the back. Colin laughed out loud. They all had the same smile, and even before flipping the photo over and reading the neat cursive scripting, he had guessed that they were Essie and her two older sisters. Even though the years had erased some of the details of the picture, it was easy to see that Essie had been the most attractive of the three.

Other photos included one with the words *Buddy and Emma Jean* written on the back. Those were the names of Essie's parents. It looked to be more of a painting than a photograph. It had probably been retouched for preservation purposes. Her father sported a dark, aged suit and had a cigarette dangling out of the side of his mouth. Her mother, a heavyset woman, wore a nice, handmade dress and matching gloves. They made a handsome couple. Most of the other photographs were of people that Colin didn't know, but one drew him in and held him. Something about the child in it looked oddly familiar. He brought it closer to his face to get a better view, then flipped it over.

Me and my only great-niece. She looks sweet, but she needs savin' or else she's gonna be the death of her Grandma Annie Belle.

Colin stood straight up, sending the box and its contents tumbling to the floor.

Chapter 29

Jennifer's Story

Her hands were so clammy that a stain of wetness could be seen on her leather steering wheel when she released it to prepare to get out of her car. Upon parking at the edge of T.K.'s property, she'd seen someone peek through one of the curtains, so she knew that her arrival was common knowledge inside the house. Jennifer had been given no time to sit in the car and collect herself.

A steady, moderate rainfall had made the drive to Stone Mountain a bit longer than normal, but she still arrived ten minutes ahead of schedule. Had Jennifer been anywhere else, she would have pulled into the driveway to put herself closer to the front door. But the homeowner's association in T.K.'s upscale subdivision didn't permit that. Vehicles had to either be pulled into the garage, or parked at street side. It was their way of keeping the driveways oil-free.

Just as she gripped the handle to open her door, the garage door lifted, and Jennifer watched T.K.'s Ford Escape slowly back out. Where was he going? Had he thought about the whole thing and changed his mind about speaking with her? Was he leaving so that she and Jerrod could have the time alone? That wouldn't do. Jennifer wanted . . . *needed* to speak with both of them. Her mind raced, trying to think what she could say or do to stop his exit. There was no time to be coy; she was in the process of preparing to blow her horn when the Escape came to a stop. T.K. flashed his headlights, climbed out of the driver's seat, and motioned for her to pull into the vacated space beside his Corvette.

Still the gentleman. Jennifer couldn't believe she'd let him get away.

From her rearview mirror as she parked, Jennifer saw T.K. pull the truck in the streetside place where her car had once been. Then he got out and jogged under the shelter of the garage, wiping water from his face.

"Thank you." The words almost got hung in her throat, but she said them. Jennifer noted the way the rain made T.K.'s Ralph Lauren polo shirt cling to the lean muscular upper body that had been gifted to him by years of running. If he didn't change into something dry, she wasn't going to be able to get through the evening without making a total imbecile of herself.

T.K. returned her gaze for a short time while he slung excess moisture from his hands and arms. "No problem," he said, then pointed toward the side door that would lead them into the house. "Come on in."

The coolness of the den welcomed them as they stepped inside. Only a few days had passed since the last time Jennifer had been here, but as she looked around, it seemed like a lifetime.

T.K. led the way from the den into the living room and pointed toward the sofa. "Make yourself comfortable. Jerrod will be down in a second."

"Thanks." He was being so cordial that Jennifer wanted to cry. She would feel better if he would just scream at her and tell her what an idiot she was.

Instead, he disappeared around a corner without another word, leaving her to her thoughts. Jennifer didn't blame him for not wanting to be in the same room with her for any length of time. She imagined that if he could find a way to breathe different air than she did, he'd do that too.

Jennifer stood slowly when Jerrod entered the room. Tears clouded her vision as she looked at her son. On the drive over, she promised herself that she wouldn't get emotional, but it was a promise that she wouldn't be able to keep. As the tears spilled onto her cheeks, she didn't try to wipe them away. "Hey, baby," she whispered.

"Hey, Ma." Jerrod looked away as if he couldn't bear to see her cry.

"Sit with me?" It was an odd sounding statement/question, but she was glad when her son complied. Jerrod's behind had barely touched the leather on the couch when Jennifer spoke again. "I'm so sorry, baby. I'm sorry for everything. I don't know what I was thinking or why I didn't talk to you first. You deserved so much better than that. It wasn't just my life that was gonna change, yours was going to change too, and I'm so sorry for not considering your feelings."

Jerrod shook his head. "I just can't believe you could do something this stupid, Ma." He sounded like he was glad to finally unburden himself of the heated thoughts he'd been holding in for days. "Everything was going so good and you just jacked it all up by bringing that no-good, trifling fool—"

"Jerrod."

The firm, one-word warning caused them both to turn around. T.K. stood in the entrance-way with his arms folded and his back resting against the wall. He'd changed into dry clothes. For Jennifer, it was a relief and a disappointment at the same time.

"Start over," he demanded.

Jennifer wiped her tears and looked back at Jerrod. It was obvious that T.K. and her son had had some kind of discussion about how the teenager was supposed to handle tonight's meeting. "It's okay," Jennifer interjected. "I want him to be honest and say what he feels."

"He can do that without being disrespectful," T.K. insisted. Then he looked back at Jerrod. "Start over, kid."

Jerrod's posture slumped and his back fell against the cushions of the sofa. As if declaring to Jerrod that he meant business, T.K. approached the fireplace that was across from the sofa and looked at the boy. T.K. spoke no words, but his eyes were intense. Jerrod sat up straight. Even Jennifer repositioned herself under T.K.'s stare.

"I just don't want him in my life, Ma." Jerrod's new tone was barely above whispering. "I been getting along just fine without him, and that's the way I want it to stay."

Jennifer's eyes dropped to her lap. "I thought the dream of every boy who had grown up without his father was to get to know his dad."

T.K. made a grunting sound and Jennifer looked up to see him shaking his head like her words couldn't have been further from the truth.

"Not me, Ma," Jerrod said. "I can't say that I ever even wanted to know what he looked like, let alone get to know him personally. Now you got me wanting to change my middle name." Jerrod kicked the airspace in front of him. "I used to like it before I knew it was *his* name too. Now I got to live the rest of my life knowing that I not only got his name, but I got his ugly face."

Jennifer reached forward and touched her son's hand. "Jerrod, you are not ugly. You're a very handsome boy. Always have been and always will be."

"Yeah. I used to think so too before I saw where I got it from," he grumbled, displeasure contorting his face. "When I get grown, I'ma change my name *and* get a facelift."

T.K. broke into a soft chuckle, and Jennifer struggled not to follow his lead. She bit her bottom lip in an attempt to maintain control, but Jerrod wasn't amused.

"Glad y'all think it's funny," he added.

"No, sweetheart," Jennifer assured him. "It's not funny."

"Yes, it is," T.K. refuted. He leaned against the mantle of the fireplace. "Disappointments are gonna come, Jerrod. People are going to disappoint you and it won't be in your control to change everything." Jennifer noted the look he shot her way when he said the words. She looked at her lap as he continued. "I'm named after my father too, Jerrod; got his *whole* name. And in order for your dad to be a lower-life individual than mine, he'd have to live in hell and be Satan's right hand man."

Jennifer's eyes found him again. T.K. had never told her much about his father other than the fact that he never knew him. She didn't know he was such a scoundrel, and she didn't know that T.K. was named after him either. As he continued to speak, T.K. had pain in his eyes, and Jennifer wanted to jump from the sofa and hold him. But she knew better than to try.

"You know what my father did?" T.K.'s eyes were locked on Jerrod, but Jennifer felt as if he were posing the question to both of them. "Not only did he abandon my mother when he found out she was pregnant, just as your dad did, but he beat her. My mother told me that his words to her were, 'If you don't get rid of this baby, I'm gonna beat him out of you.' That's what he told her.

"You see, my father wanted my mom to have an abortion to cover his adultery, cover his *crime*.

He was a married man. A chronic cheater. A pedophile that always had some underage lover on the side. Thirty-six years old when my mama was fifteen. He befriended my mother, made her think he loved her, took her innocence, got her pregnant, and then wanted her to kill me to cover his tracks. When she wouldn't abort, he figured he'd do a bootleg abortion for her. Literally kicked her in the stomach with the steel toe of his boots to try to get rid of me."

Jennifer placed her hands over her mouth. She had no idea. Devon had abandoned her during her pregnancy, but he'd never tried to harm her.

"She wouldn't press charges, wouldn't tell on him, nothing," T.K. said. "Even after all of that, Mama still loved him enough to name me after the man. Thomas King Donaldson Jr." He released a cold laugh and shook his head. "At thirteen or so, I started going by T.K. just so I wouldn't have to hear his name every time I heard mine." He moved across the floor and sat on the space beside Jerrod. "Listen, kid. Don't nobody understand what you're dealing with more than me. But one thing I've found out in life is that there are some battles that only God can fight. In this world there have always been dads who are deadbeat and dads who will beat you dead. The best way to fight it is to not become one of them. You can change your face and change your name, but the truth of the matter is you will still be who you are, and the man who planted the seed that got you here will still be the same. You get what I'm saying?"

"I do, Coach," Jerrod said, "but I guess you just better than me. I just can't do this. I can't live with him, knowing that he ditched us when he found out I was on the way. How am I supposed to play like I'm a'ight with that?"

Jennifer opened her mouth to speak, but it was as if she was no longer a part of the conversation.

"That's where we differ, Jerrod," T.K. said. "You're wrong. I'm not better than you. In fact, you're gonna have to be a better man than me. See, I didn't have to live with my dad. I don't know why your mama decided to take your father back. I don't like it any more than you do, but I can't exactly look down on her just because my mom didn't go that route." Jennifer fidgeted in her seat, but said nothing. "I believe with everything within me that if my mother would have had a choice in the matter, she probably would have taken my father back too. It was his choice to leave her; not vice versa."

"Why would she take him back after he tried to kill her baby?"

T.K. shook his head. "I don't know, kid. I stopped trying to figure women out a long time ago. Take it from me; life is easier that way."

Stillness settled in the room for a moment, and Jennifer decided that now was the time. "Jerrod, sweetheart; I—"

"I can't do it, Ma," Jerrod broke in. He shifted so that he faced her now. "I heard everything Coach said, and I already know what you're gonna say. I know Devon is my daddy by nature, but I don't want nothing to do with him. Toby's got an apartment and he's living on his own. He ain't but a few months older than me. You won't even have to pay for my junk like Toby's parents pay for his. I'll get an after-school job and take care of myself. If you want to marry him, then more power to you. I ain't gonna try to stand in your way, and I ain't gonna try to make no trouble for y'all. All I'm asking is that you don't force him on me."

"But, Jerrod—"

"Ma, every boy don't want to know who his father is, okay? Maybe every kid needs a father figure, but they don't necessarily need their daddies in their life to have that." He turned and looked at T.K., then turned back to Jennifer and added, "I got a father figure, Ma. Coach D is a better daddy to me than that man will ever be. I'm not asking you not to make Devon your husband, Ma. I'm just telling you that I can't make him my dad."

Tears glossed Jennifer's eyes once more. "That's what I'm trying to tell you, Jerrod. I came here to tell you that I'm not going to force you to live under the same roof with Devon."

Jerrod's body snapped to attention. "For real, Ma?"

Jennifer nodded. "For real, sweetheart. I'm not gonna make him your daddy, and I'm not going to make him my husband either." She felt T.K.'s eyes burn into her flesh, but she made an effort to hold her eyes on her son. "I made a mistake, Jerrod. A very, very expensive mistake. A mistake that may have cost me the best thing that has happened to me since you." Jennifer didn't even look away from Jerrod when T.K. stood from the sofa and walked back toward the fireplace. But she hoped that he knew her next words were just as much for him as they were for Jerrod. "I'm sorry, Jerrod. I had prayed for God to send me something special; a specific blessing. And when Devon suddenly showed back up in my life, I thought he was the answer to my prayers." She closed her eyes when her son reached forward and wiped away her tears with his hands.

"I messed up," she said, choking on the heavier flow of tears. "I just want you to know that I love you very much." It was then that she turned her eyes toward the man standing at the fireplace searching her. "Very much," Jennifer reiterated before looking back at Jerrod. "I promise that I'll never allow anything to come between us again, never put another man's desires above our relationship. Never. I promise."

Jerrod flung his arms around her neck and held on tight. Tears flowed from her eyes onto his shoulder.

"Forgive me?" Jennifer whispered.

"Yeah, Ma. I mean, yes, ma'am." Jerrod suddenly pulled away and turned toward the fireplace. Excitement was the theme of his face. "Coach D, ain't you got something to say? Something to *ask*?"

Jennifer glimpsed at T.K. and wondered why he all of a sudden looked like a deer caught in headlights.

Chapter 30

Elaine's Story

Her body was so sore that moving was limited. Most of the pain was in her upper body; in the area where she'd bumped her head during the fall, and in the spots where the doctors had tried unsuccessfully to insert needles before they could find a vein that was receptive. But in spite of it all, Elaine was thankful.

After Angel left with Essie's blanket folded in her arms, Elaine and Mason had requested that the doctors not allow anymore visitors for the evening. Elaine knew that their friends would understand. As long as they all knew that she was fine, they wouldn't mind having to wait another day to see her. All of them had come earlier anyway; or so Mason told her. She was sorry that she wasn't alert to see all of the love that her forest of flowers proved had been showered on her. According to Dr. Zbornak, she would soon have the chance to tell them all in person just how blessed she felt to be surrounded by such a community of supportive, caring people. But as excited as she was about her pending release, there were more pressing issues on her mind.

"So how long has it been?" she asked, holding Mason's hand in hers.

She could tell by the way her husband twisted in his chair that this was an uncomfortable subject. "I . . . I . . . I really don't know." He wouldn't look her in the face.

"You don't know, or you just don't want to tell me?"

Mason slipped his hand from her soft grip and leaned back in the chair, but Elaine could see the anguish on his face through the gap in the bed railing. He had been far more talkative when they were discussing her problems. *Her* weight loss, *her* loneliness, *her* fitness obsession, *her* self-esteem issues, *her* battle with bulimia. He didn't mind talking about any of that. Mason had even been open enough to finally validate what Essie said about him wanting Elaine to reclaim some of the weight she'd lost. But when it came to elaborating on his own personal problems, he clammed up.

"I thought we were gonna talk, Mason." Elaine was trying to be patient, but they'd never get anywhere if he was going to keep shutting her out. And this time she wasn't going to allow him not to talk about it. Essie had made her feel stupid enough for letting it go on this long. Elaine pressed the button to raise the head of her bed so that she was sitting in a slight recline rather than lying flat. She had to be in a position that would prevent her husband from hiding from her. "You're gonna have to be open and honest with me just like I was with you, Mason. Nobody else is in the room. It's just us."

"I know, babe, I know," he said. Then after a heaving exhale, he said, "It's been some months."

That wasn't good enough. Elaine pried further. "How many months?"

"Seven . . . eight . . . I don't know, maybe longer," Mason answered, rendering her speechless. "At first when it was happening, or *wasn't* happening, I thought it was 'cause I was just so outdone with you that you couldn't do nothing that even remotely enticed me."

She'd asked him to be honest, but *dang*. It was Elaine's turn to squirm now. His words reminded her of just how much pain her infidelity had inflicted on him. But if they were going to talk this through, she had to be able to take it. "So when did you realize that it wasn't just about me?"

"Real early on," he admitted. "When we made the decision to stay together and try to work it out, and especially when we rededicated ourselves to God. I knew it wasn't just about you then." He frowned and looked at the ceiling like he was searching for the right words to say. "This is so hard to explain," he said. "It was about you in a way, but it really was about me."

Elaine shook her head. He was going to have to do better than that. All he was doing right now was confusing her even more. He read her body language loud and clear.

"It's like Reverend Tides pointed out," he clarified. "I had forgiven you with my mouth, but not my heart. I wanted to forgive you with my heart, but as much as I tried, I couldn't let it go. You gave some other dude what belonged to me, Elaine. Knowing something like that is enough to put any man out of commission."

Ouch. The sting of his words caused a tear to ooze from the corner of Elaine's eye, prompting an immediate recant.

"Don't cry, babe. I didn't mean to make it sound so—"

"No, no, no. Don't apologize," Elaine said. "I asked for honesty, and that's what I want." She wiped her face with the bed sheet. "I just don't know what to say, that's all. I mean, I've already said I was sorry at least a hundred times, and I meant it every single time. But apparently sorry isn't enough, and I don't know what else to do."

"But your apology *is* enough, Elaine," Mason said. "At least it should be. If it was enough for God, it should be enough for me, and I know God has forgiven you. I just have to work through this and be able to do the same. I'm not blaming my problem on you. I know it might seem like I am, but I'm not.

This is my fault. I'm the one with the forgiveness issues, and it's those issues that's causing this problem; not you."

"So what are you saying?" Elaine held her breath for a moment; afraid of what his answer might be. "Are you saying that you may never be able to truly forgive me?"

She saw uncertainty in Mason's eyes as he reached for her hand and brought the back of it to his mouth and kissed it, right at the point where the needle was inserted. The touch of his lips sent shivers up her right arm that cleared her shoulder like a rollercoaster, and then rocketed down her spine.

"I'm trying, babe," he whispered. "I have to find some way to do it 'cause I'm looking at you right now, and I know that look." His kissed her hand again; this time longer. "I used to love that look, but now it scares me. 'Cause I know that if God doesn't help me to *truly* forgive you, I'll never again know the joy of satisfying that look."

Feeling flushed, Elaine looked away. She didn't know that her desire for him was so obvious. But then again, she had been married and celibate for more than four hundred days. As Elaine saw it, she was doing well not to leave a trail of steam everywhere she walked. The fact that the liquids that were being fed into her body weren't boiling in their bags as they hung behind her bed was nothing short of a miracle. "What are we gonna do, Mason?" Elaine felt frightened. She knew the fate of their marriage rested largely in her hands, but as much as she loved Mason, she didn't know how much longer she could live like this.

"I want to move back in the bedroom," he said. "Will you let me?"

Elaine looked at him and nodded. "Of course I will. It's what I've wanted from the beginning."

"I know, babe. But you'll have to do it with the knowledge that I can't make no guarantees. I just want to take some real steps toward putting my faith into action. All I can promise is that I'll try. God knows with everything in me, I'll try."

Elaine searched at her husband's helpless face. She saw eyes that she hadn't looked in deeply in over a year, chubby cheeks that she hadn't caressed in over a year, full lips that she hadn't kissed in over a year. At that moment, she felt divinely empowered. Like there was nothing that needed to be done that God hadn't equipped her to do. All she needed now was to get well enough to get out of this bed and into her own. And she would.

Elaine gave her husband a shamelessly seductive smile. "I have an idea," she said. "Why don't you and all of your faith move into the bedroom and leave all the *action* to me." She took her index finger and placed it on the cleft of Mason's chin, then allowed it to trace a path down the center of his neck where it lingered for a moment before coming to a stop in the middle of his chest. Mason's right eyebrow twitched, his Adam's apple bobbed, and through the fabric of his shirt, she felt his chest tighten and swell.

"Umph," Elaine grunted. "And just think. I haven't even gotten started yet."

Chapter 31

Angel's Story

"I knew you'd come," she said as she sat on the side of the mattress with a firm grip on the pink and blue blanket that was draped across her lap. When Elaine handed her the blanket and whispered the words, "Ms. Essie told me to give this to you," Angel didn't even flinch. Not once did she doubt her friend's declaration. In fact, she embraced them and couldn't wait to get home. Essie had promised to always be there for Angel, and although the elderly woman hadn't been there when Angel thought she should, Elaine's words told her that it was only a matter of time. It didn't even bother Angel when Jennifer informed her that Colin had stopped by and gotten Austin; nor did it upset her when she walked into Essie's bedroom and found a handwritten note that indicated that he'd not only found her hiding place, but had been inside.

Let's talk, sweetheart. Please don't count me out. Don't give up on us. There's so much that you don't know. So much I didn't even know until tonight. It's not what you think. There is no other woman. Never has been. Never will be. As God is my witness, I'm telling the truth. And by the time you read this note, even the association that resulted in this misunderstanding will have been severed. Completely severed. No friendship, no fellowship, no relationship is worth losing you. I'm sorry for anything I did to bring us to this point. Please come home to me so we can talk . . . and make up for lost time. I love you, Angel.

Colin's words seemed heartfelt, but they didn't explain the lipstick on his collar or the scent of some other woman's perfume in his shirt. There would be no making up if he couldn't explain that. And as far as talking goes, tonight she needed to talk to someone else. There was so much that she needed to say to Essie, but when she looked into the beautiful brown eyes of the woman who'd been like a nurturing grandmother to her, tears danced at the edges of Angel's lower lids. Essie opened her arms like she understood the words that Angel hadn't even spoken yet.

Angel leaned her head on Essie's chest and melted in her embrace. For a long while, as they sat together on the bed, all that could be heard was Angel's weeping and Essie's humming as she rocked back and forth. Essie had never been a great singer, but when she hummed, Angel always found solace. The woman's soft hand caressed Angel's arm as they swayed in gentle motions. It was the same feeling of protection that Essie had given her for most of her life. Whether it was a scraped knee, hurtful words from the school bully, a heart left broken by a disloyal boyfriend, or just the frustration of a bad hair day; Essie had always been there to help Angel pick up the pieces and offer much-needed encouragement. Yet, the one time when Essie needed her most, Angel was nowhere around. "I'm so sorry, Ms. Essie," she blurted.

Essie tightened her grip. "What you sorry for, sugar?"

"That I wasn't there to help you that night. If I had been there, you wouldn't have died. I would have been able to get you some help, been able to save you." Her words were mixed with wails and periodic gasps of air.

"Get me some help?" Essie chuckled and kissed the top of Angel's head. "Girl, I didn't need no help. It was my time to go, and I was ready to be with the Lord; to be with my Ben. You ain't got nothing to feel bad about. God called my name

that night, Angel. I had to go. I wanted to go."
She pulled Angel away from her and cupped her
wet face in her hands, forcing Angel to look her
in the eyes. "Do you understand what I'm saying? I *wanted* to go. Ain't nothing you could have
done to change what happened, and I wouldn't
have wanted you to even if you could. Besides, it
ain't like you was in Biloxi somewhere playing the
numbers or something. You were having a baby,
child. And at the time, there wasn't nothing in this
world more important than bringing that beautiful baby boy into this world."

Angel sat up straight and used the knitted
blanked to wipe her face. "I just feel so bad. I never
got to say good-bye." Angel's voice quivered. "I
couldn't even make the homegoing service."

"Please!" Essie gave her hand a carefree wave,
and the whole bed shook when she laughed. "*I*
wasn't even at the homegoing service."

Angel looked at her with inquisitive eyes.

"That wasn't nothing but a shell that them
folks had prettied up in that casket," Essie explained. "I wasn't nowhere in it. To be absent
from the body is to be present with the Lord. I
was with the Lord, child. I was too busy rejoicing
with my Savior to care who was at some funeral."

Angel tucked stray hairs behind her ears. It had meant so much to her; had been so painful to her that she'd missed out on so much. But listening to Essie made her feel as though she'd been making a mountain out of a mole hill all these months. "I just wish I could have paid my respects," she mumbled.

Essie turned and looked at her. "Honey, you gave me all the respect I could ask for when I was living right here in this house. You know how many old ladies wish they had young folks to love them and want to be around them like you did me? I had natural family that never even bothered to come and see about me. They didn't come to see 'bout me when I was living, and didn't even care enough to throw dirt on me when I was dead. But you? You was different. When your granny was living, I figured you was around me 'cause she was around me. Then when she died all them years ago and you kept coming around, I knew then that you loved me for me. Sometimes I forgot that you wasn't really kin." Essie laughed and her eyes brightened. But seconds later, the laugh was gone and she gave Angel an intense look. "But you done stopped paying your respects now."

Angel felt as though Essie had sucker punched her. What was she talking about? As much grieving as she'd done in the past year; as much hard work as she was now putting into getting Essie's house ready for the market, how could she say such a thing?

"Oh yeah, honey, you done stopped respecting me," she added, looking at Angel like her thoughts had been spoken words. "When you let my homegoing come 'tween you and your husband, you stopped respecting me."

Angel searched Essie's face. "I didn't let—"

"You hush up now and listen," Essie said. She stood from the bed and peeked through the blinds into the night. When she turned back to face Angel, she said, "I ain't got much time, so you listen to me and you listen good." She squatted in front of Angel and took both Angel's hands in hers. Angel couldn't help wonder how a woman of Essie's years could squat so easily and hold the position so effortlessly. "I'm only gonna say this to you once, 'cause I ain't got time to say it twice," Essie started. "You ain't doing right by your husband."

Angel opened her mouth to defend herself, but Essie held up her index finger in silent warning. It was a signal that Angel had seen many times in her life, and she knew that when Essie flashed it, she meant business.

"When I died, that boy stood by you. He prayed for you, cried with you, sat up sometimes all night long and talked you through your pain. When you finally snapped out of all your grief, what you went and did?"

Angel's mind searched for an answer, but Essie didn't give her time to think of one before she spoke again.

"Nothing," she said, and her tone was stern. "That's what you went and did. You ain't hardly done one thing for that boy since." Angel swallowed hard, and she stared at the pink and blue blanket as Essie continued to scold her. "You 'round here shopping for Austin, going to church, cleaning up my house, and running 'round the neighborhood with Elaine, but you ain't done one good thing for or *to* Colin in months. Now what kinda sense does that make? Honey, you ain't respecting me and you ain't doing no favors for your son or your friends if you ain't taking care of your husband." She lifted Angel's chin with her finger. "You understand me, child?"

"Yes, ma'am." All Angel could manage was a murmur.

"When I left here, there wasn't love nowhere this side of heaven that was stronger than yours and Colin's. Now you over here sleeping in my bed 'cause you think he's having an affair."

Angel sat up straight. "I found—"

"A shirt with some lipstick on the collar; that's *all* you found, and that don't mean squat." Spit flew out of Essie's mouth as she spewed the words. "Lipstick don't equal no affair, Angel. But if you don't straighten up and give that man the attention he needs and *deserves*, then you gonna lose him for real. Honey, you betta wake up and smell the coffee 'fore the percolator runs dry. You know how many women out there would kill for a man like the one you got? Handsome, hard-working, loyal, God-fearing. You got some out there who will take him just to be vengeful. They jealous and will do anything to tear you down."

"Jealous of what?" Angel asked. "I don't have a lot of friends, Ms. Essie, but the ones I have are trustworthy. I don't believe—"

"Ain't nobody said nothing about your friends," Essie snapped. "Just like you got friends, you got enemies. Some you know 'bout and some you don't. Enemies can be just like family, but they can hate your guts. Jealousy is an evil thing, and you got plenty to be jealous of. Not only do you have a good family, but you got money, child. I left you everything when I died, and there are folks out there who ain't all that happy about that. They didn't never do nothing for me when I was living 'cause they didn't know I had anything to leave them when I died. Now they're mad 'cause I left it all to you."

Angel looked at Essie. She'd never seen her explain anything with such adamancy. Her words didn't sound hypothetical. She sounded as if she were specifically talking about someone.

"Who, Ms. Essie? Who's doing that?"

"Just know that there are some evil people in this world, sugar," Essie said. "Some seem like they were born evil. Been evil all their lives." She looked away, and then turned and faced Angel again. "The point I'm making is that if they can't take your money, they'll aim for something else. Maybe something else that they know you care more about than money. If that means destroying your family, that's what they'll do, 'cause they know that money can buy a lot of things, but it ain't never been able to meet the price tag that comes with happiness."

"So Colin's not having an affair?" Angel really needed to know.

"No," Essie answered. "I ain't saying he was right for staying away deep into the night like he been doing lately, but you got to give him a reason to come home, baby." Essie finally stood up straight. "If you really give it some thought, I think you'll realize that you miss being with him just as much as he been missing being with you."

Angel looked up at Ms. Essie. Truer words had never been spoken. "What do I do now?"

Essie put her hands on her hips. "What you mean what do you do now? It ain't like you got to get on a plane, child." Essie pointed at Colin's open-faced letter that Angel had placed on the nightstand. "Your house is right 'cross the way, and he done already begged you to come home. *Go home*, Angel. Do your making up tonight. The talking can wait 'til tomorrow." She winked like that was something experience had taught her.

Angel bounced from the mattress, but a twinge of sadness set in as soon as she looked at Essie. "You're gonna leave now, aren't you?"

"My work here is done." She veered her eyes toward the ceiling, then looked back at Angel and added, "But don't you worry none, I'm always gonna be here whenever you need me. You might not see me, but I'm here. And as long as you do- ing the right thing by God and by your family, you can rest assured that I'm proud, and I'm happy. Understand?"

Angel's lips trembled, but she managed a smile. "Yes, ma'am. I understand."

Essie reached out and pulled Angel into a hug, but as soon as their bodies touched, Angel's eyes flew open. She awakened to find herself lying in bed, clutching the handmade blanket in her arms as though it were another person. She took a moment to steady her breathing and savor her experience, then Angel slung her legs out of bed, shoved her feet into her bedroom slippers, and grabbed her car keys. She ran from the bedroom to the porch, only pausing to lock the front door when she exited. Wearing only her pajamas and a pink and blue blanket draped around her shoulders, she headed to her car.

Chapter 32

Jerrod's Story

Still dressed in his church clothes—a pair of chocolate slacks and a white dress shirt with chocolate pinstripes—he stood on the front porch and waited for his mom to finish preparing dinner. Jerrod sniffed the air. It was just too nice of a day to waste it indoors. When T.K. dropped him off at home after church, Jennifer had invited T.K. to stay for dinner, but he'd declined. Jerrod was disappointed, but he understood; just like he understood why T.K. chose not to offer Jennifer the engagement ring he'd purchased for her; even after she announced that her short-lived relationship with Devon was over.

"I want you to understand that this is gonna take some time for me," T.K. had explained to him after Jennifer left for home that night. "Although she admitted that it was a mistake, that doesn't change the way or the fact that she ditched me when she thought she'd found some other guy who would marry her sooner. Don't get me wrong, kid, I still love your mom, but the mere fact that she did what she did means we have some work to do before we can make this official. Might take a year, might take a month, might take a week. But it's got to be done. You understand that, don't you?"

"Yes, sir," Jerrod had responded, and he meant it. If he were in T.K.'s shoes, he would have done the same thing, if he had stayed around at all.

His time in Stone Mountain had been good for him and it passed quickly, ending with morning worship at New Hope. The service had been a good one as always, and Toby said he enjoyed it so much that he wanted to come back next Sunday.

T.K. told Jerrod that God had given Toby to him as an assignment. At first, the notion scared Jerrod. He barely had it together himself. He didn't know if he wanted to be responsible for anybody else's spiritual well-being. But after a while, the thought that he could somehow help Toby through his struggles like Essie had helped Jerrod through his, appealed to him. Jerrod looked up in the sky. He hoped that Essie was smiling at his decision to step up to the plate and do what he could to help his friend.

The sun was shining so bright that Jerrod had to cut his sky gazing short. Something had transpired in this community in the time that he had been away. When Jerrod ran off last Saturday after the unplanned meeting with Devon, everything about Braxton Park was jacked up. His mom, her friends, his life; even the weather was messy. Now, eight days later, everything seemed back to normal.

A horn blew and Jerrod waved at Mason and Elaine as they headed out of the subdivision. Maybe things were even better than normal. He'd never seen the two of them sitting so close together in their vehicle. Elaine was so close to Mason that it was hard to tell which of them was navigating. He wondered where they were going. Maybe just for a Sunday drive.

Shoving his hands in his pocket, Jerrod leaned against one of the porch pillars and looked down at the new shoes T.K. purchased for him from Joseph A. Bank yesterday. He'd never owned a pair of brown Florsheims before. He'd never owned a pair of any color Florsheims before. They were so spiffy that all day long, Jerrod had felt the need to take them off and carry them in his hands. Shoes this sharp didn't belong on the ground.

A second horn caught his attention, and he looked up to see Colin's truck heading toward the mouth of the subdivision. He didn't question where they were headed. Colin and Angel always ate out on Sundays. Angel's window was lowered and she waved wildly at Jerrod, grinning the whole while. She had on red, and the color looked pretty against her skin. Jerrod returned her friendly gesture and watched the SUV roll out of sight.

Something had gone on with the two of them too. Jerrod didn't know the details, but Jennifer was having a three-way call with Elaine and Angel about an hour ago (like they hadn't all just seen each other at church), and Jerrod overheard something about another woman. She was somebody's relative—he couldn't determine whose—that Colin had fired from the bank. What that was all about, Jerrod wasn't sure, and he didn't want to ask questions because that would let on to Jennifer that he was eavesdropping. But whatever the problem was, the smile Angel wore on her face a moment ago indicated that it was resolved now.

Taking care not to scrape up his shoes, Jerrod walked down the front steps of his house and strolled into Essie's yard. It just didn't seem right for her house to be so empty and so quiet. That was about to end though. Jerrod also overheard his mom's response when Angel said that she and Colin had decided to sell their own house instead of Essie's. They were going to move the Stephens family into 216 Braxton Way. That news had made Jennifer happy.

Jerrod's mouth curled upward at the thought of the object of his affections living right next door. Made him happy too.

Without even thinking about it, he began climbing Essie's steps, ending up on her front porch. He walked to the rocking chair where Essie used to spend so many hours sitting, singing, and knitting. Not since the morning after her death had he stood this close to her chair. Jerrod remembered the moment well because his nerves jittered inside of him that day; just as they were doing now.

Stepping closer, Jerrod removed the handkerchief from his pants pocket and dusted the seat and back of the chair, then sat. As soon as he did, his anxieties calmed. He felt like a frightened child who had just been delivered to the safety of his mother's lap. The sensation enveloped him, and Jerrod closed his eyes and relished it. Oh, how he missed Essie Mae Richardson.

Bong!

The sound of the grandfather clock startled him. Jerrod opened his eyes and straightened his back in a single jolt. He looked at his watch. It was 3:43 P.M.; not a time that the clock would normally chime. Jerrod scrambled out of the chair and faced Essie's front door, his breaths coming faster. Every time he heard that single chime, something major happened. Like when Essie died. And when he was summoned to testify against Big Dog Freddie. And when Colin's coworker got arrested. And when Devon showed up.

"Oh, God," he panted. Something was about to happen. He could feel it in his bones.

The third horn that blew scared him so bad that he nearly lost his balance when he spun around to face the street.

"What you doing, kid?"

The relief that engulfed him at the sight of T.K. and Toby climbing from the car was almost enough to make Jerrod pass out. He had to take a minute to recompose himself before he could even answer. "Nothing," he said. "I was just over here looking around and stuff. What y'all doing here?"

T.K. was still dressed in the suit that he wore to church and he pulled the sides of his coat back and stuck his hands in his pockets. "I was on the way home and thought about Jen's invitation, and I thought I'd swing by Midtown, pick Toby back up, and come on over and take her up on it. You think she'll mind the extra company?"

A gleeful beam stretched Jerrod's lips as far as the elasticity of his skin would allow. "Are you kidding me? Mama took her lessons from Ms. Essie. She got enough food to feed all of us two times."

T.K. controlled his smile, but Jerrod could tell that his coach was as happy to be there as he was to have him there. "Good," T.K. said, then gestured for Jerrod to join him and Toby on the ground. "Come on. Let's eat."

Jerrod hesitated and looked back at Essie's house one more time. Without a doubt, he knew that this time, the clock's chime was marking a monumental moment that would lead to something to celebrate. Bolting down the steps, he joined the awaiting men.

Discussion Questions

1. The lives of the featured characters in this story began unraveling the morning after the death of a loved one. Have you ever had or known someone to have a similar experience?

2. If you read *Three Fifty-seven A.M.* you were introduced to the blanket that Essie wove. Do you believe an inanimate object such as that can be pivotal in keeping people connected to the person it reminds them of?

3. Impotence and bulimia are two topics tackled in this novel, but seldom addressed in the church community. How prevalent do you think "hush-hush" problems like these are amongst Christians, and how important do you think it is that they be addressed within ministry?

4. What was your initial opinion of Nona upon
    her introduction in the story? Did you imme-
    diately like her? Dislike her? Why?

5. Mason's rejection of Elaine was so devas-
    tating that it drove her to a breaking point,
    and her deception of him did the same. How
    could both of their long-term suffering have
    been lessened or avoided altogether?

6. How did you feel about Colin's relationship
    with his office assistant? Was it inappropri-
    ate? When Angel confronted him, was she
    being overdramatic or unfair in her assess-
    ment?

7. Should "true Christian" marriages be im-
    mune to the types of major challenges that
    the Stephenses or the Dempses faced?

8. Studies indicate that children who grow up
    with their fathers in the home are better off
    because of it. After reading Jerrod's story and
    his feelings toward his dad, what are your
    thoughts regarding the statistical findings?

9. Jennifer depicted the mindset and actions of
    many women (especially those over thirty)
    in today's society. Many of them feel in-
    complete without a man, and as a result,
    become desperate and make poor choices for
    themselves and their children. If you were in
    T.K.'s shoes, would Jennifer's lapse in judg-
    ment be forgivable?

10. What were your thoughts about Toby and the
    manner in which he was renounced by his
    family? As professed Christians, how could
    his parents have better dealt with the revela-
    tion of the teen's secret?

11. If you are a reader of the "Shelton Heights
    Series" (*In Greene Pastures*, *Battle of Jeri-
    cho*, and *The Lyons Den*) were you surprised
    to see some of the characters from that series
    in *The Morning After*? What did you think of
    the role of Reverend Tides in this story?

12. Do you believe in guardian angels? Do you
    believe in spiritual visitations from deceased
    loved ones by way of dreams and/or visions?
    Discuss why or why not.

13. Is there any part of *The Morning After* that you would change if you could rewrite the story? If so, which part would it be?

14. Know anyone suffering with bulimia or anorexia? Call the National Eating Disorders Association's toll free hotline at 1-800-931-2237, or visit them on the web at: *www.nationaleatingdisorders.org*.

15. Have a friend who needs more information on impotence? Call the Impotence Information Center at 1-800843-4315.

About the Authors

Kendra Norman-Bellamy is a multi-award winning, national bestselling author, columnist, and motivational speaker; as well as the founder of KNB Publications, LLC. She and her literary works have been featured in *Essence*, *Upscale*, *Precious Times*, *HOPE for Women*, *WOW!*, *Global Woman*, and *EKG Literary* magazines. Kendra is the mastermind behind The Writer's Hut (an on-line support group for creators of literary works), The Writer's Cocoon (a writer's workshop and an expanded focus group), and she is the founder of Cruisin' For Christ (a groundbreaking cruise that celebrates Christian artistries). Kendra is a graduate of Valdosta Technical College and a proud member of the Iota Phi Lambda Sorority. She is a wife and mother of two teenage daughters and resides with her family in metropolitan Atlanta, GA.

Hank Stewart is an Emmy Award winning poet who is a catalyst for action and a messenger of hope. He has shared the stage with Tavis Smiley, Rev. Jesse Jackson, Dr. Joseph Lowery, Congressman John Lewis, the late Rev. Hosea Williams, and the late Johnnie Cochran, to name a few. Additionally, Hank is the author of three self-published books of poetry: *The Answer*, *Second Chance*, and *Be Still And Know*, and his first work of fiction, *Three Fifty-seven A.M.*, was also co-authored by Kendra Norman-Bellamy. He is the founder of The Stewart Foundation, a non-profit organization whose purpose is largely geared toward the betterment of today's youth. Hank is the doting father of one son and resides in metropolitan Atlanta, GA.

UC HIS GLORY BOOK CLUB!

www.uchisglorybookclub.net

UC His Glory Book Club is the spirit-inspired brainchild of Joylynn Jossel, Author and Acquisitions Editor of Urban Christian, and Kendra Norman-Bellamy, Author for Urban Christian. This is an online book club that hosts authors of Urban Christian. We welcome as members all men and women who have a passion for reading Christian-based fiction.

UC His Glory Book Club pledges our commitment to provide support, positive feedback, encouragement, and a forum whereby members can openly discuss and review the literary works of Urban Christian authors.

There is no membership fee associated with UC His Glory Book Club; however, we do ask that you support the authors through purchasing, encouraging, providing book reviews, and of course, your prayers. We also ask that you respect our beliefs and follow the guidelines of the book club. We hope to receive your valuable input, opinions, and reviews that build up, rather than tear down our authors.

What We Believe:

—We believe that Jesus is the Christ, Son of the Living God

—We believe the Bible is the true, living Word of God

—We believe all Urban Christian authors should use their God-given writing abilities to honor God and share the message of the written word God has given to each of them uniquely.

—We believe in supporting Urban Christian authors in their literary endeavors by reading, purchasing and sharing their titles with our on-line community.

—We believe that in everything we do in our literary arena should be done in a manner that will lead to God being glorified and honored.

We look forward to the online fellowship with you.

Please visit us often at:
www.uchisglorybookclub.net.

Many Blessing to You!

Shelia E. Lipsey,
President, UC His Glory Book Club

Notes